PENG

© Robert Trathen

Paula Morris (Ngati Wai) was born in Auckland. She is the author of three adult novels: *Queen of Beauty*, *Hibiscus Coast* and *Trendy But Casual*; two young adult novels, published in the United States; a collection of short stories, *Forbidden Cities*; and is the editor of *The Penguin Book of Contemporary New Zealand Short Stories*. She lives in Glasgow.

ALSO BY PAULA MORRIS

Queen of Beauty

Hibiscus Coast

Trendy But Casual

Forbidden Cities

The Penguin Book of Contemporary New Zealand Short Stories

Rangatira

A novel by
Paula Morris

PENGUIN BOOKS

PENGUIN BOOKS

Published by the Penguin Group

Penguin Group (NZ), 67 Apollo Drive, Rosedale,
Auckland 0632, New Zealand (a division of Pearson New Zealand Ltd)

Penguin Group (USA) Inc., 375 Hudson Street,
New York, New York 10014, USA

Penguin Group (Canada), 90 Eglinton Avenue East, Suite 700, Toronto,
Ontario, M4P 2Y3, Canada (a division of Pearson Penguin Canada Inc.)

Penguin Books Ltd, 80 Strand, London, WC2R 0RL, England

Penguin Ireland, 25 St Stephen's Green,
Dublin 2, Ireland (a division of Penguin Books Ltd)

Penguin Group (Australia), 250 Camberwell Road, Camberwell,
Victoria 3124, Australia (a division of Pearson Australia Group Pty Ltd)

Penguin Books India Pvt Ltd, 11, Community Centre,
Panchsheel Park, New Delhi – 110 017, India

Penguin Books (South Africa) (Pty) Ltd, 24 Sturdee Avenue,
Rosebank, Johannesburg 2196, South Africa

Penguin Books Ltd, Registered Offices: 80 Strand, London, WC2R 0RL, England

First published by Penguin Group (NZ), 2011
3 5 7 9 10 8 6 4 2

Designed and typeset by Sarah Healey, © Penguin Group (NZ)
Typeset in Adobe Caslon Pro
Maps by Outline Drafting and Graphics Ltd
Printed in Australia by McPherson's Printing Group

ISBN 978 0 14 56575 8

A catalogue record for this book is available
from the National Library of New Zealand.

www.penguin.co.nz

For my parents,
Deborah and Kiri Morris

Ránga tíra; A gentleman or lady. Proper name.

From *A Grammar and Vocabulary of the Language of New Zealand*
Samuel Lee and Thomas Kendall (1820)

rangatira, *n.* chief.

From *First Lessons in Maori*
William H. Williams (1862)

RANGATIRA, a chief, whether male or female: *Te rangatira o runga i a Tainui*—P. M., 72: *He wahine pai tera, he rangatira hoki ia*—P. M., 128. 2. A master or mistress: *Kua takoto hoki he kino mo ta matou rangatira*—1 Ham., xxv. 17. 3. Fertile, rich, bounteous: *He tane ngaki-kumara, he tau-whenua rangatira*—S. T., 159. Cf. *ranga*, to arrange, to set in order; to set an army in motion; to urge forwards; to raise up, to lift; *whakarangaranga*, to extol; *rangatata*, a warrior, a hero; *tira*, a mast; a company of travellers; *ranga*, a company.

From *Maori–Polynesian Comparative Dictionary*
Edward Tregear (1891)

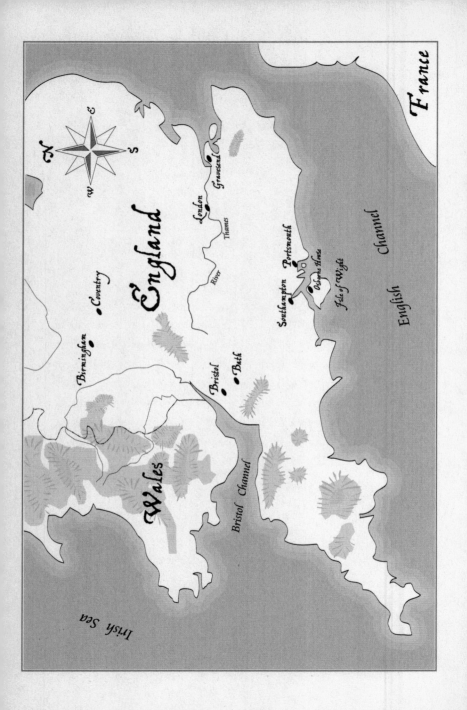

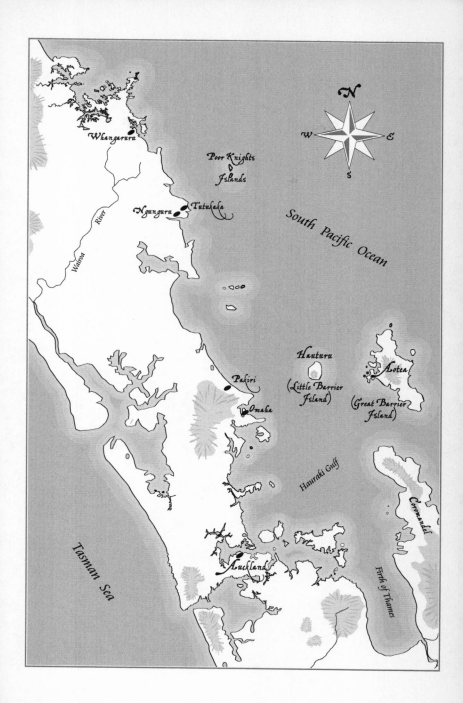

The great Nga Puhi ariki Hongi Hika – tohunga, warrior, master strategist – died of battle wounds in March 1828. As the military commander leading the Northern tribes during the so-called Musket Wars of the 1820s, Hongi gained legendary status in his own lifetime for his brilliance and for his alleged ferocity. Missionaries and other observers reported that many hundreds of Hongi's enemies were killed during battle – or afterwards, in acts of ritual cannibalism. Thousands, they said, were enslaved. Hongi was often seen wearing the helmet and armour given to him, during a trip to England in 1820, by King George IV.

This image of Hongi as bloodthirsty, merciless and vengeful grew after his death. By the 1860s, few who had fought alongside him remained. Pomare the Great died in battle the same year as Hongi, his body eaten by his adversaries. Men who were still alive – like the veteran campaigner Patuone, by then in his nineties – were seen as legends in their own right.

As a young man, Paratene Te Manu, a Ngati Wai rangatira, fought alongside Hongi, Pomare and Patuone in the Thames region and Central North Island during the campaigns of the early 1820s.

Paratene's life spanned the nineteenth century. He was one of the final inhabitants (and owners) of Hauturu, Little Barrier Island. Like Patuone, Paratene Te Manu eventually converted to Christianity and ended his fighting days. Like Hongi, he was invited to travel to England – in 1863 – and was taken to meet the reigning monarch.

This is his story.

From the North
Paratene (Broughton) Te Manu, Ngati Wai
Kamariera (Gamaliel) Te Hautakiri Wharepapa, Nga Puhi
Reihana (Richard) Te Taukawau, Nga Puhi
Hare (Harry) Pomare – great nephew of Pomare, son of
    Pomare II, nephew of Patuone – and his wife, Hariata
    (Harriet) Tutapuiti, Nga Puhi
Wiremu (William) Te Wana Pou, and his brother, Horomona
    (Solomon) Te Atua, Nga Puhi
Hirini (Sydney) Pakia, and his wife, Hariata (Harriet) Tere Te
    Iringa, Nga Puhi
Hariata (Harriet) Haumu, Nga Puhi

From the Thames region
Huria (Julia) Ngahuia, Ngati Whanaunga

From the Central and Western North Island
Hapimana (Chapman) Ngapiko, Te Ati Awa
Takarei (Douglas) Ngawaka, Ngati Tuwharetoa
Kihirini (Kissling) Te Tuahu, Tuhourangi

William Jenkins, cabinet-maker, upholsterer and native
  interpreter, of Nelson
William Wales Lightband, tanner and gold prospector; and
  his father-in-law William Brent, landowner, of Nelson
William Lloyd, gold prospector, of Nelson

In London
Colonel Robert Marsh Hughes, Superintendent, the
  Strangers' Home for Asiatics, Africans and South Sea
  Islanders
Alec Ridgway, Land and Emigration Agent for Auckland
  Province
Anthony Ashley-Cooper, 7th Earl of Shaftesbury
The missionaries: Elizabeth Colenso, Reverend James Stack
  (Te Taka), and George Maunsell
The Colonial Office: Henry Pelham Clinton, 5th Duke of
  Newcastle; and Sir Frederic Rogers

In Birmingham
Thomas Sneyd Kynnersley, Stipendiary Magistrate
Charlotte Julia Dorotea Weale (Mihi Wira), Superintendent,
  Winson Green Road Home for Girls

For he that speaketh in an unknown tongue speaketh not unto men, but unto God; for no man understandeth him . . .

I CORINTHIANS 14:2

Ko te kai a te rangatira he korero

Auckland, New Zealand
June 1886

At the Native Hostel down on the waterfront, people are always talking. At times I think they don't have anything else to do. Many of them are in Auckland to appear at the Native Land Court, to say their piece or argue about claims to this and that. Some of them are here to sell something in the market, or buy something in the shops. Some of them spend too much time in the grog shops along Shortland Street. I don't bother with that any more. Drink is a waste of money, and it steals days, turning them into dreams. I don't have that many days left to waste on dreaming.

Last time I was in Auckland, when the trees were still bristling with leaves, I was asked to pose for a photograph. I was happy to do this, even though it was quite a to-do. Someone has made pictures of me before, in a proper studio, in a proper city, so I knew what to expect. But this photographer just had a room behind a chemist's shop, and a blanket hanging on the wall. His hair was slick with oil. He insisted that I wear a peacock feather tucked behind one ear. He stuck it there himself, and his fingers were as greasy as his hair.

This feather was quite ridiculous. Then he covered my jacket with a great cloak, a kaitaka, but he draped it upside down over my shoulders. He wanted the woven border of taniko work to show in the picture, he said. I was an ancient warrior, he told me, as though this would explain why I was wearing a peacock feather and an upside-down cloak.

When I say he told me, I mean to say this – he told my old friend Wharepapa to explain things to me in Maori. I could understand his English, but I didn't let the photographer know that. I don't even let Wharepapa know that. People speak more when they don't think you understand.

One of my eyes doesn't see too good these days. I stood looking away from the camera.

'Does the old man think the photograph will insult him in some way?' he asked Wharepapa. 'Does he think it will steal his spirit?'

'Yes,' said Wharepapa, without a smile, although I'm sure he thought this was a great joke.

'Paratene Te Manu, the last of the ancient warriors,' the photographer said, almost to himself, and then Wharepapa grew restless. He fancies himself quite handsome and vigorous still, and likes to tell people of the old days when he too was a great warrior. He doesn't often say this when I'm there, because we both know that I was fighting with my second taua when he was still a gurgling baby, strapped to his mother's back. Almost everything he says about battles are stories he heard from his uncles.

The picture was taken, and there was an end to it, I thought. But this week, at the Native Hostel, one old fool tells me he's seen my face, pinned to the wall somewhere along Queen Street. I don't take any notice until Wharepapa comes thudding down the hill from his house in Parnell, seeking me out on the beach where I'm smoking my pipe. The Bohemian painter is back in Auckland, he tells me. He has taken over a small room in Mr Partridge's building, and is working from the photographs taken in town earlier this year.

'You should talk to him,' Wharepapa advises. 'Otherwise he'll paint your picture with that peacock feather. People will say you're an Indian princess.'

Wharepapa thinks this is so funny, he repeats it to everyone in Mechanics Bay. I wish I was back up north on Hauturu, tending my garden, away from the chatter and intrigues of this place.

I need not have come down, you see, after all. I sailed here with a Mr McGregor, who is here in Auckland to make deals for his timber and gum. Tenetahi, my nephew, used to bring me here in his cutter, *Rangatira*, whenever I had to speak before the land court. But the *Rangatira* was smashed to pieces in a storm a few years ago, on the rocks off Aotea. This is the island that people now call the Great Barrier. Tenetahi and his wife, Rahui, live on Hauturu, or the Little Barrier. Everything has two names these days – a Maori name, and a name that Captain Cook thought of and the Pakeha can remember. These Aucklanders here, I'm certain they were happy to hear that the *Rangatira* lay in pieces, because Tenetahi was always winning too many races in the Auckland regatta.

He and Rahui almost drowned that day, off the shores of Aotea. After the *Rangatira* was stuck on the rocks, and they saw that nothing could be saved, they found a whaling boat and began to row home. Another storm turned the waters of the gulf grey and angry, and tipped the whaling boat upside down. Rahui had to swim out to fetch a lost oar. Every time they righted the boat, it filled with water again. A man travelling with them was washed away. A boy they'd taken to Aotea to teach him how to strip blubber from a whale, he died later from the cold. They took more than half a day to row back to Hauturu. People staying at the hostel said it was makutu, some sort of spell, because of all the bad will in the land court.

The argument is over who owns Hauturu. Whoever owns Hauturu has the right to sell it, and someone or other has been trying to claim the island, and sell the island, for the past forty years – Nga Puhi, Te Kawerau, Ngati Whatua. And us, Ngati Wai, the ones who have kept our fires burning there for as long as I can remember. And who in Auckland can remember longer than I can? The court tries to make it complicated when it isn't.

In 1881 the judge agreed that we Ngati Wai were the owners, naming five people. Each of us represented one hapu of Ngati Wai. But not long after the sinking of the *Rangatira*, the judgment at the land court was given to Kawerau. That's when people started saying things were turning against us.

For us Ngati Wai, all of our mana comes from the water. Now Tangaroa was angered and Tenetahi's boat, with its boastful name, was so many pieces of driftwood. Tenetahi's mother was Ngati Kahungunu ki Wairoa, from the East Coast, and his father was a Pakeha, people said, perhaps a Portuguese sailor. He was only the adopted grandson of Te Heru and had no rights to Hauturu on the basis of descent. They said that Rahui's rights were through her father, Te Kiri, and their Te Kawerau lineage, or their Ngati Whatua lineage, nothing to do with Ngati Wai. They would say that, wouldn't they?

I'm tired of all this. I just want to live there in peace. Some years ago, I said that we should sell the island to the Queen, to end this matter once and for all. We'll live there without constant summons to court by this or that person. I wrote many letters to the court saying so, because every time we stand before a judge, he chooses a different group, and then years go by with more bad will and more arguments. More appeals, my nephew says, because he knows all the language of the court.

So this is why I travelled down to Auckland this week, for yet another appeal. If the judge restores our claim, we have decided to ask for £4000 to be shared among us all, and for Tenetahi and Rahui to keep a small piece of the island. Just a hundred acres, where we live most of the time, so we can continue growing crops and grazing, and cutting timber to ship down to Auckland. We're all agreed on this.

But now my nephew says that this is not a good week to stand before the court. If we wait until later this year, the rules are about to change. We can have a Pakeha lawyer to help us present our argument and no one can wring their hands about it, as they did last time when Mr Tole helped us. Perhaps things will be better by the end of the year, he says, because now the government is saying that times are hard. The gold rush is over. The stock market has collapsed. They don't have any money these days. We should come back to Auckland in the spring, in October.

He may be right. Matariki has risen, but the first new moon of our new year brought a tohu, a very bad sign. This is what people at the hostel are talking about today. Down on Lake Rotomahana there have been sightings of a spirit waka, its ghostly warriors paddling through the mist. Many more people talk of a strange wave surging across the lake, and of the Pink Terrace, which people travel across oceans to see, spitting mud.

We're not supposed to believe in things like omens any more. We've put aside the old ways, the old beliefs, the old fears. We have our new Christian names, the Maori words for

John, and William, and my name, Paratene, which is our word for Broughton. But we still have our old names. How can we forget the knowledge of our ancestors? For a long time I tried to tell myself that they were wrong and that only the ways of the missionaries were right. But as I grow older, in my mind I can't unpick the two. I do know that a lot of what we were told by the missionaries wasn't true.

I'd like to go home now, to be far away from all this talk of restless lake spirits, and bad omens. But Mr McGregor is down here for another five days. I might find this Bohemian painter and see what he's going to do with the picture of me pinned to his wall. At another time in my life I was expected to wear a costume, to be on display, and this made me very unhappy.

If he's going to make a painting, the Bohemian has to take away the peacock feather. I'll tell him this in English, so there can be no mistaking what I'm trying to say.

So I set off down Queen Street, walking towards Mr Partridge's shop. The street is crunchy with mud and stones, and rain starts falling again. The first time I saw this city, when my son was a small boy, none of these buildings were here. It was a settlement, not even daring to call itself a city. None of these docks or wide roads – just tracks cut into a deep bed of fern, the sea lapping up. This wide road, and the hill where horses haul the big trams up to the ridge, that was all water. Some parts of it were a stream, clogged with clumps of flax, and some parts of it were just a swamp. All you could see was the thatch of ferns and clusters of manuka trees, with their spindly arms and legs, whispering in the wind.

In later years, when it started calling itself a city, things weren't much better in Auckland. There was a church and a fort up on the point, but the whare were only replaced with shops and houses that a gust could blow down. Whenever it rained, the track along the stream turned into a bog, and to climb it was to walk in treacle. We used to laugh at them, those Pakeha, trying to press their town into the soggy hill and moving dirt and rocks to fill in the sea. We always camped down by the bay, where the Native Hostel and market stand now. Easier to get in and out.

They also tried to build a fort around the stream, to make it a canal. I say canal, but really it was a dirty gully where people emptied their piss-pots, and it looked and smelled like the prickled mud around mangroves at low tide. You had to cross it by walking on planks. At night, when people were drunk and nobody could see anything, they'd fall in. This was the best show going in Auckland for years, Wharepapa always said – that, and people tumbling off the rickety wharf they built, the one that collapsed a few years ago. Not to mention visiting the stocks and the gallows, of course, though they don't have those anywhere near Queen Street any more.

I don't usually buy my tobacco from Mr Partridge, but I know his shop. On a day like today, when it's raining, the place is crowded, and smells like a wet dog. A whey-faced boy in a stained apron points the way to the Bohemian's room, up the stairs and at the back of the building. I knock on the door with my stick, and there's a long pause before someone inside coughs and tells me to come in.

Because of the rain pelting the window, the room is quite dark. The only light is from a kerosene lamp, and a small, ashy fire in the grate. I know I'm in the right place, because it smells of paint in here, and many Maori faces are pinned to the wall. The Bohemian, sitting in a chair in the corner, is drinking from a teacup. He's peering at me through small round glasses, and with his sharp face and his hooded eyes, he looks like a bird at night, huddling in the darkness.

He places the cup on the floor and stands up to shake my hand. He knows my name, which surprises me at first, but of course he must recognise me from the photograph that was taken. I can't see the picture myself. There are so many up on the wall.

'I thought you will come,' he says. His English sounds worse than mine. 'Your friend tells me.'

Wharepapa. He has the biggest mouth in Auckland.

The Bohemian pulls papers off a low chair so I can sit down as well, and finds the photograph to show me. I look angry in the picture. My white whiskers stick through the ridges of my moko, so my face is like a frayed mat. I'm staring off to the side, my left eye milky, fuming about the peacock feather. I should never have agreed to it.

'You paint *my* face, not this one,' I tell him, jabbing at the photograph. It's strange to hear myself speaking English out loud. 'No feather.'

I smack my left ear so he understands about the feather, and the Bohemian smiles. If a ruru could smile, it would look like him. Even the Bohemian's little beard is as pointed as a beak. Just his cap, which seems to be made of carpet, is round.

'Next week I will go away,' he says. He's looking hard at my face, and then, without saying anything, he leans forward to take the photograph from my hands. His own hands are thin and veined with blue.

The Bohemian looks at the photograph for a long time. The only noise is the patter of rain against the glass, and a tired hiss from the fireplace. Then he gets up and pokes at the fire with the irons.

'I go away too,' I say. 'Until October.'

If I'm alive then, of course. I think this argument at the Native Land Court may outlive me.

'I am no more in Auckland this year,' the Bohemian says. 'In five days, my wife and I, we go. On Wednesday we sail for England. Mr Buller took some of my paintings to an exhibition in London. You know Mr Buller?'

I nod. This Mr Buller was once a judge at the land court, but not in Auckland or in Helensville. I've heard of him, but he's not one of the judges I know, like Mr Monro and Mr O'Brien, who are sensible chaps, or Mr Macdonald, who is a stupid fellow, and utterly wrong in his judgments.

'But perhaps . . .' The Bohemian doesn't finish his sentence. He looks at me and taps his chin – one, two, three. He doesn't have any of the quickness of a bird about him. The last time a painter looked at me, it was very different from this. That painter had a bush of hair, wild eyes, and thick hands that crushed the pencil he was holding. He came to our lodgings and drew me, and then another person, and then another person, wriggling in his seat all the while. Months passed before any of us saw the painting. It was very big, and no one could recognise himself in it. In the picture we were all standing in a room at John Wesley's house, a place we'd only visited – once or twice, I can't remember.

This all took place in London. I must tell the Bohemian that I, Paratene Te Manu, have been to London, and have been painted before, and that the painting was very large indeed. I won't tell him that in this painting I was on the edge of things and looked like a child trying to hide from view, rather than a rangatira, and the oldest person in the room. The only one among them to have fought alongside the great Hongi! The

English don't understand these things. Perhaps Bohemians don't either.

I hope that the Bohemian is only planning a small painting, so it need not take months and months.

'Can you come tomorrow?' he asks me. 'We meet tomorrow, and again on Monday and Tuesday, maybe?'

I agree to this. There's little else for me to do in Auckland these days, except spend money and hear people talk about bad omens, and neither of these things is good for me at all.

'You will talk to me about London, yes?' The Bohemian is smiling again. He pins my photograph back on the wall. 'I know you spent much time there, some years ago. With your friend, Mr Wharepapa.'

Wharepapa should write stories for the *Auckland Weekly News*. He likes to shout his business up and down the town. I'm sure he's told the Bohemian that without him, without the personal invitation of the great Kamariera Te Hautakiri Wharepapa, I would have never stepped onto that ship and sailed to England.

This annoys me so much that I start muttering bad words and banging my stick on the floor. The painter, who I think does not understand Maori, glances at the window as though he's eager for the day to be over. The rain has stopped and, finally, so do I.

'Tomorrow,' he says, bowing to me, and I let him help me up from my chair. This weather makes my bones creak.

When I leave the Bohemian's little studio, I walk down Queen Street towards the water, making my way back towards the Native Hostel. The canal of shit is covered over now, but the city still smells, especially when the wind blows the smoke from the big sawmills at Te To. I could cut down Fort Street, but I don't want to. Old men like me remember when this was Fore Street, when its shacks and stables used to gaze out to sea. Now it's a foul and bedraggled place, fed by the muddy alleys where harpies lurk, waiting for night to fall and the sailors to stagger along into their arms.

Here on Queen Street, a lot of the old shops have burned down or been replaced. These grand banks with their pillars and railings, these shops with the big letters outside, the trams that have to be pushed and dragged up the hill, even these flat footpaths supposed to keep your shoes dry – they're all new. If you stood in the middle of Queen Street, looking at all the false fronts, and the gas lamps, and the men hurrying about their business, you might think that this is a real city now. But it's not. I've seen a real city, the biggest city in the world. And whatever that chattering kaka Wharepapa has to say, it was nothing to do with him.

Here are the reasons I went to England. The only reasons.

I went to England because I happened to be down in Auckland in January of 1863. I was there to speak up for old Tirarau in his dispute with Te Aranui, to make sure we in the North were not going to start fighting each other again with guns. I arrived just after the big fire, the one that raged up and down Queen Street and turned the Thistle Hotel to a mound of ash.

I was near the ruins of the Greyhound, I think, watching it smoulder, when Charley Davis walked up. He had been a friend to us Maori for many years, so I listened when he asked me if I would like to join a party of rangatira people the following month. This party would be making a journey to the other side of the world to see England and some of its great factories, palaces, churches, and schools.

Our passage there and back would be paid, as would all our lodgings and expenses. He said we would see the riches and wonders of this place, and learn their language. People would assemble in churches and schools, eager to hear us talk of our customs and old ways.

This sounded very interesting, of course, but perhaps a little vanity played its part as well. When I should have been suspicious, or cautious, I was thinking how important I must be, to have Charley Davis seek me out and make such an offer. I would be among rangatira, not riff-raff, as I am all too often at the hostel.

But this was not the only reason. I went to England because while I was in Auckland for too long, busy with the affairs of Tirarau, my younger brother drowned off the Tutukaka coast, and he had died and been buried before I could get home to learn of it. And then my dear son, the only one of my children to survive to manhood, had the coughing sickness, and died just two days after I returned to Tutukaka. With my brother gone, and my son gone, I couldn't bear to stay there. This was January of 1863. My wife had been dead for six years. Everyone I loved most in the world had left me.

None of my people wanted me to go, and there was a lot of wailing and begging from my sister and my youngest brother. They tried to stop me from boarding a boat for Auckland. They said I needed to stay at home to receive mourners, as was customary. But I didn't care anything about custom any more. I wanted to sail as far away as possible, where there was nothing to remind me of all I'd lost.

So then, these are the reasons most people know – that I was invited and lured with many promises, that my brother had died, that my son had died, that I wanted to travel far away. But one thing no one knows, because, unlike Wharepapa, I don't announce all my business to the world.

I went to England because when I was a young man, still eager for fighting, I heard Hongi tell stories of his own trip there. This was the visit when he met King George, and when he helped the missionary and the professor write their book of Maori words. He returned with chainmail and a helmet presented to him at the King's armoury, and a vast number of muskets, collected in Port Jackson on his way home. I carried one of these guns on my first taua against Ngati Paoa at Tamaki, just two months after Hongi arrived back.

That was 1821. I'd been learning to fight, waiting to fight, my whole life. The night at camp, not long after the first battle, when I heard Hongi speak of going to England, I decided that I too would go one day. I wanted to see the riches that Hongi had seen, the castles of powerful men, the book-houses holding the maps of Napoleon's battles. I never thought I'd have to wait so long, or that by then I would no longer have any appetite for muskets, or armour, or battles of any kind.

And of all the stories that Hongi told, or other people told of Hongi, there was one I should have believed, more than any of the others. He said that after that voyage to England he realised a Maori could never trust a missionary. All the missionaries did was put themselves in the way of things, speaking for the Maori, trying to stop us from conducting our business in the proper and established way.

That day on the street in Auckland, when Charley Davis told me about the trip to England, I should have remembered Hongi's words. There was a good Pakeha in charge of our party, Charley Davis told me, and this man, this Jenkins, would see to everything. Jenkins wore a white neckcloth. He was a Wesleyan, and at first I thought he was a minister. He didn't say he was, but that's what I assumed.

Jenkins had worked as a native interpreter, Charley Davis said, so he knew our language and our ways. He was a devout man too, building Wesleyan chapels down in the South Island, when he first arrived in New Zealand.

I signed the piece of paper he put in front of me, and agreed to join the group travelling to England. I didn't read this paper at all, although it was written in Maori, and at my age I should know better about signing pieces of paper without looking at every word. Charley Davis said we could trust Jenkins, a fellow Christian, to take care of us, and I believed him because I wanted to believe him. But Charley Davis was wrong. We couldn't trust Jenkins, and we couldn't trust ourselves.

There's too much to this story – too much to remember, too much to explain. I will write it down, and I will write it down in English. There must be a record. So much depends, as I have discovered, on things that are written down on paper.

They that go down to the sea in ships, that do business in great waters;

These see the works of the Lord, and his wonders in the deep.

PSALMS 107:23–24

We sailed in February of 1863, and the voyage took a hundred nights.

I know about boats, of course, because this is the way I've always travelled. How else am I to move between the various places I live? New Zealand is not like England, with its straight roads and hump-backed bridges, and its trains that charge from place to place. Whenever I move from one home to another – between Tutukaka, Whangaruru and Ngunguru on the mainland, or to and from my island homes on Aotea and Hauturu – I sail.

But even in the old days when I was travelling with a taua, paddling through the waves day after day, I was never gone for more than a couple of months. Every night we would pull our waka onto the shore, to find food and a dry place to sleep, and sometimes to gather more fighting men. On this big ship, named the *Ida Zeigler*, we slept every night deep below the deck, in a small, dark room that smelled of salt and sweat. Fourteen of us down there like the lowest prisoners, while Jenkins slept higher up in a cabin by himself, with his own bed, and chairs, so I heard, and fresh meat every day.

Most of us were from the North, because a lot of Maori further south were busy getting ready to fight the government, and because when Jenkins and his friends were recruiting for the trip, a number of us happened to be in Auckland to help the court settle Tirarau's dispute. But some on this trip were not Northerners, which meant there was a natural divide between us. This is the way it's always been. The missionaries can't sweep clean our memories. Our old saying is that the only men in the south are the ones the Nga Puhi warriors chose to leave behind.

Hapimana Ngapiko, who liked a joke, and liked a drink even more, was Ati Awa from Taranaki. I didn't mind him so much at first, though I soon grew to wish that his laugh wasn't quite so loud. He had met Jenkins down in Nelson, though I never found out what young Hapimana was doing down there in the South Island, so far away from home. Perhaps he was looking for gold.

Takarei Ngawaka, of Ngati Tuwharetoa down Taupo way, didn't use his mouth for smoking, or for talking much either. It was hard to believe that his grandfather was the great tohunga Te Heuheu, known as Mananui, who was buried by an avalanche of mud at Te Rapa in 1846. I always heard that Mananui was a giant, but his grandson was short and squat. This Takarei, his Pakeha friends called him Sir Grey, because they said he looked like Sir George Grey. This is what Takarei told us, anyway. I don't know how they got that idea, because Takarei had no whiskers on his face. Maybe Sir George Grey never visited the Taupo area.

On board the ship Takarei became friends with cheeky young Hapimana. This would have amused old Mananui if he were still alive. He led the famous taua against Te Ati Awa,

Hapimana's people. He also refused to sign the Treaty because he didn't trust missionaries and didn't want to be subject to any woman, even if she were the Queen. This trip of his grandson's to England wouldn't have pleased him at all!

Takarei managed to get a berth to himself, sleeping alongside his box, which he refused to place on the floor. Hapimana had to share a berth with the other stranger, Te Tuahu, who the missionaries called Kihirini. He was Tuhourangi, from the shores of Lake Tarawera, a descendant of Rangitihi. Old Kihirini would be very unhappy to know of the bad signs this week from his native region. He was not a friendly man, preferring to keep to himself, and we all took against him from the start.

Kihirini was sturdy, and stout in the face, when we set off, so later it was a shock to see what England did to him. No one in his family would have recognised him. But I'm remembering too much, too soon. At this point, we were all in good health, and most of us were in good spirits. We had no notion of what lay ahead.

The rest of our group were from the North, more or less, if you include Huria Ngahuia in that list. She was one of the Hauraki people, and the granddaughter of Te Horeta, Hongi's old adversary. This is the man the Pakeha called Hooknose. Ngahuia was born long, long after we sacked the pa at Mauinaina and Mokoia, and at Te Totara, and this was a subject, of course, which I never raised in her presence.

On board the ship I thought she was pleasant enough, and handsome as well, though she spoke too often of her grandfather's meeting with Captain Cook, which none of us cared about. Later, once we were in England, she was more troublesome. She spoke a little English, and this was part of the problem. But one thing I will say for her: she was the only person on board who could handle Hariata Haumu.

I can't tell you much about this woman Haumu. There was something about her being related to Arama Karaka Pi, I think, so she was well-born, and came from the Hokianga. She heard some talk on our last night down at the hostel, and resolved at once to join us. Her husband, a Pakeha, had died, and she decided to leave their little daughter with her people. Jenkins and his associates knew nothing of her, I think, until she turned up on board and demanded to be taken to England as well. He should have made some enquiries before agreeing but, as we were to learn, Jenkins was not a wise man, and he often acted in haste. She and Ngahuia shared a berth that was something like a store cupboard, behind a door that led to our own dark room. That door would not last long.

There were two other women in our party, and they could not have been more different. The first was another Hariata, the daughter of Pikimaui, who fought long ago alongside Hongi. She was a sweet-natured thing and, like her husband, Hare Pomare, very young, quite fresh in the face. I knew Hare's father, the Pomare who signed the Treaty, and I knew Pomare the Great, his matua. He was a leader on my first taua, and my hapu sailed away with his when things went bad at Te Totara. Our siege of the pa was achieving nothing, so Hongi decided to trick the Ngati Maru by making a false peace. Pomare was unhappy about this, so we set off for the Bay of Plenty, where we had much other business to settle.

I say nothing to Hare Pomare, but that father of his, the one who called himself Pomare II, he once tried to sell Hauturu to a grocer on Shortland Street in exchange for a schooner. The island wasn't his to sell, and Te Kiri, Rahui's father, had to stop the sale. But there were no bad feelings over this. We owed a debt to Pomare. Some years earlier, he had given me a letter to take back to Hauturu. A lot of Ngati Wai and Ngati Rehua were on the island then to harvest muttonbirds. In this letter everyone was warned to return at once for Aotea, because Te Mauparaoa had overrun the pa there, and plundered all the muskets and powder.

This was in the days before Pomare became a Christian, when our country was still governed by the old rules and customs – though of course we were all happy for the missionaries to teach us how to read and write. Pomare's allegiances to us were deeper and more entwined than his alliance with Te Mauparaoa, so he wanted to warn us. Te Mauparaoa managed to escape, sailing back to the mainland on a raupo raft. Soon he was back living near his old ally, Pomare. I don't think he ever knew about that letter.

Hare Pomare had been raised in a world entirely different from the one his father was born into. When we sailed for England, he and Hariata were both very young and not long married. Though we did not know of it during the voyage, she was with child.

The other woman was neither young nor sweet. She was Tere, the wife of Hirini Pakia. Yes, she was high-born, like all the Nga Puhi on this voyage. As I said before, everyone there was a rangatira by birth. Her grandfather was the great Kawiti, who was both a warrior and a peacemaker. But she was not like her grandfather. She was more like her husband, a slithery eel.

As for Hirini Pakia himself, he makes as much as he can from the fact that his father was Hongi's cousin. This is the closest he can creep to glory, you see. He actually tried to stop me from boarding the ship so I wouldn't be able to sail to England. He sided with my brother and sister, saying that it was improper I should leave, and seemed determined to prevent me from going. Perhaps he knew that with me present, he wouldn't be able to tell so many tall stories of his illustrious ancestry, or boast of his family connection to Hongi. Or perhaps he was afraid I would tell Jenkins and the other Pakeha that he was not a reputable person. He stole things, and he drank a great deal, and he would do anything to get money. This was something that Jenkins would discover eventually, when we were all far from home and nothing could be done.

Then there were the two young Nga Puhi from up Wharepapa's way, Wiremu Te Wana Pou, and his stepbrother, Horomona Te Atua. They were both tall, handsome young men. They were so tall, in fact, that I felt sorry for them having to share a berth. One or other of them always seemed to have his feet dangling over the wooden shelf. Unfortunately, there was a rivalry between them that showed up whenever ladies were around to watch.

'That Wiremu Pou will be trouble,' Wharepapa muttered to me on our second or perhaps third night at sea, and he was to be proven right.

So yes, of course, Wharepapa was there. These days he stomps around Auckland, but back then he was still living most of the time deep in the Mangakahia Valley. He was not yet old, but already a widower. Before the ship was clear of the Hauraki Gulf I'd realised that he was determined to become the leader of our group.

The final member of our party was Reihana Te Taukawau. I say that he was the final person, but in fact Reihana was on board before any of us, because he wanted to choose the best berth. Unfortunately, there were no best berths to be had. We

Maori were to be crammed together, one bed on top of the next. He had to share his berth with Wharepapa, who was only invited on the trip because Reihana suggested it.

I've already talked a lot about Wharepapa, though I will never have as much to say on this subject as Wharepapa himself. Of Reihana Te Taukawau I'll declare this: certainly he was a Christian, the only true Christian among us. He insisted, in fact, that we always call him Reihana, his Christian name, which means Richard in English. In those days I tried my best to be a Christian, but sometimes I forgot or erred, or grew confused. But Reihana, he was filled with the wrath of God, and the certainty of his beliefs. This I respected.

Well, sometimes I respected it. At other times, I wanted him to stop his fist-shaking. And here I will admit something very unchristian indeed: I wanted him to stop talking about the death of his son. He only agreed to come on this voyage, he said, because his mind was blurred with grief. *My* son had died, *my* brother had died, but I didn't burden everyone else with constant lamentations. I don't grieve on and on, like a woman. But there was Reihana, always gloomy, his eyes glazed, dragging the darkness of his mood about the ship as though it were a mud-spattered rain cloak.

He was gaunt in the face and not very tall. Because he had no moko of any kind, his face as bare as a Pakeha's, he looked much younger than I was, even though only a few years separated us. He was related, as I recall, to that foolish woman Tere Pakia, and also to Wharepapa, and also to the tall brothers Horomona Te Atua and Wiremu Pou. He lived in Ohaeawai, in the far North, but you could never speak of the great battle of that name with him. He was off with the missionaries, learning to be pious, when Kawiti was outwitting the British there. Reihana's father was the chief Tu Karawa, who fought alongside Hongi and died in bloody combat on the beach at Moremonui in 1807, when Reihana was just a baby.

But Reihana wasn't raised to fight, as I was. He never fought a day in his life, not even when Hongi gathered us all to avenge those deaths at Moremonui. Perhaps that's why the fight had festered inside smooth-cheeked Reihana all those years, and made him a warrior for God.

So there we were, a group of strangers and relatives, old foes and old allies, stuck for a hundred nights in a room without light or air. Not a deck house, but below deck in steerage, down where they kept the bales of wool, kauri gum, and sperm oil. I, Paratene Te Manu, had my own bed, because I was the oldest person in the group. Above me slept Reihana and Wharepapa. The two married couples had a bed each. As I said, the brothers had to share, with their long legs dangling, and young Hapimana and old Kihirini shared as well. Takarei slept clinging to his precious box, as if he were afraid the Northerners would ransack it in the night. The two unmarried women, Ngahuia and Haumu, shared a bed beyond the door.

Because of the table and forms in the middle of the room, and all our boxes about the place, we could barely move, and not all of us could sit down to eat at the same time. At first the forms were fixed to the floor, but soon we broke them up, so we could move them about. I'm accustomed to a small house, but I was not accustomed to huddling close to so many others, and to eating and sleeping in the same tiny room.

This I did not like at all. I had to cook my own food and wash my own dishes, and I had to eat in the room where I slept. This was something I had never done in my life. In fact, I had never, in my entire life, thought of such a thing as cooking for myself.

I'm pleased to say that once I returned to New Zealand, I never cooked or cleaned a dish for myself ever again. But on this voyage I often thought of our old saying: he kuri, he tangata haere. I was a traveller now, and therefore like a dog. I would not be accorded the respect I would command at home.

Down in our dark room the women washed themselves, and we men washed up on deck. There was not supposed to be washing of any kind below deck, we learned – only our hands, at a communal pump. This rule the women ignored. We couldn't live amid our own slop, like animals. We were also not supposed to walk about the poop deck. We were told that this was for ladies and gentlemen only.

'We are ladies and gentlemen,' Wharepapa told Jenkins.

'I mean the ladies and gentlemen who sleep in the cabins,' Jenkins explained. In other words, people like him. But who was Jenkins? He wasn't even an ordained minister. He was just an ordinary Pakeha, a follower of Wesley, from Nelson. He wasn't a rangatira, or an important missionary like Mr Williams, who didn't care much for Wesleyans.

So we insisted on walking as often as the weather permitted on the poop deck. If people complained, we decided, we would pretend not to understand. But nobody scolded or frowned at us, and often they were smiling, talking away in English. I didn't know what they were saying. Unlike Wharepapa, who practised his talking every day, I didn't want to know English. This was stupid of me. It meant I had to rely on Jenkins, and his associates young Mr Lightband, who spoke quite good Maori, and Mr Brent and Mr Lloyd, who were too old to learn new things, and spoke only a little.

A hundred or so soldiers were on board, a few with their wives and children. They were very happy to be going back to

England, even though they too were sleeping below the deck. The children often visited us when they were bored playing in their own quarters. These quarters were separated from ours by a thin wall, and we could hear the rattle of their cups and plates when they sat at table, and the way they coughed or retched in the night. No doubt they could hear poor Hariata Pomare vomiting when the ship lurched and rolled through a storm, not to mention all the carrying-on from Haumu.

Sometimes the soldiers themselves would visit with us, crowding into our small, stuffy room and perching on our boxes. One of them would play the fiddle for us, to drown out the creaking of the ship, and they would bring us gifts of sugar, or delicious raspberry vinegar. The sugar we were supposed to get, to take with our tea and coffee, ran out before we rounded the Cape.

Their sergeant spoke to our steward, a dense lad, about getting us some beer, because we were thirsty all the time – too much salt pork and salt beef. But one thing they couldn't get us was fresh meat. Even though we'd seen live fowls and pigs and even sheep on board, we were not permitted to buy any, let alone cook and eat them. The fresh meat was only for the Pakeha sleeping in the cabins.

We were given hard biscuits riddled with worms for two entire weeks, and when we sent them away with the steward, he brought them back again and said there was nothing else. There was other food, a certain allowance per person – the salt meat, preserved tripe, potatoes, pickles. Nothing fresh at all, and the amounts every day quite small, so we needed the biscuits. Reihana was feeling sick a lot of the time, because of the endless sway of the boat, and biscuits were all he wanted to eat. He would have been hopeless travelling with a taua.

After we sent the steward away for a second time, I leaned towards Reihana. It was wrong to tease him, I know, but I couldn't resist.

'If we complain too much about this, Jenkins will hear,' I whispered to him. 'And then he'll be very angry with us, and have us cast into the water.'

'Can he do that?' Reihana looked even more stricken than usual.

'Yes,' I said. 'Why do you think there are so many soldiers on this ship? They're here to keep an eye on us, in case we decide to cause trouble like the Maori in Taranaki. They have orders to end any rebellion by throwing us into the waves. No one at home will know the truth. They'll just be told that we died at sea from some illness, or were washed away in a storm.'

'I knew it,' said Reihana. He smacked a hand down on the table, and raised his voice so everyone could hear. 'Nothing good will come of this trip. We are led into godlessness, by a godless man.'

'I'm led into hunger,' said Hapimana. 'By a wormy biscuit.'

After that everyone was laughing and not listening to Reihana any more, so he went and sat on a box, his head in his hands. I felt guilty, of course. That was the thing about Reihana. It was difficult to feel inspired by his Christian example, even though he was right most of the time.

The only things cast into the sea, by the way, were the biscuits. The soldiers told us to throw them away, and they would find us good biscuits we could eat. Jenkins was no help at all with this, just as he was no help when we ran out of sugar for our tea. He was up in his fine cabin eating roast beef and fresh eggs, saying his prayers in English with the other Pakeha. Not once did Jenkins come down to read the Bible with us, or say prayers.

Not once! I led the group in this every day. I had my Book of Common Prayer, with the prayers written out in Maori, the copy I've carried for years. I may not have been a Christian as long as Reihana, but a true rangatira can be both a warrior and a priest, as Hongi showed us, though he was not for a moment interested in the religion of the missionaries.

On days when the weather was fine, Jenkins would ask us to stand up on deck and practise some waiata and haka, which he thought the English might like to hear. He called these our 'special Maori songs and dances'. In other words, everything the missionaries had made us promise never to perform again.

These things don't mean much to the younger ones. They were happy to be out in the fresh air, and they liked the attention they got whenever they were singing or chanting. Some of the soldiers and their wives, and the ladies and gentlemen who had their own cabins, they would gather to listen. These people especially liked the haka I would call a ngeri, where everyone is doing whatever they feel like doing, and is a good opportunity for show-offs like Hapimana and Wiremu Pou to strike a pose and play a part.

I didn't take part in any of this. I didn't hold with all this practising of what Jenkins called 'the war dance' and 'the welcome dance'. Didn't the missionaries compel us to choose the treasures of the Gospel over the rituals of the past? Didn't we renounce the old customs when we were baptised and took on our new names?

In any case, there was no point to all this performance simply for the sake of applause from foreign ladies. A true peruperu is performed with weapons, facing down an enemy, with warriors naked apart from their woven tatua wrapped about the midriff, with weapons tucked into it. The rage we express in a peruperu is the wind that helps us leap high in the air; the fury we muster sustains us through the fight. When we summon up this rage, we're calling on Tumatauenga, the god of war, to drive us forward into battle and keep our anger burning like a ferocious fire. I don't think the young ones, like Wiremu Pou or Hapimana, had any true understanding of this. Neither did anyone watching. On the deck of the ship, all we could expect was polite murmurs from onlookers, and Jenkins frowning down at the book Charley Davis had given him, asking us why we all didn't know the 'right' words.

So I said I wouldn't leap about on deck for no reason, and Jenkins appeared to accept that. In England I could talk to the people of the old customs, and recite some of the old incantations, he told me. I made no objection to this, because I didn't want to argue with him the way Reihana did. But really, if I were to do as Jenkins asked, the English would be fainting with shock, and none of them would ever have the courage to take up farming or shop-keeping in New Zealand.

The singing up in the deck house outraged our righteous friend Reihana. He not only refused to take part, he tried to stop them altogether.

'I have never done such things in all my life,' he told Jenkins. 'These are old heathen ways. This is wickedness you're asking of us, wickedness! Brothers and sisters, I beg you. Don't practise these wrong things.'

No one paid any attention to Reihana, because they were too busy practising pukana, seeing who could make the whites of their eyes the largest and most impressive. I have to admit, that sly Hirini Pakia wasn't bad at all. He no doubt practised by gazing in the looking glass.

Jenkins was losing patience with Reihana.

'How else are we to make back the money invested in this venture?' he demanded. They were standing outside the deck house, and Jenkins' grey hair was flapping in the breeze. He was a tall man with a long nose. The young ones called him Toko Tikena, Pole Jenkins. 'Do you have any idea of how much it costs to transport you all across the sea, to feed you, and find you lodgings once we arrive? How are we to take you to the great factories and dockyards and cathedrals of England, without any money in our pockets? How am I to house and clothe you? You've already received a considerable sum. You know I have risked my all to bring you on this great trip.'

I was standing nearby when all this was going on, sharing some of my tobacco with the soldiers who were walking on the deck. These were the best times on board the ship, when I could watch it slicing through the water, and fill my lungs with fresh air. The sails of this cutter were vast, and we were speeding along, flying so fast that it seemed we would cross all the oceans in no time.

At the time I didn't understand what Jenkins was talking about. How was there a connection between singing a lament for a dead tupuna and Jenkins shouting about the cost of things? A waiata doesn't spirit coins out of the air.

As for this considerable sum we'd all received, I suppose he meant the eight pounds Charley Davis had handed over to each of us. From that we had to buy all our own clothes for the trip. In Auckland I'd bought some shirts, and trousers, and two coats, and a blanket. I should have bought sheets, for there were none for us on board the ship, and a pair of trousers had to serve as my pillow. Jenkins and his associates had bought us all mattresses, but no other bedding. I had given some of the money to my sister, because I was sure I'd be given more, as soon as we reached England.

Two coats may seem excessive, but I remember what Hongi said about his journey to England in 1820. He and Waikato arrived in the summertime, and he said it was nothing at all like our summertime. They had to get greatcoats and flannel caps. The sky was grey, and they were miserable every day. The stones of the street were too cold for their feet, and Mr Kendall, the missionary with them, had to find them boots so they could walk about. As their feet were too big for most English boots, this took some time. Hongi was very ill while he was there, and for a time was afraid that he wouldn't survive the journey home.

Jenkins had also asked us to bring cloaks with us, our Maori cloaks. Mats, the Pakeha called them. We would need to wear these cloaks when we spoke at churches and schools, Jenkins said, because no one in England would pay to see us wearing our usual coats and trousers. Takarei had three in that box of his. I knew this for a fact, because Horomona and his brother Wiremu Pou went through it one day when Takarei was up on the deck.

It's strange, I think, that the clothes of our ancestors were so desirable to the Pakeha – so desirable that Jenkins went red in the face when he discovered that there were no cloaks of any kind in Reihana's box – but the things our ancestors believed were utterly contemptible to them.

On his first night on board the ship, Reihana had a pre-monition while he lay sleeping. He lay on his back, his hand on his chest, whimpering and twitching like a dog. We could all hear him, but no one thought much of it until the next morning, not even Wharepapa who had to put up with sharing his berth.

'Brothers,' Reihana said to us in the morning, when we were chewing on the foul biscuits, the tea sloshing from our mugs.

'Brothers, listen to me.'

'Brothers and *sisters*,' said Tere Pakia, who had no patience for Reihana even then, when we were still somewhere in the Pacific. 'Aren't we good enough to hear your story?'

'It's not a story.' Reihana was glum. 'I dreamed of something last night, and it was a sign. A very bad sign.'

'It would be,' Tere muttered. She walked away, staggering because of the rocking of the ship. I thought she was going to tend to Haumu, who was crying in the small room, but she stood with her back to the door, listening.

'Last night,' Reihana said, 'I knew that I would have a premonition, and discover the meaning of this voyage. I lay down with my left hand in a certain position on my chest. This is how I always sleep.'

'He does,' confirmed Wharepapa.

'So I lay there with my eyes closed. My body was asleep, but my heart was awake. It was waiting for a sign.'

He paused to slurp his tea.

'And?' Horomona Te Atua demanded. The faces around our table were serious. Even Horomona's brother, the cocky Wiremu Pou, was listening. We all wanted to hear the end of Reihana's premonition.

'I dreamed that my left hand was twitching,' said Reihana. 'I couldn't move it away from my chest, or stop it from jerking and shaking. I was very afraid. You know what this means. Some harm will come to us.'

'These biscuits will kill us,' said Hapimana, trying to make a joke as usual, but it was half-hearted and no one laughed.

'This expedition of ours will come to no good end,' Reihana said. 'Something disastrous will happen. Death will part us. Perhaps the ship will be wrecked.'

He took a bite of his biscuit and sat chewing it, his face foggy with sadness. I did the same, then spat my mouthful onto the table. Perhaps Hapimana was right. We couldn't survive weeks of those biscuits.

It's true that times are changing, but as all the talk this week about the spirit waka attests, we still take signs, and dreams like Reihana's, very seriously. We know that they carry warnings. So we were sombre that morning, though the sea was calmer now and the day was quite fair.

That afternoon most of us went for a walk about the deck, and I stood watching the great sails billow, the westerly winds pushing us through the ocean. Jenkins was up on the deck with Mr Brent or perhaps Mr Lloyd – men we saw little of at this time, but would come to know more in London. Jenkins made the mistake, while Reihana was still in earshot, of requesting another practice. He should have waited until Reihana had returned below, as he was about to do. But no, the words were said, and then Reihana had to respond with words of his own, telling Jenkins about his dream, and the omen of the twitching hand.

'Stop saying such things at once,' Jenkins said, his voice curt. This was not the way he spoke to any of us in Auckland, I must say, when Charley Davis was present. 'I can assure you that you're in very capable hands. Captain Reynolds will see to it that the ship is *not* wrecked. The only evil to befall you will be this kind of talk, this primitive superstition. Once we're in England, you'll find that no one has sympathy with this sort of heathen belief. Civilised people don't believe in prophesies.'

When he heard this, Reihana was furious. Perhaps I'm making him seem like a man who talked a lot, and this was not the case. He was quiet most of the time, brooding over his son's death and – after this day – about the message of his dream. But he would object to the singing and so forth, and now there was something else in the air between him and Jenkins. Reihana did not like to be called a heathen, or to hear the ways and beliefs of his ancestors, of his father, Tu Karawa, dismissed by such a man as Jenkins. Tu Karawa was a great rangatira, and was not to be insulted in this way. In the old days, such an insult would provide what we called a *take*, and this would need to be resolved in some way. Words had consequences.

But these things could not be resolved on the ship. Jenkins could say whatever he wished and then walk away.

'You shall see,' Reihana said, half to himself. Jenkins couldn't hear him, certainly. 'We shall come to grief.'

The ship was not wrecked on that voyage, of course, because here I am now, more than twenty years later. But Reihana's vision was right. Many things were to part us, including death. Already our little party was starting to simmer and seethe, one complaining about the other.

That night, the murmur of sound from behind the door separating the quarters of Ngahuia and Haumu from our own grew into something else, something almost inhuman. At first, in fact, it sounded like the lowing of a cow, but soon it was clear to me that the noise was a terrible moan, interrupted now and then by a fervent, rapid muttering. This was Haumu, taking leave of her senses.

The muttering didn't stop, day or night, but darkness made her condition worse. Ngahuia tried her best, cradling Haumu, or singing softly to her, trying to calm her when she banged and kicked at the door, screaming to be free. The poor woman seemed to think she was in a prison cell. If there was still daylight outside, Hapimana would lead her up the ladder, to show her that we were all staying below by choice, not because we were shackled or under arrest, even if this was the way it sometimes felt.

But this accomplished very little, and talking to her became increasingly fruitless. Sometimes she would sit quietly, holding Ngahuia's hand, rocking back and forth on the bench. These were exceptional times, however. As well as muttering and sobbing, there were hysterical shrieks, as though she'd seen a terrible vision. One night, I looked through my book for something to say over her, a prayer for someone of troubled mind. E Ihowa, ko koe te Matua o nga mahi tohu, te Atua hoki o nga whakamarietanga katoa . . .

Her screams drowned my voice, and she wriggled free of Ngahuia's grip. The door was the object of her greatest rages, and that night she progressed from pounding and kicking it to battering it with one of the benches. The benches were nailed down when we first boarded, and we'd taken the fastenings up so we could make more room between our berths. We didn't foresee Haumu suddenly gaining the strength of three men, and using a bench as a battering ram. This happened on more than one occasion, and we had to learn to be vigilant.

On one strange day, she managed to get hold of an axe from the soldiers' quarters, notching ragged scars into the door and slicing off its handle before she could be disarmed. That was the end of that door. The crew refused to hang it again, or mend the handle. It was taken away entirely, which meant there were no barriers between us and the moaning, crying and incoherent mumbling that rose and fell with the waves each night. We prayed over Haumu daily, but nothing would take away her terror.

'This is the beginning,' I heard Reihana say to Wharepapa

one night, as they prepared to sleep. 'This was the message of my dream. Nothing good can come of this voyage into the darkness.'

Not once, by the way, did Jenkins come down to inspect the damage, or to counsel Haumu, though the soldiers' wives whispered to us that her mania was the talk of the ship. Hirini Pakia reported that some of the men were placing bets about her jumping overboard or murdering Ngahuia with the axe, but I think he invented this story to get attention. For all her madness, Haumu was more trustworthy than either Pakia or his wife. She was pathetic in her misery and confusion, not conniving.

Haumu was Anglican, as I am, but there was something about this fear that none of our Christian prayers could touch. I've seen this kind of thing before, years ago, when someone violated tapu and was punished in some way – wasting away, or terrorised by sights and sounds only he could experience. I've seen a man lying shivering by a fire pit, unable to walk or speak when only the day before he could stride up any hill.

The missionaries told us that the soul was immortal and this was something that we too believed. But in the English religion, all these souls were corralled into heaven or hell, like the cabins and steerage on a ship, without any means of escape. We knew that a spirit could transform into a malignant force which must be respected and appeased. I couldn't help but think that Haumu had offended the spirit of one of her ancestors, perhaps, and that there was nothing any of us could do to change her situation.

During the day, the younger ones tried to distract her from her miseries. We all wrapped up in our coats and blankets to peer through the fog at the ice mountains of the Drake Passage and then, after the weather cleared, the green prow of Cape Horn. This was the tip of the continent of South America. Now there was a new ocean to navigate, the Atlantic, where storms blew us towards Africa and then back towards the coast of Brazil, where the days simmered with heat. As we crossed the invisible line into the northern part of the world, it felt as though the whole ship was cooking in an oven.

For many days the wind deserted us, and we bobbed in the ocean, sails limp. The women in our party had wondered if Haumu's fear of the storms was causing her misery, but these long days of stillness did nothing to help her. None of us could sleep in the damp heat, so we knew all too well that her moanings and mutterings continued every night.

At times I thought we would never arrive in England, or perhaps that England didn't exist. I began to wonder if the place Hongi had spoken of was a dream he'd had, a warning to us that I'd misinterpreted. Week after week passed, and although we'd travelled so much further than our ancestors, those greatest of voyagers, we were still waiting to arrive.

'Perhaps you will wear this pompom cloak?' the Bohemian says. Like the English, he wants to see us Maori in a cloak, not a coat. He drapes a ngore around me, and it's soft against my skin. I don't mind wearing this, as he requests. I can't see any peacock feathers lying around the studio, waiting to fly into my hair.

The Bohemian is named Mr Lindauer, and he wants to know what I should be called. Do I prefer Paratene or Te Manu? This question takes me some time to answer, because I never really think about this. Te Manu is the name I was given at birth, and Paratene is the one suggested by the minister, Mr Williams, all those years ago. I think it was 1838, or perhaps 1839, when I finally agreed to be baptised.

As I've said, Paratene is our word for Broughton. Bishop Broughton had just visited from Australia, and he was a man of great importance, so I was happy to take his name. Tane, of course, had more than one name, though you couldn't speak of such things with our missionaries. They were always vexed by any mention of Maori gods. We used to joke that the only people they liked less than Maori gods were Catholic priests.

I try to explain about my Christian name, and the Bohemian grins. He was born with another name as well. Now, he says, he calls himself Gottfried.

'When I was a child my name was Bohumír,' he says. He tells me about walking to Vienna when he was a young man. Vienna is an enormous city, like London, and it took him six days to walk there from his father's house. 'I go to study to paint, at the Academy. In Vienna everyone speaks German. My teachers. The students. The people who will pay me to paint their pictures. So I change my name to a German one, Gottfried.'

These two names of his mean the same thing, I discover. The greatness of God, the peace of God. I wouldn't mind having a name that meant the greatness of God. Instead I'm named for a bishop who's been dead for a long time. Soon no one will have heard of him, and it will be so much for the name of Paratene Te Manu.

'Please, will you look here?' the Bohemian asks me, and I oblige him by fixing my gaze on a picture on the wall, fastened just behind his head. From this distance, the picture is blurry. However long I stare at it, I can't make it out. This doesn't matter. The important thing is sitting here, looking straight ahead. In this painting I will not crouch on the edge of things, or avert my eyes. People will look at it, and see my moko, and know who I am.

Be not forgetful to entertain strangers: for thereby some have entertained angels unawares.

HEBREWS 13:2

W e arrived in England but we were not yet in London. We were told to wait on the ship sitting in the port of Gravesend, in the care of Mr Brent, while Jenkins went ahead to find us lodgings. Jenkins had already bought us more provisions, and we were very happy to eat fresh meat again, and to pour fresh milk into our tea.

While Jenkins was away, we spent much of our time on deck, watching the lowering of barrels and livestock onto the dock, and longing to be away from our cramped berths. It was here, with the seagulls swooping above us, that we were introduced to our first English visitor, though he was a person who had spent many years in New Zealand. This was the Reverend James Stack, or Te Taka, as we called him, beaming a great smile and shouting greetings to us in Maori as he clambered up the plank. Te Taka was my age, and knew Northland and the Nga Puhi well, for as a young man he had lived in the Hokianga, and in Whangaroa when the area was under attack by Hongi.

He asked us many questions about this trip to England, and our purpose in coming here, and frowned when Reihana talked of all the practising of waiata and haka.

'We are told we must learn the heathen songs for the English,' Reihana complained. 'We are to walk the streets dressed in heathen cloaks.'

'My friends,' said Te Taka, his face solemn, 'I beg you not to do this. As Christians you will be welcomed to this country, and embraced by its people. As heathens you will be gazed upon and laughed at. This is no way for rangatira to go about. I will speak to Brent about this.'

Reihana was very pleased with himself after this conversation, and urged us all, at that very moment, to cast our cloaks into the sea and let the people of England drag them out of the water to use as fishing nets. I knew then that Reihana had done very little fishing in his life, if he thought a dogskin cloak could serve much purpose in the water. None of us did as he said, of course, for we didn't want to anger Jenkins so soon after arriving, and the cloaks we had brought were valuable. My kahu kuri was woven for my father. To wear it was to announce my importance, like the Queen placing a crown on her head and taking up her sceptre.

I don't know if Reverend Stack talked to Mr Brent that day, or if anything came of such a conversation, for the subject of our cloaks was not mentioned again for some time. There were too many other things to concern us, like the trip by steamer into London itself. How to describe such an arrival? We had crossed oceans and seen almost no other ships, but on the river that wends through London every possible vessel might be seen, clustered so thick in the water that you might cross from one shore to the other without once getting your feet wet. Entire fleets were berthed in the great docks and basins, a thick wood of bare masts. We couldn't see the city for the boats sailing in and out, and I imagined the whole of London as one vast dock, with all life lived on the river.

At the docks, the ships dangled men. They hung from ropes, or perched on planks of wood, scrubbing or hammering. Among the forest of masts they were small brown birds, or grubs, perhaps, swarming over the bark. Later, when we walked out at night, I saw men sleeping out on the river, bundled up in small boats or exposed on the lumpy mounds weighing down the hayboats. Some had tied themselves on, for fear of slithering down in their sleep and plopping into the dark water.

We were taken to a place called Limehouse, near the great West India Docks, where the coal barges showered the wharves with their black dust and the air was thick with smoke. On some days, we would discover, the smell was even more pungent, when the foul odours from the tanneries across the river swept in on the wind. This was the area we would stay in London, Jenkins told us, until other arrangements could be made. When we drove to our lodgings, we quickly lost sight of the river, for immense warehouses blocked it from view. These buildings were so tall, and constructed so close together, that the narrow streets below were untouched by the sun.

The warehouses were like great churches with men, not saints, framed in the arches and crevices. In the open mouths that gaped on every storey, men reached into the air for the bales swinging from hook and chain, or they sat, legs hanging, looking down out onto the cobbles below, or at the grey wash of river before them.

The house where we would sleep was not far from the river, on a street unusually wide, as I would soon find out, for this part of the city. The building was large, with many arched windows and smoking chimneys, and that day we all thought it imposing and highly respectable. It made the Native Hostel in Auckland look pathetically ramshackle, like a shelter built for boats rather than men.

This building was the work of the Church Missionary Society, we were told, and a Maharajah of India, and was a favoured project of the late Prince Albert. Because it was a new building, its bricks were not yet entirely black with soot, like so many of the other houses we saw. The name of this place, Jenkins told us, was the Strangers' Home for Asiatics, Africans and South Sea Islanders.

But when we stepped inside its wide hall, and saw the other inhabitants sitting about on benches, playing cards or talking with each other in strange tongues, Hapimana gave it a new name. This place was Te Whare Mangumangu, the House of Negroes. There we were to meet many Lascar sailors, waiting for another job on a ship, and also Arabians and Persians and Africans, and men from the many islands of the Caribbean. Very few of us could speak to each other, for they did not know any Maori and some did not know any English, but it was a friendly sort of place, and only Takarei worried that things would be taken from his box. A sign hanging in the hall said 'Glory to God' in ten different languages which, according to Mr Lightband, included Russian, Chinese, Hindee and Portuguese.

We were to stay in some grander places in England, but when we arrived in London this was the finest house any of us had ever seen. It was possible to have baths in this place, and to wash our clothes. Hot-water pipes warmed all the dormitories. The lavatories were indoors, and at first we were all unsure about this. Mr Lightband conferred with Colonel Hughes, who was in charge of the place, and assured us that the Queen herself had an indoor lavatory. She wished that all her subjects could enjoy such clean and convenient bathing facilities.

'Not clean,' said Kihirini gruffly. We were all surprised that he knew any English words, and also surprised to hear him speak. He'd said so little to any of us on the voyage over. All he ever did was tell Hapimana, who shared his bed, to stop talking.

The alternative, Mr Lightband explained, was to use one of the outside lavatories in a nearby yard, but these were shared by the hundreds of people who lived in the tall houses surrounding each yard. The yards and alleyways of Limehouse were not safe places, he said, and they were certainly not clean. There were many dangerous people, and dangerous diseases, lying in wait for us Maori.

In Limehouse I saw some people – men, women, children – simply crouching in the street, like dogs. Perhaps they too had been warned against seeking out the lavatories in the yards.

Mr Lightband was relieved we were staying at the Strangers' Home, for he was the keeper of the company purse, and he said the cost for each of us, for board and lodgings for a week, was just eight shillings. This seemed a great deal of money to me at the time, but I knew that London would be much more expensive than Auckland, and we were yet to spend our days worrying where these shillings were to be found.

Reihana pronounced the Strangers' Home to be low-class, for some people there could not afford lodgings of any kind, and were only kept there by Christian charity until they could be returned to their native land, or by earning pennies sweeping the streets. He also complained that the beds were filled with people who were not Christians, but worshipped other gods. I told him I liked the chatter of different tongues, for it reminded me of Babel, where the Lord stepped in to confound the language spoken there, so that we might all speak with different words and scatter ourselves across the earth. If He hadn't done this, how would our ancestors have found New Zealand? Where would we Maori live now – in the hot desert of the Holy Land?

Colonel Hughes, a kind and Christian man, insisted that the doctor inoculate us all against the smallpox, for it was raging in Limehouse, he said, and throughout the East End. I was to grow far too accustomed to the sight of sufferers of this painful and disfiguring disease. They were everywhere in the streets of London, their faces blotched with red sores, or pitted as though stabbed with a small knife. Some were blind, able only to beg in the street, and many looked as though they longed for death. There was no smallpox at the Strangers' Home, the Colonel told us, and no cholera, either, or Irish fever. We would be quite safe there, as long as we took care wandering the alleys, yards and courts of Limehouse after dark.

'I am not afraid of the English,' Wiremu Pou said, but he never went out without his brother, and once I saw him slip a patu into his coat pocket to use, I assume, if ruffians attacked him.

I must admit that I was a little overwhelmed, if not exactly afraid, for I had never seen so many white faces in one place, and these faces were much whiter than those of the Pakeha in New Zealand. Some looked like ghouls, staring at us wherever we went, their eyes pale in their wan, half-dead faces. Young Hariata Pomare did not like walking outside the Strangers' Home at all, and whispered that we should not stay in that neighbourhood too long. There were too many Pakeha here, and what if they decided to surround us and kill us? Reihana told her that they would surely kill the godless Lascars first, and Wharepapa assured her that the warriors among us would fight to the death, and see off any number of the pasty English, but she was not comforted.

At first I did not wander much alone, not even during the day, but I could not help but be drawn to the river. One morning I awoke early, and found young Hare Pomare downstairs, smoking on the front steps. Hariata had been awake half the night with sickness, he said. She was sleeping at last, but he was wide awake and restless.

We walked down to the shore, following the smell of the river more than anything, for it was impossible to see until we were nearly upon it. Though it was not long after dawn, many people were out in the streets already – fish merchants pushing their carts and apple vendors filling their baskets, girls sorting bunches of lavender or piling their trays with oranges, men trudging towards the warehouses or the ships. Many people lay asleep in the streets, leaning against walls, slumped in doorways, and on the very stones of the narrow alleys. Whole families, in some cases, lay collapsed in a heap, a baby crying with hunger while its mother and brothers still slept. Many of them were so filthy they looked as though they had rolled in ashes and dust.

We reached a rickety wharf, where steps led down to the river itself. It was low tide, and the muddy shore was dotted with figures, burrowing in the mud. Most of these people were children, bare-legged and already filthy, but some were old women, older than I was. Often I've bent over to scoop pipi from the damp sand, but I've never had to scavenge for rubbish, like the old women I saw down by the river that day. One was so feeble, she toppled over into the mud, overwhelmed by the wash of waves from a passing boat.

'What do they look for?' Hare asked me, for we could see they weren't digging up shellfish. At first I thought that the children were helping the kuia, or were somehow under their supervision. But the more I watched, the more I realised that the children were in competition with these old women for the bent nails and pebbles of coal that could be pulled from the riverbed. The children were more bold and more agile, unafraid of getting their rags soaked through, even early in the morning, before the sun had warmed the water.

When we next saw Reverend Stack, I told him about this sight, and he said the people we saw were called mudlarks. They made their living from things pulled out of the river, like pieces of wood or rope, or lumps of coal. Sometimes these were stolen from the boats moored nearby. At the most, he thought, these mudlarks could earn a few pennies a day from the things they found and sold, and in the winter they made a desperate sight, standing shivering in the icy water for hours without shoes or a coat.

This was new to us, like so much in London, and surprising to us as well, for London was a wealthy city, the centre of a great empire. It was one thing to run about with no shoes on in Tutukaka, where it was warm for much of the year and shoes would be an encumbrance, but this was a dirty place and a cold place, even now in the summertime. This was something, I suppose, we had not expected to see in England. Perhaps this was part of the education Jenkins wished for us, or perhaps, as he was English himself, it was unremarkable to him, like the billowing clouds of smoke that hid the sky.

As well as Reverend Stack, we were visited by someone else who spoke Maori. This was Mrs Elizabeth Colenso, a lady whose name was known to us all, and who we would grow to like and respect very much. At this time she was in her middle years, neat in her appearance and firm in her manner, with two grown-up children who had accompanied her to England two years earlier. She had dark hair, which she wore in the style of the Queen, and took out small spectacles whenever she had to read.

Of course, we knew the stories about Mrs Colenso and about her husband, for these stories travel about, and there's little we Maori enjoy more than talking and writing each other letters. The missionaries used to think that we all crowded into their schools to hear the word of God, when really everyone wanted to learn how to read and write the alphabet, so they could talk to their friends in distant places.

The Reverend Colenso, her husband, was known to us as the printer of many Maori books, including the Book of Common Prayer and much of the Bible. Some years before our visit to England he was dismissed by the Church Missionary Society, and left by his wife, after it was discovered that he had another wife, a Maori girl, and that together they had produced a child.

This kind of thing went on all the time in the old days, up in the Bay of Islands. Not with missionaries so much, but with Pakeha men who had a wife here of one race, and a wife there of another, and children of various descriptions running all about the place. We Maori often had more than one wife, so we would laugh at the fuss the missionaries made about such things. But, of course, these were the old days, when much was wrong. Now that we live in modern times, and hold to Christian ways, we must only have one wife at a time, even if we don't like her much.

In London Mrs Colenso was engaged in work on a new Maori Bible, one that would be complete for the first time. She was checking it, line by line, to make sure of each Maori word for, as she told us, she believed she spoke better Maori than English. Unlike Reverend Stack, she was born in New Zealand, and grew up on a mission far from any other Pakeha. She promised to take an interest in our affairs in London, and told us to summon her whenever we needed her. In London, we would not need to light a fire or wait for a passing boat. We could drop a letter in the post box and it would be with her within an hour or two, for the post boxes were emptied eight times a day!

The next time Reverend Stack returned to the Strangers' Home, the only person he wanted to see was Haumu, the woman who had lost – and not yet recovered – her senses. He and Jenkins had agreed that she must be sent away to live at a place called the Grove Hall Lunatic Asylum. This was not far from Limehouse, I believe, but was in a place named Bow. We would not be permitted to visit her there, however, for poor Haumu needed complete rest. Mr Lloyd asked why she could not rest at the Strangers' Home, where the cost was only eight shillings each week, instead of at Grove Hall, where the sum was much higher, but Te Taka, in his booming voice, declared that she must go and Mr Lloyd dared not quarrel with him.

Ngahuia wept saying goodbye to her, in part because Haumu seemed to have no idea that she was being taken from us. We stood on the steps of the Strangers' Home to farewell her, but she sat in her cab next to Jenkins, entirely oblivious. Mrs Colenso had given her a new workbag, and she was preoccupied with rifling through it, pulling out all the coloured silks and holding them up to the light.

I wish I could say that this was the only time someone left our party while we were in England, but Haumu's departure was merely the first. I won't talk of such unpleasant things now. In those early days in London, we were all excited. Jenkins bustled around making plans for us, and soliciting invitations. We were in London just a day or two, as I recall, when he took us to a service at St Paul's Cathedral. This was the greatest church in the whole of England, and it was to be our first place of worship in London.

I was pleased that we were going to an Anglican church, because we had been worried on the ship that once we arrived in England Jenkins and his friends would try to turn us all into Wesleyans. Reverend Williams would not be pleased at all if he knew our guide to England was a Wesleyan. The Church Missionary Society looked down on them, for reasons we didn't understand. Perhaps it was that the Wesleyans were against everything, including playing cards and smoking, though it must be said that Jenkins had supplied us with much tobacco for the voyage over.

Outside, the walls of St Paul's were black, but inside the huge columns were as white as whalebones and, in the candlelight, the golden ceilings glittered. We couldn't understand the words of the service, but followed along in our own Maori books, even singing our own Maori words to the hymns. The other people attending the service were much taken with us, clustering around us after the final procession to stare and ask questions of Jenkins. One lad reached up to stroke Wharepapa's face, tracing his fingers in disbelief along the grooves of the moko. Wharepapa said nothing, but the look on his face was so fierce that the boy's mother snatched his hand away, and dragged him off through the crowd.

This is the thing I haven't written of yet, when I speak of our first weeks in London. We were all agog at the many sights of the city, for it was all new to us. But the city was agog at the sight of us, and wherever we went, even if it was just onto the street outside the Strangers' Home, we attracted much attention. Children ran around us, pulling on our coats and leaping up at us like bumptious dogs, and their elders were little better. People wanted to stare at us, and call out to us, and touch us as we passed. Some seemed almost angry with their shouting. Girls giggled and shrieked, and darted to the other side of the road. Those of us with moko attracted the most attention. We grew so accustomed to seeing people turn from us in disgust, or run from us in terror, that I asked Wharepapa if they thought we might have the smallpox.

'We don't have red spots,' he said. 'We have green lips.'

When we left St Paul's that day, a huge crowd followed us along the street – encircled us, I should say, so that every way we turned we saw gawping faces. We walked along the riverside, to look upon the great fish market at Billingsgate, but although I could smell it I could see almost nothing, so numerous and determined were our entourage. We came upon London Bridge, and it was Jenkins' intention that we should cross it, to walk to the other side of the river. The bridge was so thick with people, and horses, and carts, and coaches, that it would be much quicker to cross the river in a wherry.

We had to take care not to be crushed up against the railings, or under rolling wheels. The crowd clustered around us, and we barely needed to move our feet to be carried along. Towering carriages passed, the whips of the drivers tickling the tops of our heads. And the noise of it was an angry storm: policemen's whistles, the whinnying of horses, shouts and jeers and cries, the rumble of barrels rolling off their cart. A dog, riding high on a stack of crates, barked down at us, startling Ngahuia so much she let out a shriek.

Before we were even halfway across the bridge, Jenkins called to us to turn around, for there was no point in trying to venture further. I felt as though I was back in battle again, besieged, pressed on all sides. These scenes were only to grow worse, I must say, once Jenkins insisted we go about wearing our Maori cloaks, with shark teeth hanging from our ears, for this meant people in all directions would know from a distance that we were foreigners, and rush to see the strange sight.

We had started to hear talk among our Pakeha of a Mr Ridgway, with whom Jenkins had met several times at that gentleman's office in Leicester Square. This Mr Ridgway had spent much time in New Zealand, and his job was to persuade the English, especially the ones with money, to move to the province of Auckland. Jenkins returned from his first meeting with Ridgway highly pleased and agitated, for he said Ridgway had many influential friends in London, and meant to write to them to announce our arrival.

One of these friends was no less a personage than the Duke of Newcastle, who was in charge of the Colonial Office. Such names and offices meant little to us at the time, but we were to come to know them very well, and to depend on them for much help, though of course we had no inkling of that yet.

Ridgway, Jenkins warned us, was koroke – that is to say, a little strange in his manner, and maybe his head – so when he visited us at the Strangers' Home, we were very curious to meet him. We stood around one of the long tables in the back room, looking out over the yard where washing hung from the line, spotted with soot. Mr Ridgway walked around the table to greet us, shaking hands with all the men, and kissing the ladies' hands, which pleased them very much.

We all started laughing, for he was a strange kind of man, loud in his voice, with red hair as frizzy as a rata bloom, and a very intent stare. He was hearty and friendly, Mr Ridgway, but there was an intelligence, a wiliness, in his eyes that told us all he was not a buffoon. He also had a certain manner of looking at Jenkins, in particular, which I observed at once, as though Jenkins was the koroke one.

Mr Ridgway was a great friend to New Zealand, he told us, and to the Maori people, and he would do all he could to ensure we received all the attention and respect we were due in England.

'None of these casual exhibitions your friend Mr Jenkins speaks of,' he said, shaking Jenkins by the shoulder in a rough but friendly manner. Jenkins did not look pleased, and neither did Mr Lightband, who was translating for us. 'You must be recognised as ambassadors, yes? Honoured guests of the British people. Don't you fear, I will see to it.'

The morning after this visit, Mrs Colenso called to take Hariata Pomare, Ngahuia and Tere Pakia shopping for fine dresses. These new clothes were the gifts of Mr Ridgway. From that day forward, Ngahuia would not hear a word about Mr Ridgway being koroke.

We liked Mr Ridgway, and we liked the promises he made, but these did not deter Jenkins and his associates from their plans. There were many places to see, Mr Lightband told us, but not enough money in the coffers to take us about, especially if we were to travel beyond London. Before many days had passed, Jenkins told us that we must all dress in our cloaks, and attend our first meeting. This would take place in a religious meeting house, and the people coming there were considering emigration to New Zealand. Jenkins would talk, and we would give a speech or two, and then perform haka and waiata for the audience. This was to be our first public engagement in London and, he said, would bring us much attention.

Wharepapa, I think it was, questioned performing haka in a place of worship.

'This is not right,' he told Jenkins. 'We will sing, perhaps, if it seems to us the right thing to do. Paratene will suggest a hymn.'

I'm afraid I don't remember very much of this first public meeting, or whether we sang a hymn or not. We were to attend so many hundreds of them that often one is the same as the next in my memory. I seem to remember that the audience was small, but very attentive, and I suppose we dressed in cloaks and carried the weapons we'd brought from New Zealand, so we might show them to the English.

I do remember, quite distinctly, that Reihana argued with Jenkins about the wearing of cloaks. He was given a korowai to drape over his usual clothing, and he complained that he had not worn such a garment in many years.

'These things harbour fleas,' he said, offending Mr Brent, who had brought this particular cloak with him from Nelson. It had cost him 'more than a bob or two,' he said, protesting that no fleas had ever been near it.

Reihana agreed, at last, to wear the korowai, but he argued with Jenkins all the way to the meeting place. Hadn't Mr Ridgway told us such 'exhibitions' would not be required? How could Jenkins think of us performing the devil's own haka in a place of worship? Why should we be asked to do anything we did not wish to do?

'Because we all need money!' exclaimed Mr Lloyd, who always grew impatient very quickly. He didn't seem to like London. He always looked worried.

Mr Ridgway was as good as his word, securing us an appointment with the Duke of Newcastle at the Colonial

Office. The meeting was short, but we liked the Duke, with his nest of a beard and bright eyes. Wharepapa spoke for all of us when he asked the Duke if we would be able to meet the Queen. Jenkins translated the words, and told us that the Duke said he would do all he could. Unfortunately, the Queen was still in deep mourning following the death of her husband two years earlier, and she was very little in London.

I think this meeting may have taken place in the Grosvenor Hotel, for by this time Jenkins had told us to pack our boxes at the Strangers' Home. We had lived there for two weeks, and now could undertake the move he had promised, to far superior accommodation in the west of London.

This move was the cause of another argument with Reihana. We climbed out of our cabs, astonished by the hotel's size and grandeur. Inside, marvelling at its vaulted ceiling and marble floors, I wondered if this building had once been a church. We were all quite overawed, I think, for even Ngahuia and Tere Pakia ceased their usual chatter, and we all stood about the lobby rather than sit in one of its many armchairs, for fear that we would be chased away.

Reihana was not so overawed that he could not argue with Jenkins.

'Why have we come to this place?' he demanded. 'What was wrong with our old place, which cost eight shillings? This must cost many more shillings, perhaps even a guinea. It's too grand. We will be brought to ruin.'

I was surprised to hear Reihana say this. He'd complained that the Strangers' Home was beneath us, and now he was complaining that the Grosvenor Hotel was too far above us. It was true, however, that we'd heard much from Mr Lightband about needing to make money, so I too was wondering how

Jenkins and his associates could afford this place.

'Tell that old man to be quiet,' Ngahuia whispered to me. She was wearing her fine dress, of green silk, and she fancied herself quite a lady in an establishment such as this.

'How is this your concern?' Jenkins demanded of Reihana. 'What is it to you if this place is grand? You're not paying for this. We are paying.'

'I'm telling you to be cautious,' said Reihana, standing with his hands on his hips, looking up at Jenkins, who was much taller than he was. 'We're worried that too much money is being spent, and by and by we'll all be brought to ruin.'

'I'm not worried,' Ngahuia said. She glared at Reihana, but he ignored her.

'You don't have to worry about any such things,' Jenkins said, his face red with anger. He hadn't learned to ignore Reihana, the way the rest of us did. 'We have money for your food and your rooms here. Let *us* worry about how *our* money is spent.'

'I don't like to see money thrown away,' Reihana told him. Mr Brent, who had flopped into an armchair, nodded, but I don't think Jenkins noticed. Reihana turned to the rest of us, his back to Jenkins, and spoke in a very mocking tone. 'My friends, great must be the riches of our Pakeha! They have such riches they can keep eighteen of us in London, all living in a grand style, without any fear of running out of money!'

Jenkins started talking before Reihana could say another word, his voice echoing through the hotel lobby.

'If you are to meet the Queen, which I believe you all desire, then first you must be raised to a great height. Do you understand? She will not see you if you are low, like the Lascar sailors wandering the streets of Limehouse. She must see that you're rangatira. After you meet the Queen, we can come down from this great height, and spend less money.'

'Better not climb to such a great height,' Reihana mumbled. He always wished to have the last word. 'Better to keep only a little high, and then we will not waste money, and have to fall very low.'

Young Mr Lightband walked up, jingling numerous keys, and Wharepapa took Reihana by the arm, walking away to another part of the lobby. We were all tired of his warnings. Now I must admit that he was right about many matters, but at the time it seemed as though he lived only to vex and goad Jenkins, and to make us anxious when we wanted to enjoy ourselves.

There was much pleasure to be had in this neighbourhood, which was not so crowded and dark as Limehouse. On many days we went out walking in one of the parks. On fine days, so many gentlemen and ladies were out on their horses, riding nowhere in particular, that the ground looked as gritty and brown as a beach. The ladies wore shiny black hats and their skirts billowed to one side when they cantered. I thought I had seen some ladies ride this way in New Zealand, but I wasn't sure. In London, when you see so much of a thing, it begins to be the natural thing, the right thing. The way this business should be done, rather than the way it is somewhere else.

This hotel was very close to Victoria train station, so we had the great excitement of seeing a train for the first time, and climbing aboard it. Such a racket, and such steam, like a volcano erupting! It rushed towards us, smoking and hissing, and Hariata Pomare had to be pushed trembling up its steps, because she thought it was a demon. When the train took off, rattling along its tracks, we all clung to our seats, for fear of being thrown off. Often in the clipper I thought we were moving fast through the water, but that was nothing like a train.

That must have been the day we went to see the Crystal Palace, which was high on a hill to the south of London. This house of glass made St Paul's look small, and we spent many hours there looking at its fountains and statues, and observing noisy machines that could spin cotton.

'Such wonders!' Tere Pakia kept saying, though she told Jenkins that she found the naked statues shockingly indecent. Hapimana and Takarei agreed with her, though I observed they could not remove their eyes from a marble trio of women called the Three Graces. These Maori had short memories, I thought, but then I wondered if they were simply too young to remember our own ways, before the missionaries made us cover ourselves with cloth.

We met no princes or dukes at the Crystal Palace, which seemed to disappoint Jenkins, but we did hear one young lady sing the song of the Queen of the Night. Her name was Carlotta Patti, a name and a voice that I remember all these years later as though we heard her song yesterday in one of the theatres of Auckland. Her skin was as creamy as those of the Three Graces, and her bosom, if I may be a little vulgar, was like the prow of a ship. Sadly, she walked with a pronounced limp, and Wiremu Pou, that chancer, asked Jenkins if he should carry her from the stage. Jenkins told him that this would alarm the lady, and he would be sure to be arrested.

None of us, I can truly say, had heard anything like this lady's voice, unless it was in the trees of New Zealand, in the early morning when the birds awaken. When she finished singing, we clapped and shouted, and Wiremu Pou thumped his taiaha on the ground to make even more noise. He carried it with him everywhere in the streets of London, to draw attention to himself and, perhaps, to spite Reihana.

Wharepapa could not contain himself.

'Come back!' he shouted to the lady, forgetting that she was Italian and could not understand any Maori. 'Come back, lady! Yours is no human voice! You have the voice of a bird!'

Perhaps someone explained Wharepapa's words to her, because this Carlotta Patti limped back onto stage, smiling and bowing, and sang something called the Laughing Song. This we all liked very much as well. Wharepapa was so smitten with her, I wondered if he intended to make her his next wife. On the ship, he had talked a great deal about his loneliness. Indeed.

It's late now, and I'm getting tired. There is so much to tell of London, which is like many cities stitched together, containing great multitudes, like Babylon. Perhaps there is just one more day I should mention now, for it was a remarkable day for all of us — especially, I think, for Jenkins.

A statue had been erected in honour of the late Prince Consort, and this was to be unveiled at the Royal Horticultural Gardens in South Kensington. We could walk there from our hotel, and so we did, all sweltering in our cloaks, for the day was warm. Tere Pakia, who could be very simple, was very anxious that the statue not resemble any that we saw at the Crystal Palace. Wiremu Pou and his brother, Horomona Te Atua, couldn't resist teasing her.

'The Queen herself wished him to be carved in stone, entirely naked,' Wiremu told her. 'He had a moko on his buttocks, just like Paratene.'

'No!' Tere's eyes were wide as saucers.

'She would like her subjects to see him as she alone did when he was alive,' said Horomona, 'without a stitch of clothing.'

'It's indecent!' squeaked Tere, who looked as though she were about to cry. 'I won't look on it! I'll cover my eyes!'

Then both brothers fell about laughing, so their game was up, and Tere smacked at them with her bag.

Of any day we spent in London, this day witnessed the greatest crush of people. London Bridge would have collapsed under the weight of everyone there to see this monument unveiled.

'There must be thousands of people here,' Jenkins told us, leading us with some difficulty towards a place arranged in advance with the Duke of Newcastle. As usual, it was hard to move at all for all the people gathering to stare at us.

After this day was over, I heard Jenkins gushing to Mrs Colenso that all eyes had been on us, and that everyone was delighted with our presence.

'The best people in London were there,' he said. They spoke in Maori, for she always insisted on it if any of us were in the same room. 'We were singled out for attention, all most flattering. Everyone wished to meet us. We are important people here in London now.'

I said nothing, for the day had turned out well. But when we first arrived, I did not see many smiles. Many of the fine ladies and gentlemen looked at us with cool eyes, turning away lest we thought they stared. No one wished to meet us. One lady snapped open her fan, as though to hide her own face. Some gentlemen, I thought, looked quite hostile, especially when we reached a seated area near the platform, and I wondered if they would push us away. We were not important people. We were strangers with green lips.

All this changed after the procession of great people had passed by, and the Duke of Newcastle stepped forward to bid us all good day. He murmured some words to Jenkins, who then rounded on us, spitting with amazement. The Prince of Wales had expressed a desire to speak to us. The Prince of Wales! The Duke would lead us forward, and we were to bow and say how do you do.

This moment of bowing before the young Prince and Princess passed very quickly, and I was conscious only of the sun beating down upon us, and the surging chatter of voices. The Prince was shorter than I thought he would be, and his skin was quite brown, though his hair looked almost golden in the sunshine. He said a few things in English, and then the audience was over. Jenkins was almost jumping out of his shoes with pride and excitement.

'You must come to Marlborough House,' he said. 'This is what the Prince of Wales just said! We must all go to visit him at Marlborough House. Happy, happy day!'

After the Prince of Wales and his party moved on, everyone – even the finest of people – wanted to shake our hands. Everyone wanted to be seen with us, and they clustered around Jenkins issuing invitations to this and that. The Prince of Wales had shown an interest in us, so we were no longer strangers in this great city. The ladies and gentlemen of London were ready to turn their faces our way.

The Bohemian tells me he is from a town called Pilsen, and that this was the only place he knew as a boy. His uncle was a bishop in the south of Bohemia, but until the Bohemian was a grown man, he never travelled to see this place. Pilsen was everything the Bohemian knew of the world until the day he set out to walk to Vienna.

I can't imagine such a life. I was born on the island of Aotea, and have always spent part of the year there. The only exception to this is 1863, the year I'm writing about, when I was only in Tutukaka, Auckland, and England.

The chief home of my parents was on Hauturu, and it was to this island that we always returned. When I was young, the karaka grew in a great shiny grove all the way to the water's edge, and our whare stood hidden in the trees – karaka, ti tree, puriri, pohutukawa, all alive with the chatter of tui and korimako. I remember the trench between the boulders for our waka. We covered them with nikau fronds, so they too were hidden from sight. In those days there were always plenty of kumara and fernroot, as well as fish. We used the bay on the north-west side to keep our pigs, in a pen formed by the cliffs and the sea.

But all the while we had fires burning in other places: Tutukaka, Ngunguru, Whangaruru. We moved with the seasons, or when we needed to trade, or when a hui was required of us by tikanga, custom. This is something the judges in the Native Land Court often find difficult to understand. They would like us all to stay put, and to have one piece of land, with written-down deeds. They want to look at our tatai, our genealogy, in one dimension only. We must account for ourselves like the sons and grandsons of Jacob going into Egypt, in one straight line of names.

The Bohemian's father worked in the orchards of a great man's palace, and when he was a boy the Bohemian was his father's apprentice. When he arrived in New Zealand, he told people that he was a gardener.

'But when I worked with my father I was drawing, not digging,' he says, his eyes moving back and forth from the canvas to my face. 'My first paintings were of flowers and plants.'

'You must see Hauturu,' I tell him. Perhaps when he returns from England he can pay us a visit. I'll show him the best place to catch fish, off the south-eastern bluff. 'You can paint the trees and the birds.'

The Bohemian smiles.

'I must paint people, not trees,' he says. 'There is no money in this country for pictures of flowers. In New Zealand people want to see their own faces, or the faces of men like you, rangatira.'

Almost all of the paintings the Bohemian has sent to Mr Buller in London are of Maori. It's more than twenty years since I was there, and still the English want to look upon Maori faces. They can't read our moko, just as they can't read our Maori books. What do they see when they look at us Maori? What will happen to us when they grow tired of gazing upon us, and look away?

Behold, the nations are as a drop of a bucket, and are counted as the small dust of the balance; behold, he taketh up the isles as a very little thing.

ISAIAH 40:15

I'm not very good at remembering dates. In the land court they want to know the dates of things from many years, when this is not how we thought of them at the time. When they asked me to speak of Mauparaoa's attack on Aotea, I couldn't remember the month and the year. All I knew was that I think it happened at some point between the death of Arama Karaka Pi and the arrival of Hobson in the Bay of Islands.

But there is one date I do remember from the English trip, and that is Saturday the thirteenth of June, 1863. This is the day we were taken to Marlborough House, to be presented to the Prince and Princess of Wales.

This house was tall, much larger than the Strangers' Home, and built of brick. It was surrounded by high walls so no one could look in from the street or shoot at the Prince and Princess. We couldn't travel there in cabs, Jenkins told us, for only private carriages would be suitable arriving at such an address.

We drew up on the gravel, where many young men in scarlet coats were waiting to open our doors and help the ladies down. An old General with a forehead like the moon greeted us, and led us into a narrow hallway, where we could swathe ourselves in our Maori cloaks. Not even Reihana complained that day, so overawed was he by the place and the occasion. Beyond the heavy doors lay our audience room, which was called the Saloon. The General told Jenkins that this was the finest room in London, and Jenkins whispered this information to us, as though it were a secret.

Double doors opened, as if by magic, to the Saloon, and we were ushered in to wait. Truly, this was no ordinary room. We we all stood, mouths agape, turning and pointing, for there was so much to see and admire. Up and up the room went, with paintings high on the ceiling, just as we'd seen in St Paul's. The walls were hung with tapestries framed in gold, though at first I thought these were paintings as well, so rich and vivid were their colours. I could see Ngahuia struggling to resist stroking their surfaces, her fingers twitching, the way the fingers of English people twitched when they wanted to touch our moko.

The floor stretched before us, black and white tiles, as polished as river stones, and a carpet of many colours that Jenkins told us was Turkish and therefore very fine and costly. Chairs with velvet seats were set against the wall, but of course we didn't sit down. We stood scattered about the carpet and gazed around us, in awe of the wonders of this room. Even the fireplace had pillars of marble.

At one end of the room, above our heads, hung some kind of verandah – I had never seen one inside a house before – though this room contained no stairs. Painted all around the room, so high that gazing up at it for too long would make my neck stiff, were scenes from a great battle. In breathless murmurs Jenkins, quite cowed by the place as well, said this battle was in France, and it had been fought and won by the Duke of Marlborough.

This, I suppose, is why the house was named in his honour.

I didn't even hear the click of the doors that admitted the Prince and Princess to this room. One moment we were looking up at a picture of the Duke in his red coat riding a black horse, and the next we were looking straight into the face of the Prince of Wales. He was smiling and easy with us, and I recall that his eyes were blue as the sky, and bulged. I would say they bulged like a lizard's, but I would never compare a great man to such a vile and malevolent creature.

The Princess of Wales was very thin and very young, close in age, I would guess, to Hariata Pomare. Her skin was an unearthly white. She had a shy, sweet smile, and seemed lost in that grand gilt-edged room. Later someone told me that she did not speak English very well, for she was just a new bride and had not lived long in England, but we had no idea of this at the time, of course. When it came to English we were quite hopeless ourselves.

The Prince had a number of questions for us, conveyed to us through Jenkins. What was our opinion of London? What were our feelings about the war in New Zealand? Were the Maori people of the North more disposed to like the English compared with the Maori of the Taranaki? Had we visited the Arsenal yet, or seen the Crown Jewels? Had we visited the Zoological Gardens, quite his favourite place in the city? What were the strangest sights we had come upon so far?

These are some of the questions, the ones I can remember. The Princess did not ask questions, but she smiled at us most angelically, and afterwards Wiremu Pou said she would be the most beautiful woman in the world if she were not so very skinny.

Many voices answered the Prince's questions, everyone

taking care not to speak for too long. I took my turn. The Prince had discovered from Jenkins that I was the oldest member of the group.

'Your fighting days are behind you now, yes?' he wanted to know. 'But how many times did you go to battle?'

'I fought with eight taua,' I told him. This notion of a taua took Jenkins some time to explain. 'But when I was baptised as a Christian, my days of warfare ended.'

The Prince seemed well satisfied with this answer, and asked if he might study my face more closely. I submitted to this, of course, and Jenkins told me that His Royal Highness was quite a student of the art of moko. He had grown very interested in the subject during his recent tour of the Palestine, and had even considered risking the ire of Her Majesty by acquiring a tattoo himself.

This was quite baffling to all of us, for we knew that the Palestine was the birthplace of Our Lord Jesus Christ, and the missionaries always told us that God frowned on moko, and regarded it as a sinful heathen practice. No wonder the Queen would be angry.

Jenkins told us that the Prince wished us to return on another day, to visit the Queen's Chapel next door. Then the Prince nodded to Jenkins, who bowed very low, and we realised that our interview was at an end. It seemed improper to me that we would just leave this house without the customary presentation of gifts. We would never visit a great chief in New Zealand without offering a gift or some kind of tribute.

I stepped forward, unlacing my kahu kuri. This was the most precious and valuable thing I brought with me to England, so it was right and fitting that I should offer it to a prince who will one day be king. I laid it on the Turkish carpet at his feet and bowed. Many of the others in our party then followed suit. Reihana and Tere Pakia laid their cloaks at the feet of the Princess, who looked a little startled. Reihana couldn't wait to get rid of that cloak, even though it wasn't his. It was the one that Mr Lloyd had carried from New Zealand in his own box.

Wharepapa presented a whalebone whakapapa stick, a very fine gift indeed. I heard Hirini Pakia saying to Jenkins that he would give the Prince and Princess a piece of land, which I thought a wily way of avoiding presenting anything at all.

The Prince seemed quite gratified with these gifts, and Jenkins jabbered away to him in English, explaining each item and its significance. He was so moved, in fact, that he instructed the old General to escort us through some of the other apartments, and to show us the wedding gifts. These were all on display still in the dining room, towers of crystal and silver laid out along the great table, glinting in the sunlight. Each room we saw was more elegant than the next. Thinking himself unobserved, Hapimana stroked the white marble of one fireplace. Cows were sculpted on its lintel, perfect in every detail. They looked as though they were carved from milk.

'This isn't a house,' Ngahuia whispered to me, peering up at the huge chandelier suspended in one of the drawing rooms. 'It's a palace.'

We were even taken outside to inspect the lawns and gardens. These were very tidy and serene, hidden from the bustle of the Mall by a line of trees. When we strolled back towards the house, we could see the Prince and Princess in an upstairs window, looking down upon us and waving. We waved back.

The honour of this visit was great. We all felt that. Even the more bumptious of our party acted in a dignified and quiet way. Considering what they were to get up to later in our trip, this was both fortunate and surprising.

We passed once again through the Saloon, all pausing to gaze around its painted walls one final time. Jenkins was not quite right in saying they depicted a battle in France, and he admitted to this, once the General had explained things. The paintings represented a series of different places. One was Blenheim, which Jenkins said was not the Blenheim in the South Island, but a place in Germany. The different panels on the wall told the stories of the Duke's various battles.

'Like your taua,' Horomona Te Atua said to me. 'You should paint the walls of your whare when you get home.'

I was one of the last to walk back out to the carriages, because I was struck by something in the last panel that I hadn't noticed before. The Duke and some of his gentlemen sat on their horses, while their fires of destruction blazed in distant fields. They all looked very fine in their hats and coats, though the style of their costume was quite old-fashioned, and not at all the kind of thing gentlemen wear in London these days.

Standing near them, clutching the bridle of a horse, was a young Negro boy. He too wore a fine coat, but no hat, and no curly wig. My first thought was that he was a whangai, an adopted child perhaps from a lower branch of the family, but I don't know that the English have this custom. He was probably a servant, a trusted one who could be taken to battle, like the slaves we sometimes took with us on a taua to cook our food. It was a strange sight in such a house, that small dark face painted on the wall. Where did that boy come from? How did he make his way to England, and into the Duke of Marlborough's house?

There was no time to ask these questions, for everyone was hurrying to climb into our carriages. Our friend the Duke of Newcastle had invited us to eat luncheon with him at the

Clarendon Hotel, and this alone would have been excitement enough for one day.

Wharepapa, Ngahuia and I rode away in a rattling carriage with Jenkins, who sat staring back out the window until the walls of Marlborough House disappeared from view. His long body was tense, and when he turned to face us he was almost manic in the eyes.

'This is the greatest day of my life,' Jenkins raved. 'Truly, the greatest day. Who would think that I should have such honour?'

None of us spoke, but Wharepapa and I exchanged glances. I have no doubt that we were thinking the same thing. The invitation was to us. The honour was ours. Jenkins was there to interpret our opinions and messages, not to offer up thoughts of his own. Of course, his vision had made this trip possible for us, but the Prince of Wales didn't go about inviting obscure Wesleyans visiting from distant colonies to chat with him in his Saloon. Not for the first or the last time, I wondered at the hubris of Jenkins. Pride goeth before destruction, and an haughty spirit before a fall, yes?

I'm sure that the Clarendon Hotel was a fine and important establishment, for if it were not, the Duke of Newcastle would not have chosen to make it his London residence. But I remember thinking that after the beauty of Marlborough House his private apartment there seemed a little mean and over-cluttered with furniture.

The Duke had invited some other ladies and gentlemen to luncheon, and, to our great astonishment, one gentleman had brought with him a young Maori boy of about fifteen. Hare Pomare recognised him at once, for they were cousins. If we were in New Zealand, Hare would have moved towards this boy to greet him, but we were all conscious of protocol, and that we must wait to be first introduced to the older and more important people in the room. The boy's eyes were wide with excitement at seeing us there, and we were all fidgeting, eager to talk to him.

Jenkins at first was annoyed by Hare Pomare tugging his sleeve and whispering, because the Duke was talking. We had to wait for Jenkins to ask the Duke's permission, and the Duke to grant it, before the boy, whose name was Wiremu Repa, might step towards us, desperate to be embraced and to press his nose against each of ours. I had not seen this boy before in my life, but it was very affecting, I must say. Tere Pakia began to cry, and soon we were all sobbing. This poor boy! How long had he lived alone among the English? Years and years he'd spent at school here, without ever seeing one of his own people.

The English ladies and gentlemen stood watching us in some dismay. The English do not cry in a public place unless they are very low sorts of people, drunk and without dignity. They don't choose to show their affection, or their happiness, or their grief in this manner. We Maori like more of a carry-on, I suppose. Wiremu Repa clung to Hare Pomare as though he was in fear of his life, though I'm sure he was very well treated by Sir Frederic and Lady Rogers, his guardians there in England. They seemed very fond of him, and solicitous, making sure he ate as much as possible at luncheon. His health was delicate, it seemed, and he told us he had not been well since the last English winter.

'You have to leave before the cold weather,' he told us. 'It's miserable. You won't like it at all.'

Once we were sitting at the table, the English people looked relieved, for all the crying was at an end now, and we were all intent on making a good meal. Some of the ladies and gentlemen seemed much more interested in watching us eat than in cutting up their own fish.

'They want to see if we can eat with a knife and a fork,' Wharepapa muttered to me.

Wiremu Repa chattered to us in Maori and to the rest in fluent English. I wished that he could travel with us everywhere, for he told us much more than Jenkins ever did.

'They're not sure if you've ever seen a melon before,' he told us. 'And that lady is impressed that you say grace before every meal, and know how to drink your soup.'

Jenkins was unaware of all this interpreting, for he was talking away to the Duke of Newcastle at one end of the table.

'This gentleman says that New Zealand is to become the Great Britain of the Southern Hemisphere,' said the boy, mashing strawberries into his pudding. 'He has read it in the newspaper. The lady next to him says that London has all sorts of exotic visitors. Hindus, Turks, and Aborigines. It's exciting, but she wonders where it will all end.'

'At Te Whare Mangumangu,' Hapimana said with mock solemnity, and we all laughed.

'When I finish school I want to be a missionary,' Wiremu Repa told us, quite earnestly, 'or fight against Taranaki!'

Even though I could tell that such a slight boy would never be fit enough to fight, we all applauded him, startling the English ladies. Everyone was in such high spirits, such good cheer that day. We had met their Royal Highnesses the Prince and Princess of Wales, and we had found young Wiremu Repa.

When I say everyone was in good cheer, I exaggerate a little. Reihana instructed the boy to tell the gentlemen seated nearby that Europeans always spoke of the extermination of the Maori, and predicted it would happen soon. What did they think of that?

'They say that these are the sentiments of boastful Europeans,' Wiremu Repa reported back. 'The French, perhaps. These are not the words of the English.'

Despite this reassurance, Reihana did not appear satisfied.

Of course, no such event could be complete without a fine speech from my friend Wharepapa, which Jenkins rose to translate. Everyone seemed to approve of it very much. I can't remember exactly what he said, for Wharepapa gave fine speeches every day of the week, even if there were no English people around to listen and nod and murmur their appreciation.

On this occasion he talked about us coming to England to seek knowledge for our own country, just as Wiremu Repa had come to learn at one of its schools. The English people, he said, would be as an elder brother to the Maori, guiding and instructing us. One thing I will say for Wharepapa – he knows how to flatter his listeners. No wonder they were all so eager to declare him the leader of our party!

We were sad to bid the boy farewell, but Sir Frederic Rogers promised that we would see him again. We stood outside the hotel waiting for our carriages to draw up and, as usual, a crowd gathered around us to stare and giggle. Some respectable-looking ladies edged as close as they dared to Wiremu Pou, who for some reason fancied himself dashing and quite a catch. He smiled and said 'hariru' to them, and they screamed as though he had threatened them with a knife. This looked like an elegant street, with many fine people sashaying by, but urchins still ran about everywhere. The street was thick with them, like a rotting log swarming with beetles. One must have slipped his hand into Hirini Pakia's pocket. When we were back in our own hotel, he discovered that all his coins were gone, and his new handkerchief too.

In the carriage, Jenkins was most agitated again. Later I said to Wharepapa that he would not last long in England, for all these excitements would strain his heart and he would collapse.

'The Duke of Newcastle will give us letters of introduction,' he said, slapping Wharepapa's knee. 'Do you know what this means? We will be able to tour the entire country!'

'The Duke has promised this?' Wharepapa didn't mean to sound sceptical, I think, but Jenkins was affronted at once.

'Do you think I'm a liar? He said these things to me today, when we talked at luncheon. You have no reason to doubt my word.'

This is what Jenkins said. This is what he swore was true. I won't rush ahead with my story, but I will say this. At the time, we didn't doubt him, but we were not entirely sure.

Certainly, we had little time to think about Jenkins' plans and promises. After our visit to Marlborough House, our lives in London were very busy. We had very little time for walks or even for letters. One of our first appointments was with a society photographer, Mr Heath, on Piccadilly. Jenkins told us that the Prince of Wales wished to have a photograph of us, so we were all to go to the studio and pose in our native costume.

This, Jenkins told us, was yet another great honour. Mr Heath had taught the famous Dr Livingstone how to use a camera, and was the last person ever to take a photograph of Prince Albert. The Queen liked these pictures so much that she asked Mr Heath to serve as photographer at the wedding of the Prince and Princess of Wales.

This was all well and good, but none of us liked posing for these photographs. We had to stand around for many hours in our cloaks, brandishing weapons and not talking. It was very dull. The only excitement was when Ngahuia made a fuss because she wanted some photographs taken of her alone in her fine new dress. Mr Heath, who had very curly hair – which intrigued us very much – and was very polite and patient, was happy to oblige, though Jenkins had a few sharp words to say to her.

He had retrieved my kahu kuri from Marlborough House for the purposes of these photographs, for apparently the Prince wished to see me wearing it. I made Jenkins promise that it would be returned to the Prince as soon as the long day in the studio was over. I was asked to crouch between Mr Brent and Mr Lloyd for one photograph. I don't know why I wasn't permitted to stand up. My legs grew very tired, for Mr Lloyd kept moving his hand and spoiling the photograph. This is how I know all about the taking of pictures – this very long day with Mr Heath. Although Mr Heath was an Englishman, and knew little about the Maori, he never suggested one of us wear a peacock feather in our hair, or turn our cloaks upside down.

After this day was over, Mr Lloyd told us, in much excitement, that the Prince would not be the only person to look upon these photographs. They would be made into visiting cards, which were all the rage in England. People bought these, and gave them to each other. These cards were so fashionable, they must be called by their French name, cartes de visite. See how I remember these French words after all these years? This is because they, like so many other things, were to become the source of many, many disputes with Jenkins.

'Is it too long now?' the Bohemian is asking me. 'You are tired, yes? Maybe we stop now and you come back tomorrow.'

'No, no,' I tell him. 'Continue.'

We don't have much time if he's to sail to England in a few days. I have to try to keep my eyes open, and not let the ngore slip from my shoulders. In any case, I was deep in thought rather than tired. I was thinking that while the English in London showed us so much magnificence and hospitality, the English in New Zealand were busy fighting the Maori in Taranaki and the Waikato.

'May I ask you a question, sir?' The Bohemian is dabbing at the paints on his palette, messing them together. 'Your moko. How old are you when it is made? When do you get the moko and become a warrior?'

He makes this sound as though a moko is the business of a day, like a haircut from one of the barbers here in Auckland.

To become a warrior is something that begins many years earlier. I was a newborn baby when my father handed me over for the karaka whati ceremony. This was a baptism of the kind the missionaries wanted to stop, for it was a ceremony for boys who would be taught the arts of war. A tohunga prayed over me, dedicating me to Tu, so I would be strong and quick, able to ward off attacks by many different weapons.

Then, when I was growing up, there was much to learn. I was sent away when I was still a child to learn how to conduct myself in war, and how to understand and observe all the necessary rituals and practices, including haka. I also spent months of every year receiving instruction in the use of the tao, for spearing, and various kinds of striking weapons, such as the mere, the patu, the pouwhenua, and the taiaha, with its long tongue. Particularly difficult to manage was the tewhatewha, but I liked this most of all. There was something to the heft of the blade, and the quivering of the feathers, that lent the weapon greater presence and authority. I was never able to use one in battle, unfortunately, because by the time I was ready to fight, many of us were carrying guns.

I try to tell some of this to the Bohemian. It would be easier to act it out, but I have promised to remain still in my chair.

'So in the battle you don't fight with Maori weapons?' He sounds disappointed.

'Yes, yes, we carried our Maori weapons as well,' I tell him. 'We liked the ones that could be carried easily in our tatua, to keep our hands free for the gun.'

Although the Bohemian must have spent much time with Maori, I think he was looking at them, not talking. He doesn't know at all what a tatua is. I describe to him the way it was folded to form a sharp valley. Into this valley we could plunge a patu or mere, to be removed when the time came for hand-to-hand combat.

At a battle, no one in our taua wore anything but a tatua. We needed to be fast and unencumbered, ready to fight. The missionaries said it was indecent, of course, but they thought this about everything.

When we're asked now to wear our native costume – as we were in England, and as I am today in the Bohemian's studio – nobody ever means a tatua. I laugh aloud at this thought, the ngore slipping from my shoulders. Imagine Reihana Te Taukawau in a tatua!

It's late in the day now, and both the Bohemian and I have grown tired. I still haven't answered his question about my moko. I still haven't told him that despite the karaka whati ceremony, and the years of instruction, I was not a warrior until my first taua. I was not a warrior until I showed I had the strength and skill to kill a man, and the courage to do it.

Can two walk together, except they be agreed?

I don't remember the order of all these things because, as I said, once the Prince received us Jenkins was sent many, many invitations and he wanted us to see and do as much as possible. Now I began to understand why post boxes must be emptied in London eight times a day, and why the rich employed so many footmen in bright coats, for on some days invitations were delivered to our house every hour.

Our presence was requested in a private box to hear the opera at Her Majesty's Theatre. We attended a military review, and numerous receptions and parties, sometimes several in the course of a day. One day we were at a party at Stafford House, hosted by the Duke and Duchess of Something or Other, and another day we were taken to the City Road Chapel to view the much simpler home of the late John Wesley, venerated above all men by Jenkins. All these things we did without complaint, for they were very interesting, even if dashing about here and there in London could take up hours of each day, and sometimes we all longed just to sit about the house and read, or write letters.

We had an especially good time at the invitation of Lord

Ranelagh. This gentleman was holding, in the gardens of Beaufort House, something the English call a fête. Again, this is a French word, and it meant that this was a pastime of the most fashionable kind. A fête, we were told, was an outdoors party with games and tests of strength. We do this kind of thing in New Zealand as well, of course, but it is not that special or unusual a day, so it doesn't need a French name.

The lawn of Beaufort House was speckled with small tables, all crowded with tea things. Ladies in pale dresses twirled their parasols and twittered around us, especially when Wiremu Pou and his brother Horomona Te Atua demonstrated great prowess knocking coconuts off their stands. They were also very impressed, and perhaps a little shocked, when Ngahuia and Tere Pakia demonstrated prowess of their own at a game called Aunt Sally. This game required them to throw a ball at a doll's head, and to smash the clay pipe from its mouth. Ngahuia was particularly good at this. She was Old Hooknose's granddaughter, after all. Perhaps she was imagining that one doll was Mr Lloyd, and another was Mr Brent, telling her to ask her friend Mr Ridgway if she wanted more money for clothes.

'Lord Ranelagh compliments you on your vigour,' Jenkins told her in a mocking tone, but for a change Ngahuia did not take offence and stomp off with her nose in the air. She would not take tea until she had smashed every clay pipe and triumphantly carried away some kind of trifle as a prize.

I must record, however, that the afternoon didn't begin at all auspiciously. Lord Ranelagh had paid some fellows to stand under the trees and serenade everyone. These singers had painted their faces black. We had never seen such a thing, and didn't like it at all. When we complained to Jenkins, he said it was an English custom, and done only to amuse.

'An English custom?' demanded Wharepapa. 'To disguise your face in this way, and pretend to be someone else?'

'The English should not pretend to be Negroes,' Reihana said. 'This is not an amusing thing.'

We couldn't understand this behaviour at all. I still don't understand it. Eventually we agreed that it was just an English joke, and we soon forgot about it, I must say, setting off to smash coconuts and drink tea instead. But it made me think of the Negro boy I saw painted on the wall at Marlborough House. I still think of this sometimes today, wondering if the young man was really black-skinned, or if he was just an Englishman in disguise.

Amidst all this whirl of activity, we were told we must move again, this time to a large furnished house on Weymouth Street, paid for by the company purse. Reihana objected to this, and Jenkins objected to this objection. Reihana brought up the story of his dream on the ship again, and Jenkins insulted him again about the beliefs of our ancestors. And on it went.

Jenkins did not listen much to Reihana, for he had met with another great man, the Earl of Shaftesbury, and like Mr Ridgway the Earl was insistent that we should be treated as honoured guests.

'The Earl suggests that your expenses should be covered by the Colonial Office, shipping agents and the New Zealand Emigration Society,' Mr Lightband told us, and Mr Brent's face was rosy with pleasure. He and Mr Lloyd always liked to hear that someone else would be paying for us.

Apart from Reihana, none of us questioned the wisdom or expense of moving into the house on Weymouth Street. We were too busy seeing the sights of London. As the Prince of Wales had suggested, we visited the Woolwich Arsenal, and the guards of the Household Cavalry, and the Queen's Chapel at Whitehall. At a great printing house we observed the progress of a two-volume Bible in Maori, and learned that our own Mrs Colenso was hard at work checking the translation. At the Bank of England, Wharepapa was asked to sign a note, which made him big-headed for the rest of the day.

The Prince of Wales had excellent taste, I think, for when we visited the Zoological Gardens I agreed at once with his verdict: this was the best place in all of London. Many other people must have agreed with him as well. Thousands were there the day we visited, from all classes of society. At times the crowd was so thick, I feared we would see no animals at all. It was easier to smell the foul odour of the monkey house than to spy any of its inhabitants, so dense and immoveable was the audience pressed up to its bars.

Many people sat sprawled in low chairs around the bandstand, and others followed an elephant being led through the grounds, children swaying high on its back. But all the distractions of the gardens did not deter a crowd gathering around us Maori, as usual, staring and pointing at us as though we too were on display.

Still, we were able to glimpse all manner of wild animals, most never seen in New Zealand: the towering giraffe, bloodthirsty wolves and tigers, the fat taniwha known as a hippopotamus, which swallows cabbages whole and lies beneath the water with only its bulbous eyes and twitching ears visible above! We would have great sport with such a beast if he lurked in the river at Ngunguru.

More elephants would soon arrive from the Zambesi, Jenkins told us, thanks to the aid of Dr Livingstone. Kiwi had been brought here on ships from New Zealand, and could be found at the Ostrich House. I don't remember us visiting them, though I would much rather have visited the Ostrich House than the Reptile House. I have no wish to look upon pythons and lizards, for they endanger the soul as well as the body. Really, I would advise the gentlemen in charge of the Zoological Gardens to spend their money on more of the great white bears, or on more of the leaping kangaroos of Australia, than on a single twisting snake.

A deaf fellow might not realise he was in a Zoological Gardens, because sometimes the only indication was the distant roar of an angry carnivore, or the screeching of monkeys. Much of the gardens were simply that, gardens, where people promenaded under a canopy of colourful parasols, looking at the flowers and other plants. Near the canal, suspended between trees, were perches for parrots of every conceivable colour, a splendid sight. The parrots squawked, dangling from their perches or biting at them with their sharp beaks, though none flew away. Some of the denizens of Parrot Walk could speak all manner of words, we were told. However, many of the words were not suitable for the ears of ladies, as the parrots had been taught by sailors and Arabians, and other unsavoury characters.

Greatest of all the beasts was the lion, and along the Carnivore Terrace we saw cage after cage of them, with nothing between their mighty jaws and our hands but a row of bars. They were enormous creatures, some with feathered beards and all with giant golden paws. One of them was locked alone in a cage, too fearsome to be at large among his family. He shouted at us, making the most ferocious face, his mouth open wide enough to consume a man's head. The young men among us responded with pukana and whetero, showing the lion their tongues and the whites of their eyes, and this seemed to enrage him further.

'Let the lions be brought out,' I suggested, 'so we may fight them!'

Of course this was not an entirely serious request, for we had no weapons with us, and the angry lion might run off with a lady clamped in his jaws, rather than stand and fight. Lions may be like Pakeha, with no notion of our rules of combat. But fighting a lion would have made quite a show for the English people – much better than a band with tootling trumpets, or singers with black paint on their faces. Jenkins shook his head.

'The Queen will be most displeased,' he said, 'if you kill her lions.'

'They would all be killed,' boasted Wiremu Pou. He had never killed anything larger than a sandfly, I'm certain, in all his life, but I said nothing to cut him down to size. Perhaps I should have said something. There were many occasions during this time in England when I could have stepped forward and had my say. Too often, I think, I was neglecting my duties as kaumatua, as rangatira. For if no one leads rash young men, they decide to lead themselves.

On this day, however, we were still one group, and our only leader was Wharepapa, appointed by himself. I remember these weeks in London, when all but Haumu lived together in one house, as a time of few disputes. We didn't like wearing cloaks when we walked the streets of London, but this was the only complaint from most of us. With all these excursions going on we had little time for public meetings, and this pleased Reihana, in particular. Even our Pakeha did not seem too disappointed, for although we were not making money at meetings, we received invitations for almost every meal, and some of these meals were very sumptuous indeed.

This happy time did not last. Trouble began the day we

learned that the men with black faces at the fête were not the only dark-skinned performers entertaining the people of London with their singing and dancing.

Mr Lightband opened the newspaper one morning and cried out in horror, thrusting the paper at Jenkins so he could share in the dismay.

The object of their unhappiness was an advertisement for the Alhambra Theatre in Leicester Square, very near the offices of Mr Ridgway. Coming to this theatre in the month of July was a group managed by a Mr Hegarty, lately of Sydney, Australia. This theatrical troupe was known as the Maori Warrior Chiefs.

Jenkins and his associates were most disheartened, fearing confusion between our two parties.

'If only we could set out now on our tour of the provinces,' Jenkins said on more than one occasion. He was always writing letters and making plans for this tour, talking about us visiting all the great cities of England. 'But we must wait for the word from the Duke of Newcastle.'

No word came. Days passed, and still the letters of introduction were not delivered to us, and when Jenkins visited the Colonial Office, he returned empty-handed. He and our other Pakeha were constantly coming and going, off to make arrangements or seek support for our tour of the provinces. They wanted to get us as far away as possible from these so-called Warrior Chiefs.

It was on a morning when they were all out that Mr Ridgway visited, bringing more troubling news with him. Some of our party had gone with Jenkins that morning, and the rest were busy writing letters that Mr Lightband promised he would take to a ship's captain the next day. Wharepapa and I set ours aside to sit with Mr Ridgway for a while in the front parlour.

'What do you know of Jenkins' scheme?' he asked us, his voice low.

'His scheme?'

'This plan of his, to take you here and there, and have you perform on a stage.'

'Oh!' said Wharepapa. 'These are our meetings. The English fill a church, and Jenkins speaks to them about New Zealand, and we make speeches and sing a farewell waiata.'

'How many of these meetings has he asked you to attend?'

We told him that we had gone to many parties so far, but not so many meetings. Often we were asked to sing or speak at these parties, we said.

'Some grumble about this, especially as Jenkins insists we wear cloaks when everyone else wears their evening clothes,' Wharepapa told Mr Ridgway. 'When we went to a theatre to see an opera, he told us that the manager would not give us tickets for the box unless we wore cloaks.'

'We had to wear them to the Zoological Gardens,' I reminded him. That day was hot, and none of us wished to drape ourselves in cloaks. Wiremu Pou kept tugging at his rain cape, and asked why he should wear such a garment when the sun shone and the sky was blue. Those in our party without a moko felt the intrusion more keenly, I think, for if it were not for their cloaks, they might slip through the crowd without attracting so many stares and remarks.

'No wonder Jenkins wants this,' Mr Ridgway said, his voice thick with contempt. 'Have you seen the handbill he has produced for your tour of the provinces?'

He pulled a copy of this handbill from inside his coat, and told us what it said. We were described as 'Warrior Chieftains' who would perform native war dances.

'This is the group of Mr Hegarty, no?'

'It is *your* group, I am sorry to say. This is beneath your dignity, sir,' he said, nodding at me, and Wharepapa and I agreed at once. At one time in my life I was a warrior, but those days were long ago. Wharepapa was very annoyed.

'When we sing to the English, it's because we wish to pay tribute, or farewell them. We're not the blind man who plays his fiddle in the street, begging for coins.'

'Or the puppets in Punch and Judy,' said Mr Ridgway, his nods so vehement he himself resembled a puppet. I was thinking that we must do all in our power to prevent Reihana from learning of this handbill, for his anger would be great, and then we would all suffer his rage and lamentations. 'The Duke of Newcastle will be most unhappy when he sees this.'

Wiremu Pou wandered into the room at this moment, yawning and stretching, for he had little taste for quiet mornings spent writing letters. He sat down just in time to hear Mr Ridgway's question about the contracts we'd signed.

'Contracts?' he asked, confused. I wasn't sure of Mr Ridgway's meaning either.

'Jenkins says you all signed an agreement with him,' he said. 'Back in Auckland, you signed papers, saying you would take part in his lectures.'

'Our lectures,' nodded Wharepapa. 'These are our meetings. We tell the English people about New Zealand, and make our observations about England.'

'No, no,' said Ridgway, frowning. 'You see, Jenkins is the one giving the lectures. Illustrated lectures, he calls them. You're just illustrations, there to be dressed up and shown off, and to make faces and dance. He vows that you all agreed to this. You're the entertainment, you see. A spectacle. You stand on the stage or

113

platform in your cloaks and feathers, brandishing your weapons, and everyone looks at you.'

'But we speak,' Wharepapa insisted. He glanced at me and then at Wiremu Pou for confirmation.

'We each have our say,' added Wiremu Pou, plucking at the threads of a cushion. He was always as restless as a child, and could never sit still.

'Like the lions in the Carnivore Terrace have their say,' said Mr Ridgway, his face grim. 'Who can understand the words you speak?'

'Jenkins tells them.'

'You can trust him?'

Wharepapa and I looked at each other.

'Gentlemen, I am very unhappy to tell you this,' Mr Ridgway said, 'but you are presented to the British public not as people but as exhibits. Like the machines you saw at the Crystal Palace. Like the statues and fountains! Jenkins and his friends are counting on people paying to see you, for without this money their whole scheme is bankrupt. He may talk of education and enlightenment, and of the great benefit to you of this trip, but his real aim is making money. You're to be exhibited so they can make money.'

'If they make money by showing us off, then they must give us money,' said Wiremu Pou, looking aggrieved. 'I hear the Maori group at the Alhambra are given three pounds a week. Three pounds each!'

'Have you received money from Jenkins or Lightband yet?'

'Not since we left Auckland.'

'All we agreed there,' said Wharepapa, now in great agitation, 'was that we would be taken to England to see the country, and to learn of the deeds and works of the English. Jenkins said they might come to hear us while we talked of matters concerning New Zealand. That was all.'

'Did they say they would give you money?'

'We talked of money, yes. Jenkins told me our passage would be paid, and here in England all our board and lodgings, and all our travelling expenses. When the English assembled to hear us, they would each pay one shilling, perhaps two. These monies would be placed in a bank and when our travels were at an end, they would be divided up.'

'How would it be divided?'

'The Pakeha would take most of this money, to repay them for the amounts they subscribed back in Nelson. They would take five parts, and we would take one.'

I was very surprised to hear Wharepapa say all this. I didn't remember any talk of five parts this, and one part that. From the look on the face of Wiremu Pou, he knew nothing of it either.

'I heard no talk of placing money in a bank!' he cried. By this time he was no longer yawning or lolling in his seat. 'No talk of them taking most of the money, or of us waiting months to be given our share. And how can we be sure they tell the truth about how many shillings are earned or spent? What if they tell us that once our passage is paid for, there is no money left for us? They may go back to Nelson rich men, and we will return home in shabby clothes, with nothing to show for this trip but stories no one will believe.'

For once I found myself agreeing with Wiremu Pou. How could we truly know how much money was taken at these meetings? All we ever heard the Pakeha say was how little we had. Yet one week we were staying at a fine hotel, and the next we moved to this house on Weymouth Street. We should have stayed at the Strangers' Home, just as Reihana had said, rather than spend all the money living like dukes and duchesses. If Wharepapa was right, and we were to add up all the shillings spent at the end of our trip, there would be little left for us.

But what was I doing, worrying about who would get the money? When we sailed, I knew nothing of this money. The first time I heard that we would be expected to earn money was on board the *Ida Zeigler*, when Reihana and Jenkins were having one of their arguments. On that day in Auckland when I signed the piece of paper in Charley Davis's office, I agreed to go to England, and for my passage and board and tickets for trains, and such, to be paid for by Jenkins and his friends. There was no talk of shillings and banks and dividing everything up. There was no talk of needing to earn money by going on show – to sing for our supper, as the English say. Perhaps there was an English version of the paper I signed, one with different words, like entertainments, and shillings, and Warrior Chieftains.

'Money is taken, and we are shown to people like the lions at the zoo,' I said to Ridgway. And, I thought, like the lions, we have no notion of how much money, or how great the cost of our cages and legs of mutton.

Mr Ridgway didn't argue with me. He sat back in his chair, tucking the handbill into his pocket. Wharepapa looked unhappy. Wiremu Pou threw his cushion on the floor with disgust. He was angry, and this anger would not go away. It would fester and grow into something ugly.

M any of the hours with the Bohemian are spent in silence. I like the peace of this, listening to the fire or the rain, unable to make sense of muffled shouts from the street or downstairs in Mr Partridge's shop. There is time to think, so when I return to the hostel I can write it down in my book.

But the more I think, the less clearly I remember, and the less certain I am. Perhaps Mr Ridgway couldn't speak Maori at all, and I had to wait for Wharepapa to translate each line for me. This is quite possible, yet the conversation with Mr Ridgway occurred early in our trip, when Wharepapa was not yet fluent in English. Mr Ridgway must have been able to speak to us in Maori, for I remember understanding everything he had to say that day. At least, I think it was that day, or that evening, not long after we read in the newspaper of the Maori Warrior Chiefs. Really, I don't know what I remember and what I was told, or what we pieced together afterwards when the place and our memories of it were distant.

Once we were home in New Zealand, Wharepapa and I talked of these matters on many occasions, but after some years had passed, we no longer spoke of the bad things. When we told others of the trip to England, we talked about meeting the Queen, and her son, the Prince of Wales, and of hearing the lions roar at the Zoological Gardens. These are the things people wanted to hear. Not about the way we were obliged to put on a show, and stay much longer than we wished, all because we signed a piece of paper without reading it properly. And certainly not about this one who went mad, and this one who died, and this one who ran away, never to be seen again.

Then said he, What have they seen in thine house? And Hezekiah answered, All that is in mine house have they seen: there is nothing among my treasures that I have not shewed them.

ISAIAH 39:4

All our arguments and anger had to wait, because the morning after the visit from Mr Ridgway, a note arrived from the Duke of Newcastle. This didn't contain the letters of introduction Jenkins expected. This note was something far, far better. We were all to be taken to meet Her Majesty the Queen.

Victoria herself had suggested we be taken to her house and presented to her. We were all very, very happy about this. Jenkins had tears in his eyes when he told us, and he was not the only one. Ngahuia and Tere Pakia sobbed for so long, the maid asked if she should send for a doctor.

Only two of our Pakeha were permitted to attend us, and after much discussion and banter it was agreed that these should be Jenkins and Mr Lightband. We were to travel down to Osborne House on the Isle of Wight that Saturday. The Duke of Newcastle would accompany us, and he would bring the Nga Puhi boy we'd met, Wiremu Repa.

We rose early that day, for first we had to catch a train to Southampton, which took several hours, and then we had to make our way to the dock, and sail across the water on the

Queen's own yacht, the *Fairy*. I was so happy to see the waves again in a blue sea, and to breathe in fresh air. In London we spent too much time inside a succession of stuffy rooms, where all manner of foul odours and gasses were trapped, and often when we were walked outside, the sky was grey with smoke or rain. I rarely heard the wind in the trees, or the sound of birds. Instead, day and night, came the sounds of horses clopping, whistles blowing, and men shouting. Out on the water, the waves slapping the boat, I could close my eyes and imagine myself at home again. The journey to an island reminded me, naturally, of my home on Hauturu, though this journey was much more swift, and we didn't have to climb over wet rocks to land.

Three of Her Majesty's carriages waited for us, and they were the kind of carriages with their roofs cut off, so we could all shout to each other, and enjoy the breeze dancing in our hair. We passed the Queen's bathing machine, which was quite a contraption, requiring much explanation from Jenkins, and drove along an avenue of trees towards Osborne House. This was another house that was really a palace, and quite different from any house we had seen in London. It was as yellow as butter, unscarred by soot, and surrounded by broad green lawns.

We were greeted by one of the gentlemen of the Court, and shown to a waiting room where we could tidy ourselves, and unpack and fasten our cloaks. There was little time for this, for soon we were led into the Council Room, where the presentation would take place. I don't remember much of this room, I must admit, for my heart was beating fast and I felt a great churning in my stomach.

I remember the red carpet beneath my feet, and the portraits of the Queen and her husband on either side of the door. They looked very young and happy, and the Queen was wearing a pale dress and a blue sash. Sunlight poured in through the glass doors, and I felt very hot in the cloak Jenkins had given to me. We were positioned in a sweeping line, for Jenkins told us this would not be an informal meeting, as it was at Marlborough House. We could not be strolling about gawking at pictures when Her Majesty entered the room.

Again, we had little time to wait. No sooner were we arrayed, than the Queen emerged from another door. She was dressed all in black, as was – and is – her custom. I can tell you that she is a very small lady, and quite round, with a face of alabaster, and blue eyes of great intensity. She looked at us all most sternly, but I don't wish to portray her as unkind or unwelcoming. There was a gravity to her, a great sorrow, unmistakeable to anyone standing nearby. The room was light and sunny that day, but the Queen was dark with gloom. With her were two shy young princesses, Helena and Beatrice, and Prince Leopold, a very serious-looking young chap, and four members of the Royal Household. All but the youngest lady – Miss Byng, as we were to learn later – wore black. Miss Byng wore a very dark grey, which gave her the appearance of a fledgling.

The Duke of Newcastle introduced Jenkins and Mr Lightband, and they both bowed very low. Mr Lightband was so overawed, he could barely speak. Then we were introduced, one by one, with Wiremu Repa last of all. We made our salutations in Maori, approaching to kiss the Queen's extended hand.

She addressed us all in a high, clear voice, and when she finished speaking Jenkins, stumbling over his words, told us what she had said.

'Her Majesty gives you her salutations,' he said. 'Salutations to the Maori people of New Zealand. I am happy to see you in this country. It is my aim to do you good, and to see that you at all times obtain justice. I hope you will be pleased with what you see in England.'

We were told that Her Majesty would be glad to hear whatever we desired to say, so Takarei said a few words, then Hare Pomare told her we were afraid that the Pakeha in London would kill us. Mr Jenkins laughed when he said these words to the Queen.

'I will not be pleased if my Maori people are killed,' she replied. 'I am not willing that New Zealand should be destroyed.'

I think we were expecting her to ask us questions, as the Prince of Wales had done, so when she said nothing we all stood about in stupid silence. The Queen bowed to us, and left the room, all her children following in an orderly line. We were all very disappointed with this, for most of us had said nothing to her but 'hariru'. Tere Pakia started sniffing, and, after Jenkins conferred with the Duke of Newcastle, the Duke left the room, away in search of the Queen. A few minutes later, to our great relief and happiness, she and her children walked in once again. This time she smiled at us.

'Please,' she told Jenkins to tell us. 'Say whatever you wish to say.'

Wharepapa and Reihana spoke, and then Kihirini stepped forward. He was not usually one for making speeches, so we were curious about what he would say. We were especially curious as his face was so mournful, his eyes already brimming with tears.

'We stand here in this place,' he said, speaking slowly so Jenkins could keep up, 'and our hearts are very heavy, very heavy indeed. Seeing you and your children here, all we can think of is Prince Albert, your dear, beloved husband. How great is your loss! How can we express to you, our Queen, how much affection we feel for you, how much of your sorrow we share!'

He talked in this manner for some time, until we all swayed with sadness, feeling the truth of his words. This was a beautiful house, golden and bright in the sunshine, built by the Queen and Prince Albert to live in peace. But now it was a place of great unhappiness, the Queen's sorrow heavy in the air.

The Queen herself was quite moved by Kihirini's speech, and tears blurred the sharp blue of her eyes. Even the Englishmen in the room seemed greatly affected. When Jenkins nodded to me to step forward, I knew that very little more was necessary.

'Be generous to the Maori people,' I said to her, and when Jenkins said the words in English, the Queen bowed her head.

'Yes,' she said. 'I am kindly disposed to the Maori race.'

Ngahuia took the greenstone heitiki from around her neck, and handed it to Victoria, curtseying deeply like the finest lady at Court. We were all very pleased with this gesture, and the Queen looked very pleased as well. She smiled at us all most benignly while the brothers, Horomona Te Atua and Wiremu Pou, stepped forward to lay their cloaks at her feet. Then, once again, she withdrew from the room, and this time we understood that there would be no further audience.

However, our day at Osborne was not yet over. We were led along corridors to have luncheon in a dining room only for the ladies and gentlemen of the Royal Household. This was such a fine room itself, with a table so large, we wondered how grand the Queen's own dining room must be. Perhaps it had a mile-long table, like the one in Marlborough House?

Luncheon was very good, with so many courses I lost count – soup, fish, a cold sirloin of beef, and so on. I was seated next to Miss Byng. Mr Lightband, on her left hand, talked away with her, and because Miss Byng had much to say, and a voice loud as a tui's, young Wiremu Repa, to my right, was able to tell me everything she said.

'The Queen hardly ever sleeps at Buckingham Palace,' he reported. 'Her Majesty prefers Windsor and Osborne, and likes Balmoral in Scotland most of all. Miss Byng and the other ladies prefer Windsor because it is near London, and their friends can visit. It is quite dull for them here at Osborne. There is nothing to read, and Miss Byng doesn't care for lawn tennis. On foggy days, there are no steamers, and that means no letters. Their rooms are very small. They are usually here until the end of August, when they go to Scotland, always returning here for Christmas. The Queen loves an open carriage, like the ones we rode in today. She will ride out in them even in a snowstorm, and sits outside on the terrace at Osborne every night, for she never feels the cold. Balmoral is ice-cold. The Queen doesn't mind. The Queen and her children all enjoy sea-bathing. All the ladies must wear black, but the younger ladies may wear white or grey now, unless a member of the European monarchy dies. If this happens, they must all wear black dresses and black gloves and jet adornments for six weeks. The Queen takes the keenest interest in death, and likes to talk of coffins and winding sheets. The Court has been in mourning since March of 1861, when Her Majesty's mother died. When the Princess Alice married last year, in the dining room here at Osborne, she had an all-black trousseau. At the wedding of the Prince of Wales this year, the ladies of the Household were permitted to wear grey. They always eat luncheon at two on the dot, with tea at half past five, and dinner three hours later. The Queen's favourite fruits are oranges and pears. The Queen does not care for mutton. The Queen cannot bear to listen to talk of the Indian Mutiny. A Zulu chief visited her, and Her Majesty was most disappointed that he was not in native dress. The Queen dislikes all oratorio, especially Handel's *Messiah*. Football she considers barbarous. Cricket balls she considers too hard. The Queen does not care for thunderstorms. Miss Byng is about to be married.'

The conversation was only lost to me when Wiremu Repa turned his attention to his plate. He spent some time nibbling at juicy slices of a huge pineapple, even though this was not one of the Queen's favourite fruits. Wharepapa was making a great show of pocketing the stones of the peaches and apricots, saying that we would plant them in New Zealand, and name the trees 'Victoria'. Hapimana and Takarei, I observed, were giddy by this time with claret, and if I had been able to see Hirini Pakia, I'm sure that he too was making steady progress through great quantities of sherry or wine.

After luncheon, Mrs Bruce told us that the Princesses Helena and Beatrice had offered to show our ladies around their private apartments. This was a great treat for the three women in our party, and off they went, returning some time later clasping photographs of the Royal Family, given to them on the Queen's instructions. Hariata Pomare, who was weeping, had to be supported by the others. Mrs Bruce had informed Her Majesty that Hariata was expecting a child, and the Queen had taken a keen interest in this news.

Jenkins was instructed to inform the Duke of Newcastle when the event was near, so all the proper attentions might be paid to Hariata. When the child was born, the Queen wished to be godmother. If the child was a girl, she would be named Victoria. If the child was a boy, he would be Albert. Hariata and Hare Pomare were quite overwhelmed with this honour. Even Ngahuia was too impressed – at this moment, at least – to be jealous and petulant.

When our carriages were announced, we were delayed a few moments. The little Princess Beatrice and her attendant had hurried outside to say goodbye to us. The Princess permitted our ladies to kiss her hand, and asked if Hapimana might give her the feather from his hair. Even when we climbed into our carriages, we were reluctant for this great day to end. Every window we could see was crowded with people – ladies and gentlemen, maids and footmen! They all wanted to look upon us before we drove away back to the dock. We all stood up and gave three loud cheers, in the English manner, to bid them farewell. Such a day! I will never forget it, not in all my life.

Other days in England, unfortunately, I would be quite happy to forget. We returned to London from Portsmouth I think, where hundreds of people gathered at the station to shake our hands and watch us leave, but the next day it seemed that all the triumph of that visit existed long, long ago. Mr Ridgway turned up again, not to hear our tales of Osborne House and the Queen's preference for oranges, but to squabble with Jenkins. He was in a foul humour, for he had attended the Alhambra Theatre to watch the Maori troupe perform.

Mr Ridgway wanted to tell Jenkins, in the most forceful language, that nothing of this kind must happen to us. We must not be asked to perform wherever we went, and we should be permitted to wear our own clothes, not native dress. When Jenkins snapped at Mr Ridgway, saying that he had the support of the Duke of Newcastle, Mr Ridgway turned almost as red as his hair.

'You know nothing of the Duke of Newcastle!' he shouted. 'He is as opposed as I am to your lecture project, and is quite determined you abandon it. He and the Earl of Shaftesbury are planning a public appeal for funds. They will donate money themselves so the rangatira may return to New Zealand before the winter. England is no place for Maori in the winter. Look at the boy Wiremu Repa! He cannot last another winter here.'

On and on they argued, for Jenkins had no intention of taking us back to New Zealand so soon. We had been in England only a few months. He had already spent far too much money, and donations alone wouldn't begin to reimburse him or his associates.

'So you say you have made no money?'

'None at all.'

'For shame, sir!' Mr Ridgway was very angry. 'I do not believe this for an instant. From now on we shall not call you Jenkins. We shall call you Gehazi.'

This was a terrible insult. Gehazi is the servant of Elisha, who takes silver from a man and then lies to his master so he can keep the money for himself. Jenkins was most upset, and would not speak any more to Mr Ridgway that day.

We didn't understand why the great men of England were so eager for us to return home, and wondered if we had offended them.

'Jenkins has offended them,' Wharepapa said, 'for all he speaks of is money.'

True, there was a great deal of talk about money in our house, for it was very much on the minds of all our Pakeha. A day after Mr Ridgway's visit, Jenkins told us we must give up the house on Weymouth Street and return to the Strangers' Home.

'I knew we had no money,' Reihana said, triumph flickering in his eyes. 'We should not have stayed at the hotel. Now we must go back to the house for poor and fallen people.'

I didn't mind the Strangers' Home, though we must sleep in the same rooms with many other people unknown to us, and from unknown places. But I must say that I did not care for many of the sights in the streets of Limehouse. One night after our return there, I went out late in the evening for a walk, just as the sun was setting. This was the best time, I'd discovered, to walk in the streets without attracting a crowd. I walked for an hour or so, wandering further from the Strangers' Home than I'd intended. In that time I saw policemen carrying a dead body from the doorway where he or she had been found. I saw a boy, no more than seven or eight years old, use a knife to slice away a man's pocket, so the coins within tumbled to the ground and his younger brother and sister, barely able to walk, scrambled to reap the harvest. Men pushed their way out of the door of a public house into its skittle-ground, smashing bottles against the walls so they could instantly set about lunging at each other. Only yards away a crowd laughed and clapped at the antics of a juggler, paying no attention to the anguished cry of a man with a scarlet slash across his face, dropping to his knees on the cobbles of the court.

A group of Lascar sailors staggered past, arm in arm with the women who always preyed upon the men just off a ship. We had learned of this in the Strangers' Home, where such women were forbidden to take one step into the hallway. These women had adorned themselves in the sailors' hats and belts, and the merry group were all – Lascars and women – extremely drunk. I stepped into the shadows to avoid them, and almost stood upon a young woman draped in rags, sitting in a sorry heap upon the ground. She held out her cupped hand to me, no doubt asking for money. The palm of her hand was black with coal dust, as though she had been crawling through the streets. The whining baby clawing at her breast was rank with its own filth.

Just days earlier we had walked through the apartments of

a royal palace. I wondered if the Queen knew of these goings-on in her own capital, or if the ministers we met knew of the degraded lives so many of the English must lead. Why were so many English missionaries in New Zealand, when the work to accomplish here, in London alone, was so mountainous an undertaking? The poor souls in this city were much worse off than the poorest of the poor in New Zealand, for they had no hope.

When I returned to the Strangers' Home that night, the first person I saw downstairs was Mrs Colenso, which was odd. She usually visited us on a morning, and had said once that she did not care to venture anywhere near Limehouse after the sun had set. She seemed flustered, another unusual circumstance, for Mrs Colenso was always calm and sensible.

'Paratene!' she cried when she saw me walking towards her. 'Thank goodness. I was afraid that they'd lured you away as well.'

I had no idea what she was talking about, and told her so.

'Have you not heard?' she asked. 'Wiremu Pou has left you all. He has decided to join the Maori troupe performing at the Alhambra.'

I couldn't believe this. We had heard from Mr Ridgway that this Maori troupe were no-account fellows, and they were not invited to Marlborough House, or Osborne House, or courted by members of the aristocracy. Why would Wiremu Pou throw in his lot with them? He was angry with Jenkins, I knew, but this was a bold and reckless act.

'Their manager, Mr Hegarty, has offered him two pounds a week,' Mrs Colenso told me, adding that Mr Hegarty had also promised to pay his board and lodging somewhere close to the theatre which, Mrs Colenso said, was 'sure to be disreputable'.

I doubted that Wiremu Pou would mind that, as long as

he had plenty of shillings jingling in his pocket. This was not the end of the story, however, for Mrs Colenso had more to tell. When Wiremu Pou returned to the Strangers' Home to pack his box, Hirini and Tere Pakia had learned of the offer and decided to leave as well. They would perform on the stage, 'in a degraded fashion,' Mrs Colenso said in despair, and would bring our whole venture into disrepute.

'And now Hapimana and Ngahuia say they will leave as well,' she told me, shaking her head. 'Reverend Stack is talking to them at this very moment in the Colonel's office, to make them see sense. This is all very, very bad.'

'Te Taka will persuade them to stay,' I said, though I wasn't sure of this at all. Just the mention of money was enough to turn Ngahuia's head, and Hapimana was a silly young fool. In the end, as I recall, it was Mrs Colenso who convinced them to stay. She said that both the Queen and the Prince of Wales would be most displeased to hear of this, and that if Ngahuia and Hapimana left to become stage performers neither of them would be admitted into the homes of the British aristocracy ever again.

By the time Mrs Colenso and Te Taka left that night, their rebellion was over. But Wiremu Pou, and Hirini and Tere Pakia, were long gone. I wasn't sure that night, or for many nights afterwards, if we would ever see any of them again.

The Bohemian is a foreigner, I suppose, the way I was a foreigner in England. But our situations are quite different. Here he can come and go as he pleases, and he makes a living painting us Maori for one or other of his patrons. In England we had no way of making money, unless we were performing on the stage of the Alhambra at the behest of its owner Mr Wilde, or performing at schools and town halls at the behest of Jenkins. When Mr Ridgway came to see those of us still living at the Strangers' Home, to enquire if we were happy about travelling to Bristol with Jenkins, what could we tell him? What choice did we have? How else were we to live?

The Bohemian stares at me now, dabbing at his canvas. He looks at me the way the English looked at me, intent and fascinated, consuming me with their eyes. He isn't quite so curious, of course, and he never seems horrified. He's seen many rangatira in his travels around New Zealand. We're not animals from the Zoological Gardens in our own country, and certainly not a dying species, whatever the newspapers say.

This is one reason it was such a relief to return to New Zealand, and to hide myself away whenever I could on Hauturu. The Queen would live forever at Osborne House on the Isle of Wight, if her courtiers would permit, and I understand that. In London people gawp at her, and sometimes they shoot at her as well. No one shoots at me on Hauturu – not any more, now we don't have to fear taua from the south.

The island is really Hauturu-o-toi, because Toi-te-huatahi, the great explorer, named it. His grandson was lost at sea, so Toi searched for him, following the path of the stars from Hawaiki south across the ocean. He didn't find his grandson, but he found Aotea and Hauturu, and decided to stay for a while. His grandson eventually turned up safe and sound in Hawaiki, as the young will do, oblivious to the fuss they've caused.

Hauturu is not like other islands. It's a place of secrets and resistance. The mountain always wears a cloak of cloud. Some say that an atua lives up there, and when it descends, disguised in grey swirls of mist, no one is safe. The waves crash and the winds blow, warning us of its descent.

The island is guarded by its sheer ridges and slashed with deep gullies, which is why it was easy to defend. The streams only flow during the rains of winter. There are no beaches, and if the wind blows from the south-west, it's impossible either to land or to leave. Toi himself couldn't find a landing place, so he sent a slave, guarded by Toi's beloved dog, Moi-pahu-roa, to find a suitable spot.

Perhaps the dog was reluctant to swim ashore, or perhaps the slave just wanted to escape his watch. For one reason or another, near the wet boulders near Titoki point, the slave dashed the dog's head with a sharp rock. He'd forgotten that the dog was Toi's property and therefore tapu. Before his eyes, the dog turned into a slab of stone. You can see it there now, lying in the water, as flat as the boulders near it are round. It's still tapu. If anyone strikes that stone, he will die within one month.

The slave was frightened, so he ran away through the trees and disappeared up the mountain. He should have stayed and faced Toi's punishment. Instead he was taken by the patupaiarehe – sprites, they call them in English – and held there forever. You can still hear his voice in the whistling wind when a storm lashes the island, crying out to Moi-pahu-roa for forgiveness.

When I was a small child and first heard this story, I was afraid of this voice. But when I was in England, and the only voices around me were shrill with petty complaints, I thought of Toi's slave trapped where the tree-tops brush the clouds, and longed to hear his lament.

For what is a man advantaged, if he gain the whole world, and lose himself, or be cast away?

LUKE 9:25

It pains me to write this down, but the rebellion in London was not really over at all. No sooner had some of our party run away, than the rest were demanding money from Jenkins. We knew he was engaged in making arrangements for a tour of provincial cities, despite the absence of four of our original group, who were to be abandoned to their fates in London. Haumu was to be left behind in her asylum, and the three who had absconded, Mr Ridgway had told us, were living in lodgings near the Alhambra Theatre, in a very low-class part of town.

By this time, we were attending fewer balls and receptions, and spending more of our time earning shillings. Jenkins had arranged quite a programme of 'illustrated lectures' in the chapels and meeting rooms of London, and therefore we had observed him and his associates collecting money from the people who attended, counting up coins afterwards. Occasionally Mr Lightband, who usually took charge of the counting, looked happy, and talked of a good night, or a most beneficial afternoon. But we had no fixed idea of how much money was spent and how much was earned, and Jenkins refused to discuss these matters with us. Money was no concern of ours, he said.

But ever since that upstart Wiremu Pou had announced how much Mr Hegarty was paying him to prance upon the stage of the Alhambra with the so-called Maori Warrior Chiefs, money had become the subject of many of our conversations. Too many, I must say. These conversations grew louder when we learned that Jenkins had commissioned a large map of New Zealand. The purpose of this was to help him illustrate these illustrated lectures, for apparently we, wearing our cloaks and brandishing our weapons, were insufficient. It was at this point, I think, that everyone grew angry. When Jenkins called one morning at the Strangers' Home, in part to discuss some private matter with Colonel Hughes, we could not wait for his meeting to end. We all crowded into the office to press our case.

'Why should the Maori troupe be paid to walk once a night onto the stage at the Alhambra?' Hapimana demanded. He was no longer laughing and joking all the time, and I suspect he regretted not running off when he had the chance. 'You ask us to perform at every event we attend, and now you say we must go to Bristol, where we must perform at churches and schools and all manner of meetings. We should be paid every week, just as these Maori Warrior Chiefs are. If you don't pay us, we will leave.'

'You will suffer very badly if you leave,' a grim-faced Jenkins warned him. 'I won't suffer, but you will. The English won't invite you to their great houses if you're no longer seen as a rangatira.'

'What is the merit of visiting great houses, if we must live like paupers?' Horomona Te Atua took a leading role in this argument, as I remember it, because he was very unhappy about his brother's defection. Horomona told me he tried to dissuade

Wiremu Pou from leaving, but his brother was stubborn, and quite determined. 'So many of our expenses now must be paid from our own pockets, when this was never the agreement in Auckland.'

This point was quite true. I sold some land before I came away, so I would have a little money in my pocket when I was in England. But none of us had expected to be asked to give the cook money, or pay when the coal was delivered, things we had to do on several occasions before we returned to the Strangers' Home. I think that Takarei had paid the butcher's bill three times. We from the North didn't care so much about this, for we had decided that Takarei had more money than any of us. I don't know why we thought such a thing. We were always imagining things about Takarei, for he was not one of us, and spoke so little to anyone but that foolish jokester Hapimana.

The result of this meeting was much angry talk among Mr Lightband, Mr Lloyd, Mr Brent, and Jenkins, and finally, at the insistence of Wharepapa, another meeting, this time at the offices of Mr Ridgway with a lawyer present. Mr Ridgway also invited Mrs Colenso and Reverend Stack to attend, so we would not need to rely on Jenkins and his friends as interpreters.

This was my first time in Leicester Square, and it was not at all as I expected. I thought it would be an elegant and well-tended place, like so many of the squares we had seen in the west of London, with their fine railings and green lawns. Leicester Square looked more like a dry wasteland, strewn with so much rubbish it might have been a dust-heap. Its straggly bushes were good for little but offering scant shelter to a great number of mangy cats, and also to the drunk and the destitute, who lay about in great numbers, groaning or sleeping, or stretching out feeble hands to beg for coins. Men staggered from low-class eating houses and dancing saloons, some singing raucous songs, unaware of the barefoot urchins who ran among them, no doubt picking their pockets. In the centre of the square stood a statue of a man on a horse, but this statue was missing both its arms and one leg, as though someone had hacked at the figure with an axe.

Horomona Te Atua could not take his eyes off the Alhambra Theatre on the far side of the square, and I must admit that I was very taken with the sight as well. I hardly knew it was a theatre until Wharepapa told me, for with its minarets and arches and dome it looked like pictures the missionaries showed us depicting King Solomon's palace. This was the theatre where the Maori Warrior Chiefs performed each night, and I wondered how could they make their voices heard in such a vast place. But seeing its size and beauty, I no longer wondered why Wiremu Pou had decided to join them. He had always fancied himself a prince of the realm.

Mr Ridgway's office, up several flights in a dark building, was not large at all. We pressed against windows and walls, and there were chairs for Mrs Colenso and Hariata Pomare alone. Ngahuia pouted because of this, and stood in the corner with her arms folded.

Here we were given new contracts in English to sign, and Mrs Colenso read them over and talked each point through with us, to ensure we understood the meaning. We would continue with our tour, under Jenkins' leadership, and the company would pay each of us one pound five shillings a week. For reasons I can't recall, Mr Ridgway insisted on an entirely separate agreement with Ngahuia, which we all suspected gave her more money. She was quite a favourite of his, and that day they stood conspiring in the corner until she was smiling and simpering once again.

Jenkins was most unhappy about all of this, and accused us all of the blackest ingratitude.

'We have been treating you like lords, and introducing you into the best society!' he complained. He stood by the door to Mr Ridgway's office, as though to bar us from escaping. 'We show you things to instruct and improve, and as a reward for our kindness you throw every difficulty in our way, and put us to great trouble and expense. We have made great losses on this venture, and you do not seem to care at all.'

Wharepapa was offended by this speech, and made a great point of saying that he and Reihana would abide by the agreement made in Auckland. They would wait until the end of our trip, and take their share then, whatever that share might be.

'We do not ask for money each week,' he said, and his face was most haughty. He does this face well, Wharepapa. I've grown quite accustomed to it over the years. 'If you offer it to us, if you beg us to take it, still we will turn away.'

This was all very fine, this talk, but we all knew that Wharepapa was the one who had visited Mr Ridgway to speak of these matters. Wharepapa was the one who requested the services of the lawyer, to ensure these new contracts were proper English law! As for Reihana, he might proclaim that he did not want to be given money each week, but he never hesitated to ask Jenkins for money whenever the need arose, however small that need. Reihana would ask Jenkins for money to have his coat brushed and mended, when the rest of us would find the required coins in our own pockets. We used to joke that Reihana would ask Jenkins for the money to have his shoes blacked or to buy a penny-ice. He was determined *not* to have money, I thought, for he liked to suffer, and to make a show of it.

I'm afraid that this is not a very Christian thought on my part, and perhaps I should not have written it down. Let me be more charitable, and conjecture that Reihana was simply a man of principle, who wished to abide by the original agreement because he could not say, in good faith, that he had misunderstood the paper he signed.

More accusations and recriminations went on for some time, to the obvious enjoyment of Mr Ridgway. From time to time he would nudge Ngahuia and then shout out warnings to Jenkins.

'The Duke will be very interested to hear this!' he would say. 'The Earl of Shaftesbury will be shocked to learn of such a statement!'

Soon Mr Brent, so disheartened by the financial losses Jenkins kept mentioning, declared his intention to return to New Zealand at once, and to leave Jenkins and Lloyd and even Mr Lightband, his son-in-law, to 'get on with it', as he said. In New Zealand he could earn money rather than just spend it, so home to New Zealand he would go.

This was not the only announcement. Hare and Hariata Pomare were told that it was the express wish of Her Majesty the Queen that they move as soon as possible to the house of Mrs Colenso. This lady and her daughter would take care of them until the child was born. The Queen herself would pay all their expenses in London, and their passage home. They were so happy with this news that they both cried with joy and relief. Poor Hariata Pomare was tired, I think, of traipsing here and there to parties or meetings, or to tour great buildings, for she felt unwell almost every day.

We were not much longer in London after that meeting, as I recall, but there were several important events that I must write down. I can't remember the order of them, but I know they all occurred before we left to catch the train to Bristol, herded to the station by Mr Lightband because Jenkins had travelled ahead of us, to find us lodgings and to make arrangements for our public appearances there.

The first thing I must speak of was the visit from a Mr Smetham, an artist, who had been commissioned by the Wesleyan Missionary Society to paint a picture of us. After we returned to live in the Strangers' Home, he arrived one morning to make sketches of us. He was a strange fellow, this Mr Smetham. I recall a wildness to him. He was like one of the cats skulking under the bushes in Leicester Square. He drew very quickly, spending very little time with each of us. I remember Wiremu Pou laughing, saying Mr Smetham pressed the pencil so hard it looked as though the paper would rip.

It was definitely Wiremu Pou who said that, for I remember him miming the actions, and nudging Horomona Te Atua so his brother would laugh as well. And I remember Tere Pakia talking on and on, saying that we had photographs of ourselves and now we would have a painting as well, and that she wondered which would look best. So this Mr Smetham must have visited us when we first returned to the Strangers' Home, just before those three fools ran off to join the Maori Warrior Chiefs.

Mr Smetham could not speak any Maori, of course, but Mr Lightband was there to explain things. Mr Lightband told us that although our likenesses were taken at the Strangers' Home, the painting itself would show us standing in the house of John Wesley, a place we had visited in July. During that visit we were taken to see the chapel and various graves, and then shown to the room where Wesley died. We all took our turn sitting in his chair, for the minister who showed us round the house seemed to expect it. John Wesley was a figure of great mana for Jenkins, who looked close to tears that night. In the cab going home he told us that it was the most happy evening he had spent in England. I remember that, for Ngahuia mocked him for it later. She said that Jenkins was a fool, and that the happiest evenings in England, in her opinion, were the ones where we promenaded about ballrooms and were fed on champagne and delicious jellies.

I did not see the sketch Mr Smetham made of me, and now I know that I should have asked that day to look upon it. Artists can make mistakes on their canvas as writers can on a page, and then what can be done? There is no way to argue with a painting, except to make another painting. And when we are all long dead, strangers will look upon these paintings, and they will not know which one is true and which is false, or if they are both false in different ways.

But now I must return to those last days in London, for there was more excitement to be had before we left for Bristol, and I soon forgot Mr Smetham and his wild eyes. Hare and Hariata Pomare were about to move away from the Strangers' Home, and with Mrs Colenso had fixed on a day of departure. I was sad that they would not be travelling with us, for they were both fine young people, but I knew that living quietly in London – if such a thing is possible! – would be preferable, especially for Hariata. I was also sad, I think, because I knew that the Queen's eye was upon them. She would not let anything untoward happen to them; she would not let them starve or live in a degraded way. While they remained with us, I believed that the Queen's gaze would encompass us all, and that we would never be permitted to sink too low. Once we parted from them, I worried that we might lose the Queen's interest, and protection.

Hare Pomare wished to remain in London for an additional reason. He had recently paid a visit to the home of Sir Frederic Rogers, to see young Wiremu Repa. The boy had left his school and was preparing to return to New Zealand. Hare went for the evening but stayed the night for, he told us, he could not bring himself to leave. The boy was terribly ill, breathing with difficulty, and sitting up in his bed like a pale ghost. Pomare was afraid the boy would not last the night, and insisted on sleeping in a chair in Wiremu Repa's bedroom. That night, when Sir Frederic and his wife left the room, the boy wheezed out what they'd been saying. Sir Frederic had told his wife he wasn't at all sure that 'six-foot-three of savage' would fit in their armchair!

Hare returned to the house every day to visit the boy, and to tend him in his illness. Later we were to hear that Wiremu Repa finally sailed for New Zealand some time in the autumn, the English autumn. Many months after that Mrs Colenso told us that the boy died before reaching New Zealand, and had been buried at sea. We were all very unhappy to hear that news, though by that time everything we heard seemed to make us unhappy.

Before we left the Strangers' Home, Hare Pomare received another invitation, though perhaps it would have been better if he hadn't. On his return from a visit with Wiremu Repa, a Captain John Reid was waiting to see him. This Captain Reid had once lived in New Zealand, more than thirty years earlier, and had known Hare Pomare's father. These days he was a land steward on a large farm outside London, but he spent much time here with his family, in their house in Marylebone. Would Hare and Hariata, and all their Nga Puhi kin, be so kind as to pay the Reid family a visit?

Of course, all of us from the North went – Reihana,

Horomona Te Atua, Wharepapa and I. We had no Jenkins there to argue that we should be speaking at a meeting and passing around a hat. The Reids lived in one of a neat row of narrow houses, and though there was nothing grand or impressive about the premises, it was most enjoyable to be in a house where Maori was spoken. Mrs Reid arranged a great spread of food, and their two daughters, Mary Ann and Elizabeth, seemed to be sweet-natured girls and most attentive, quite unafraid of us. The girls spoke no Maori at all, of course, for they were born and raised in England. Elizabeth, the older girl, had worked as a maidservant for her father's employers, but had been sent home to recuperate from scarlet fever, or some other malady. She had very yellow hair, and a pretty smile.

Wharepapa enjoyed the visit more than any of us, for Captain Reid knew his part of Northland very well, and they had much to talk about. We only had a few days left to us in London, and Wharepapa managed to visit the Reid household every one of those days. Mr Lightband grew quite frustrated with us, for one afternoon, when we had a long-standing tea engagement at the home of a Wesleyan minister, he could only muster four of our party to attend.

Our last night in London I remember particularly clearly. This was the evening that Ngahuia announced she would not travel with us to Bristol. She had no desire to leave London, where she was the pet of numerous ladies, and where there were many shops, parties, and amusements. She didn't want to move from one lodging house to the next, or to stand on platforms and exhibit herself, especially as she was now the only woman in our party, without any sort of companion or confidante. The ladies of London would take care of her, with Mr Ridgway's assistance.

She said all this to Mr Lloyd, who had called at the Strangers' Home to settle our account. He was furious.

'You cannot stay here alone, you stupid woman!' he told her, raising his voice so everyone in the large hall could hear, though only we Maori could understand.

'Haumu is alone in London,' she said, pouting. 'Tere is alone.'

Mr Lloyd looked at her as though, like Haumu, she had taken leave of her senses.

'Hariata Haumu is in a sick house, cared for by many nurses,' he shouted. 'Tere Pakia is with her husband, under the protection of Mr Hegarty. You cannot stay here alone!'

We were all there to hear this argument apart from Wharepapa, who had gone out alone that evening. Reihana tried to persuade her to come with us to Bristol, warning her that London was a wicked place filled with degenerates, and she was sure to come to no good, but Ngahuia would not listen. When Hapimana stroked at her arm, she threw him off.

'Don't touch me!' she hissed at him, and then turned to address the rest of us. 'This is what he did to Haumu on board the ship. He said he was comforting her, but I know what happened. This is why she lost her mind!'

Between Hapimana's frantic and indignant denials, and Ngahuia's sobs and foot-stamping, we made quite a spectacle in the Strangers' Home that night. A gaggle of Lascars, smoking their pipes before the fire, watched with some interest. Mr Lloyd was unmoved by any of Ngahuia's talk, and said that they would not pay for another night's accommodation for her in that place. She was to come to Bristol with us the next day, or be left to her own devices in London – which, he said, was 'the most expensive place on earth'.

Ngahuia vowed that she did not care, and that she would

stay on at the Strangers' Home without us. But some time later, when we were in Bristol, we heard that Colonel Hughes had not allowed her to stay. He doubted her ability to pay her bill, did not usually house young women with no chaperone, and, I suspect, was weary of her hysterical carrying-on. In fact, I suspect he was weary of all his Maori residents, for we seemed to be constantly in his office, arguing with Jenkins, complaining about this and that, or dashing off at night to join theatrical troupes.

Ngahuia, that stubborn girl, had to throw herself on the mercy of Mr Ridgway, who found her lodgings elsewhere in Limehouse with a Miss Hobson. Strange that this is a name I remember, when I never met this lady at all, and yet the name of the Mayor of Bath, who was so good to us, is gone from my memory!

My tale of our last night in London is not yet over, for it was an evening of much incident. At that time of the English summer, the days were very long, and none of us wished to be going to bed while it was still light. Horomona Te Atua and I walked out without any particular destination in mind. As I said, I liked walking in the evenings in Limehouse, for we were not followed or stared at too much, many people assuming, I think, that we were some of the many hundreds of Lascar sailors staying in this area.

For a long while Horomona Te Atua was silent, and then he took me into his confidence. Firstly, he knew where Wharepapa was that night. Wharepapa was up to no good with Elizabeth Reid, whose father had been called away to the countryside. They had planned an assignation.

I say 'assignation', but Horomona used more plain language at the time.

The second thing he wanted to tell me was that his brother, Wiremu Pou, had sent him a message asking him to come to the Alhambra Theatre that night, to see his first performance with the Maori Warrior Chiefs. Horomona had been struggling with this all day. Mr Lightband would not approve, not least because he didn't want any more of us to abscond, and visiting the theatre might put this idea in our heads.

'But this might be the last time I see my brother in this country,' said Horomona, looking quite miserable. Wiremu Pou was a coxcomb, and he had left us despite the pleas of Horomona Te Atua, but they were still brothers. With Hare Pomare staying in London, Horomona would be the only young man in our party. The only young Nga Puhi man, I mean. He had very little to say to Hapimana Ngapiko.

Horomona Te Atua thought he had enough money for a cab to Leicester Square, but didn't like the thought of going alone to such a strange place, and sitting by himself without any friends. So of course I agreed to go with him. I must admit to a profound curiosity about what occurred behind the huge doors of such a place, and I was also interested to see these so-called Maori Warrior Chiefs in action. For a moment I was concerned about unwelcome attention once we reached Leicester Square, for it would be brighter and more crowded with people there. Horomona Te Atua had no moko, and in his trousers and coat he was simply a tall young gentleman with a dark complexion. My moko, however, was etched deep into my face, and there was no way to disguise it, unless I were to wear a high collar and a false beard!

Horomona reassured me that night was about to fall, that it was sure to be dark in the theatre, and that everyone there would be either confused by drink or absorbed by what was happening on the stage. In all of these points he was quite correct.

Leicester Square was no more respectable at night than it was during the day, people thronging its drinking dens and pot-houses, the hurdy-gurdy boys making a racket outside the theatre. A monkey scampered over my foot, and I had to clutch Horomona Te Atua's arm to steady myself. We paid sixpence each to enter the Alhambra without exciting much attention, and inside I only noticed a few stares. It was infernally hot, smoke thick in the air, and there was a stale, unpleasant smell of gas fumes and spilled liquor.

The theatre had numerous storeys, each propped up with decorated pillars. Most people sat down below, but our tickets were the cheapest, and we could only wander the gallery, where there were no chairs. Many other people promenaded about here, drinking and conversing, as though the acrobats on the stage were of no interest to them. Dozens of ladies walked about or leaned against the railing, each more bawdy than the next, with their painted faces and raucous laughs. One draped herself against Horomona in a startling fashion, shouting with mock outrage when he shook her off. Even on the streets of Lime-house I had not observed so many brazen bawds in one place.

We could not enter the main floor of the theatre, but we could look down upon it. This area was crammed with tables where people sat eating oysters and chops, and drinking wine as though it were water. The audience, as far as I could see in the gleaming gaslight, was largely comprised of gentlemen and girls, and not the kind of girls we met at the soirées and receptions to which Jenkins escorted us. These were the kind of girls who dangled on a gentleman's knee, or threw pieces of bread at the stage, cheering when they hit one of the performers.

The acrobats tumbled away to rowdy applause, and were

replaced by a singer who was nothing like Miss Patti, the lady we heard at the Crystal Palace. I couldn't understand the words of her song, but many in the crowd seemed to know it, and their voices soon drowned out the orchestra. Horomona Te Atua leaned over the railings, gazing at the fantastic sights of this place. I wasn't sure if he was shocked by the decision his brother had made, or envious.

After another performer, doing some kind of comic turn that included falling over and stealing a cymbal from the orchestra, the curtains opened again, with a roll of the drums, to reveal the so-called Maori Warrior Chiefs. How the crowd roared at their first glimpse of these men! Horomona and I pressed against the railings, trying to make out Hirini Pakia and Wiremu Pou. Even at such a distance, we soon fixed on the latter, for he was the youngest man of the six before us. Hirini and Tere didn't take the stage that night, perhaps because they had yet to learn the different parts of the performance.

The six men on the stage wore flax kilts but no cloaks. They had no heitiki, no ornaments of any kind, and they carried no patu or taiaha in their hands. Their half-naked appearance seemed to excite the crowd, as did the four haka they performed, each louder and more vigorous than the next, and some with words I recognised from Charley Davis's book. They began with what looked like a tutu ngarahu, but without weapons this was meaningless, and each haka ended with the high leap of the peruperu, no matter what kind of haka had proceeded it. No one in the Alhambra knew or cared about such things, of course, and they quite obviously preferred the haka to anything else. After the haka, the men on stage, quite out of breath, performed a maudlin waiata, while the audience chattered and grew restless.

After this, the Maori threw a ball here and there, and then wrestled each other for a while, which the crowd seemed to like very much. One man in particular was very strong, overcoming all his opponents, including the man who was so tall he towered over the rest, even Wiremu Pou. Three of the men had moko, though I couldn't make out the detail from such a distance.

Within twenty minutes, perhaps less, it was all over. Horomona Te Atua had talked of going to what his brother had called the Canteen, a place on a lower floor where champagne was served, and the dancers who would appear later in the evening entertained their admirers and cast about for new ones. But as soon as the performance was over Horomona seemed to lose heart, suggesting we returned at once to Limehouse. Seeing his brother on the stage was sufficient. Perhaps if he had truly believed that he would not see Wiremu Pou again in England, Horomona would have sought him out that night. At that time, I think, he imagined his brother's flirtation with a life on the stage, playing before such a rude and drunken crowd, would be short-lived.

We were invited to take this trip to England because we were rangatira, but in England, I think, we lost sense of what that meant. When I was a child, I learned what would be expected of me – a certain dignity, the ability to lead, the observation of protocol and custom, a respect for mana and tapu. An understanding of utu, the reciprocity on which our society depended so our lives would be in balance and our ancestors would be appeased. But in England we were little better than slaves, led and directed by others, and displayed in public places like trophies of war. Perhaps this was why some of our party were chafing to be free, even if they could only find another kind of captivity elsewhere.

Jenkins accused us constantly of ingratitude, and now I think that, in part, he was right. We were shown many wonders, and spent so much time wheedling and complaining, and wishing ourselves somewhere else. He was expecting humility from us Maori, when all we had was pride. This was what was left to us, now that the old ways of doing and seeing things had been swept away. In England we had the attitude of rangatira without any of the mana. The more that attitude angered our Pakeha, the more I wondered why they chose to bring us. If they'd just wished to instruct us, they could have done that in New Zealand. Was there nothing we could teach the English? Were the English to have all the authority?

These men up on the stage, they called themselves chiefs. But this was simply a show. No one in the audience knew who they were, or cared to know. If these men were truly rangatira people, as Wiremu Pou certainly was, this was beneath them. The moko on their faces were so much decoration. The words they spoke were meaningless, like the squawking of the birds on Parrot Walk, or the grunts of a child struggling to be understood.

'Wharepapa says you were a friend of the great Hongi,' the Bohemian tells me. He's making us some tea, because we've both been still for too long, and I need to sit for a while by the fire.

'Not a friend,' I say. 'Not an enemy, not a friend. I fought with and for him, as so many of us did at that time.'

How to explain this? These days I'm a rangatira, old and respected, with photographs and paintings, and people like Wharepapa bandying my name about the town. Back then, when I was young, Hongi was an ariki, a paramount chief, and when we were summoned to fight alongside his people, we went. There were always debts and alliances to be honoured. Sometimes we were lured with gifts. Besides, a taua was an opportunity to resolve disputes of our own along the way.

The Bohemian pulls up a low chair for me near the fire, and drops sugar into my tea. He knows how to make it the way I like. He only has one spoon and no saucers, but I don't mind.

'In my studio in Pilsen, my patron was a doctor, Dr von Meyer,' he tells me. 'This is when I was a young man, after my studies in Vienna.'

The Bohemian always has one patron or another. Here it's Mr Buller and Mr Partridge. He's told me that this is important for artists, for otherwise they might starve, like us in London without Jenkins.

This Dr von Meyer was once physician to the Sultan of the Ottoman Empire, and from him the Bohemian learned many interesting things. For many centuries the Sultans of that place were guarded by a group of the very best soldiers in the empire, and these men were called Janissaries.

'They were boys from Christian families,' the Bohemian explains. 'At a very young age, they were removed from their families and villages forever. They could be Christians no more. They were taught how to fight, and all their loyalty was to the Sultan.'

I sip my tea and rest my boots against the grate, for my feet are cold. The Bohemian keeps talking, asking me if this was the way things were done here. I don't understand what he means.

'When Hongi took slaves,' he says, 'was that not the same thing? They were young men who could fight for him?'

'No, no, no.' I would drum my feet against the grate, but I don't have the energy. The Bohemian understands nothing. The men of a taua are tapu in a way a low-born slave could never be. A slave could gather food for us, or cook, but never fight alongside us.

I mean, of course, that we *were* tapu. I speak of things as though they're going on now, but these were the old days. Sometimes slaves would be taken to resolve a dispute, or perhaps some would be killed so honour could be restored without having to harm other rangatira. Sometimes, when we were away from home on a taua for a long period of time, slaves would be killed because we needed to eat. Sometimes they were killed after we returned home, taken as utu by the family of a slain warrior, or killed for our feasts.

Some prisoners taken during a battle were a different sort of captive, a rangatira who was useful for a marriage alliance, or for trade. These are not the kind of slaves the Bohemian is talking about. I don't know why he brings all this up. It's unseemly. No one speaks of this any more.

As I said, these were the old days, before the missionaries persuaded us that so many of our ways were wrong – everything from our moko to our songs to the way we slept in our houses. Tapu was wrong. Slavery was wrong. We were supposed to release slaves, and if we couldn't do that we should at least promise not to kill them. This is why so few of the old-time rangatira agreed to convert. The loss of tapu and mana was too much to bear.

I tell the Bohemian the story of Toi, whose slave killed his dog and was punished, because the dog was tapu.

'You can't fight alongside slaves,' I say, 'because you can't trust them.'

This is all I will say on the subject of slaves.

'But these Janissaries, *they* were trusted when they were slaves,' the Bohemian insists. 'When they began to admit men who were not slaves, there was a problem. These new men had much ambition. They wanted to own land and have power, and tell Sultans what to do. Dr von Meyer told me that the old Sultan was very unhappy about this. He decided to kill all the Janissaries. So he did.'

'He killed all of them?'

'Yes, many thousands of them. Now there are no more.'

People say terrible things about Hongi these days, but nobody accuses him of killing thousands of his own men. This was not the way things were done.

I place my teacup on the floor and tell the Bohemian that I have to go back to the hostel now and rest. I will not be able to write much tonight. Some days I feel too old for everything. But I must try to write something, to shake the past from my head. It's so much more vivid than the present. Its voices are loud, crying out to be heard.

Through wisdom is a house builded; and by understanding it is established:

And by knowledge shall the chambers be filled with all precious and pleasant riches.

PROVERBS 24:3–4

Off we set for the city of Bristol, expecting to stay a week. Such was our popularity there, however, that eventually our visit was extended to a month. We were told that the city was smaller than London, but it still seemed a huge and busy place, its streets bustling with people, though certainly the river did not smell quite so foul. Bristol had a grand train station with a vast vaulted roof, the steam from the engines drifting about like clouds, and hundreds of men were building a bridge that stretched high above the river. There was no bridge as high and daring as this in London.

We stayed in lodgings on Queen Square. On warm days we could walk in the square, and sit in the shade of its many trees, and from my room I could look out at the statue of a king sitting upon his horse. This was a much finer place than Leicester Square, I can tell you, and the statue had not been set upon with an axe. Kihirini did not like it here, because he heard that many hundreds of people had been killed in Queen Square some years before. The place was tapu, he said, refusing to walk there or sit with us.

We didn't care one way or the other, for by now he was little company. He complained of exhaustion, and then swollen knees, and Jenkins had to call the doctor. 'More money,' said Reihana, still gloomy despite the sunny weather. Kihirini's illness was rheumatic fever, the doctor said, and he was to stay in his bed as much as possible, and not attend any public meetings.

For it was in Bristol that our life of meetings and lectures really began in earnest. Jenkins was very pleased to be in this city, because he was a Wesleyan, and John Wesley had built a chapel here, and because at last he could have his way and give one illustrated lecture after the next about New Zealand, with us – and his new painted map – serving as illustrations. There was no Mr Ridgway here to chastise him, or to report his activities to the Duke of Newcastle. Instead there was the Mayor and his council and hundreds of ladies and gentlemen, all eager to invite us to receptions and make speeches, and nearby there was another city, Bath, where the Mayor and other dignitaries were all equally happy to see us. Jenkins told us that every day he received letters from the great manufacturers of the county, inviting us to tour their premises.

Like London, Bristol and Bath had their own Zoological Gardens and museums, as well as assembly rooms, guildhalls, churches, and great houses. We visited the hospital and gaol and the baths, the newspaper offices, a house were orphans lived, a house where the blind were cared for and taught. If ever we doubted the greatness of England, or thought it just confined to one city, we realised the falseness of this in Bristol.

When we walked in the street, scores of children followed us, wishing to tug on our coats or shake our hands. After church services, ladies clustered around us, begging for our autographs. Horomona Te Atua was a particular favourite, for he was much taller and more handsome than Hapimana. This went to his head a little. Some ladies said he resembled an Italian tenor, or a dashing pirate. But Mr Lightband told us that everywhere we went, English people were amazed to find us so agreeable and dignified in our bearing. They expected us to be savages, you see, eager to pounce on the English and beat them to death.

In the Zoological Gardens, so many people pressed round us that the only escape was to launch some small boats out on the lake, and row them around while the ladies called out and applauded from the shore. This was my favourite thing in Bristol, I must say. The lake was small – what I would call a pond. But to be on the water is preferable to being always in a crush of people.

We visited many manufactories as well, seeing machines that spun flax, and others that wove floor-cloths. The men and women and children who worked there stepped away from their roaring machines, calling out to us or staring with their mouths open. They had never seen anyone like us, and we had never seen anything like these places. A small child would at once tend several machines that whirred and shouted, even though these machines were large enough to gobble him up.

We were given many gifts in Bristol, and shown much hospitality. After we inspected the floor-cloth works, the Mayor took us to the manager's office where we were handed glasses of wine and cigars, and each presented with a book printed with colour pictures of many different floor-cloths. Horomona Te Atua and Takarei returned from a visit to a brass foundry with stories of the way boiling hot metal was poured from giant spoons. Horomona was given a copper kettle engraved with his name, and Takarei received a portrait of the Queen in polished brass.

Best of all, in one manufactory we each were given a pair of new shoes. I had never in my life had more than one pair of shoes at a time. We were ashamed that we had nothing to give these people in return, apart from the cloaks Jenkins insisted we wear to all meetings and visits. These, he said, we must stop giving away, lest we have none left before the month was out. I had already given my dogskin cloak to the Prince of Wales, and after that day had to borrow one of Takarei's rain capes to wear here and there in London, or else wear something brought to England by one of the Pakeha. Takarei was already obliged to share his cloaks with Hapimana, and was very ill-humoured about lending his treasure to others in our party, especially someone from Northland.

When Hirini Pakia ran off to join the Maori Warrior Chiefs, he left his kaitaka behind, so usually I wore that. In Bath I presented it as a gift to the daughter of the Mayor, at the end of a big evening meeting at the guildhall. Even Jenkins did not have the cheek to ask for it back, though he threatened as much.

'He'll send you home now,' Hapimana joked when we were clambering into the omnibus waiting for us outside the guildhall. 'The last person here will be Takarei, because he has more cloaks than anyone else.'

Wharepapa was also running out of things to give, for he had presented his greenstone mere to the Mayor of Bath. He suggested we dig a hangi pit in the garden of one of the Reverends, so the ladies could taste our food rather than just hear about it. This garden, by the way, was bigger than any garden I've seen in New Zealand. It had stone walls, and towering trees, and a lawn that stretched as far as I could see. Several hundred people were there that day, and because they all wanted to taste the fish and potatoes cooked for them, we soon ran out of food. One kete was filled with mussels and cockles, and these were especially popular with the little gang of charity boys employed by the Reverend that day to play upon their fifes and drums.

I supervised the digging of this pit, by the way, and the laying in of the coals, but I did not take part in the cooking and serving of food. Reihana took his part with much gusto, which impressed me. This is what I mean when I say he was a true Christian. I could never claim such a title for myself.

Wherever we went, many people asked if we had cartes de visite, and if Jenkins, Mr Lloyd, or Mr Lightband heard these requests, they would produce small photographs of us and hand them over in exchange for coins. Some of us didn't like this at all. I had no objection to giving these cards to people, but selling them was another matter. It did not seem proper. When our photographs were taken in London, it was at the request, we were told, of the Prince of Wales. We didn't know these pictures would be stuck onto cards and hawked in the street. I raised the issue with Mr Lightband. He was most apologetic, but said it was an English custom and besides, we needed every penny. Even with our reduced party, he was barely able to cover everyone's expenses.

For this reason our group had to give many lectures, with Jenkins talking, then each of us in turn speaking, then the group singing or performing a haka. Reihana would speak, though he never took part in these performances. At first I would not perform either, but after a week or so I stood to sing the waiata or hymn along with the others. It seemed churlish and ungenerous to stay in my seat. There was no harm in it, I think, especially as the ministers present at these lectures never objected.

Wharepapa had plenty to say at these events. He was often

introduced as 'the leader of the chiefs', a title he liked very much. In the Victoria Rooms, an elegant place that looked like a church, he talked for so long, and with such violent emotion and gestures, that one lady fainted.

At that particular lecture I was sitting on the platform next to Horomona Te Atua, who was often subject to melancholy now his brother was gone. True, the attentions of young ladies cheered him up, and his understanding of English was improving every day, because so many were eager for him to practise conversation with them. This was a cause of much jealousy on Hapimana's part, for Horomona Te Atua was generally agreed to be the more distinguished of the two. Not only was he much taller than Hapimana, he had a more dignified bearing. There was nothing dignified about Hapimana Ngapiko, as I will tell in a moment.

At the lecture in the Victoria Rooms Wharepapa was proclaiming the things he proclaimed everywhere. Since we arrived in Bristol, he had become quite the statesman, with much to say about the war in Taranaki. This was their own foolish business, he said, and nothing to do with us. It was all the fault of the so-called Maori King. Quite right too. We all murmured in agreement.

Our troubles in New Zealand, Wharepapa said, could be blamed on two things. Firstly, blame lay with the Roman Catholics, who had come up with this wrong idea of a Maori King. Secondly, our problems were the fault of intoxicating drinks, which were ruining the country. This latter idea Wharepapa trotted out a lot, because it always received warm applause, especially from the ladies. Jenkins liked it as well, for he was a Wesleyan, and they are against everything that brings a person pleasure or relief, unless it is a great deal of prayer and the loud singing of hymns.

I often wondered that Takarei didn't take offence at Wharepapa's speech, because we were all convinced he was a Roman Catholic. We didn't know this for certain, and perhaps we were wrong, for we had no particular evidence for this suspicion. We could have asked him, I suppose, but none of us ever did.

The part of Wharepapa's speech about intoxicating drinks was designed to cause offence, this time with Hapimana in mind. Because of Hapimana, we were all asked to sign a pledge not to drink. Hapimana had been making a fool of himself in the streets of Bristol, carousing with no-good people. One night he was escorted back to his lodgings by a policeman, and his landlady complained to Jenkins. We were all annoyed with him about this, because it made us look like low-class Maori, and because the outcome of it was this pledge written out by Mr Lightband. Apart from Reihana, all of us liked to drink a beer or take some wine. We were not Wesleyans, after all.

Perhaps it was at this lecture in Bristol that I made my speech about the Sabbath, or perhaps it was at a lecture in Bath. On many days we had two or three of such events, the afternoon meetings attended by hundreds of people, and the evening lectures by thousands. Soon we barely knew the name of the town or the hall.

I think this particular evening we were in Bath, for I remember the broad smile on the face of the Mayor there, and also that I began my speech by praising his beautiful city and the kindness he had shown our party. Then I talked of how surprised I was to see that so many English people wore two hats on the Sabbath – that is, they wore their hats to church, but they also carried baskets about on their head, selling goods in the street as though it was any day of the week. I was very surprised to observe the Sabbath desecrated in a Christian country like England.

While Jenkins interpreted my speech for everyone in the audience, I thought of my final taua, when we all agreed not to fight on Sunday. No one was a Christian, but we didn't want to upset the missionaries who were anchored in the bay, and there was also much discussion of not angering their God. He was very powerful and, we'd heard, vengeful. It was safer to declare the day tapu and wait for the next day to resume our siege.

Once I was baptised in the Christian faith, I observed the Sabbath for different reasons, of course. It seemed strange to me that rangatira who rejected this faith would respect the Sabbath, when so many English Christians did not. I received no satisfaction on this point, however, as Kihirini Te Tuahu seemed eager to stand up and have his say.

Perhaps this was an evening in Bath, for Kihirini liked to come to that city to take the waters, hoping that they would make him well again. That night he talked in his wheezy, cracking voice about how as a warrior he had slain hundreds of men, with both our native weapons and the muskets of the Pakeha. Yet now, he said, the only weapon that mattered to him was the Word of God. After Jenkins relayed his words, the audience clapped for a long time.

I said nothing about this, but I truly doubt that Kihirini slew hundreds of men. I, Paratene Te Manu, would not make such a claim, and I am older than Kihirini and fought with more taua. He would be the greatest living warrior in New Zealand if this story were true, which I doubt. The missionaries liked to tell such stories, of untold hundreds killed, and thousands enslaved, and so on, but they were watching from a distance, or often not there at all.

Almost everyone took their turn to speak that night. Hapimana, not at all chastened after the encounter with a police constable, said there were far too many poor people in England, and he felt very sorry for them. They should go to New Zealand where they could till the land or work in a mine. He also said that his favourite thing in England was the public house, but Jenkins frowned at him and did not appear to relay his words to the crowd.

'Let's play a joke on Wharepapa,' Horomona Te Atua whispered to me. In London Horomona left the jokes to Wiremu Pou, but perhaps now he was stepping out from his brother's shadow. 'Watch his face while I talk.'

He stood up and paced the platform. We were happy to hear, he said, that Her Majesty the Queen did not wish to oppress the Maori people, and instead wished for them to be equal to her British subjects. But the laws in New Zealand were not truly uniting the English and Maori people.

'I think,' he said, pausing so that Jenkins could catch up with his words, 'that to unite our countries, our two races should marry together.'

There was much laughter from the audience at this, and some applause.

'You may laugh at this suggestion,' said Horomona, pleased at the reaction. 'But these are my thoughts. Marriage between the English and the Maori would improve both peoples.'

Everyone in the big room seemed to like this, once Jenkins had explained the words, and some gentlemen shouted out 'hear, hear!'

'Some of our Maori women have married English men,'

Horomona continued. 'But as yet English ladies have not married our Maori men. Surely the Bible teaches us that we must do unto others as we would be done by? Surely it teaches we must love one another? We could not do either of these things in a better manner.'

There was much applause now, and cheering.

'Ladies, you must follow the example of Maori ladies,' he said. Even Jenkins was smiling now, and Mr Lightband and the Mayor were laughing most heartily. 'This is all I have to say on the matter.'

I looked over at Wharepapa, who wasn't smiling at all.

These were good places, Bristol and Bath. In October, not long before we were due to travel north, Jenkins went away to London for a few days and returned with much good news. He'd visited Hare and Hariata Pomare at Mrs Colenso's house, and found them in good health and spirits. He'd also visited poor Haumu at the Grove Hall Asylum in Bow and discovered that she was much improved, her disposition quite restored.

She had not been trapped inside all these months, as we feared. Haumu had been taken on a picnic in Epping Forest, and on an outing for private patients to Southend, and she had behaved impeccably on both occasions, according to her nurses. Now she wanted to join our party again, and Jenkins had agreed to this at once. I think this was at Mr Lightband's urging, for he said the asylum was a costly place, and it would have been cheaper to keep Haumu all this time at the Grosvenor Hotel.

Jenkins' third visit in London had been more dramatic, for it involved much arguing with people he referred to as the henchmen of Mr Ridgway, a harridan of a landlady in Limehouse, and a vulgar seafaring man displaying the most base of intentions. But this visit too had been successful in the end, for at last Ngahuia had been persuaded to rejoin our party.

In many ways Ngahuia was a foolish woman, more foolish than she should have been at her age – around thirty, I think, at the time. But it was not right for her to be living in London without any protection, especially as she spoke only a little English. Her place was with us. As for Haumu, she should not have come on this trip to England at all, but she could not be abandoned to the company of the disturbed inhabitants of the Grove Hall Asylum. She and Ngahuia would be companions for each other, as they were on board the *Ida Zeigler*, except this time, we hoped, there would be no cries in the night and no broken doors.

So this was our happy ending in Bristol. Our farewell gathering was in the Broadmead Rooms, and this too ended with much laughter and applause. Crowds of people crammed in, cheering at the end of every speech. The plaintive voices of the women helped our waiata soar to the rooftops, moving some in the crowd to tears. Then the Mayor said he had heard of the strange Maori custom of rubbing noses, and declared himself anxious to see it. Wharepapa said he would be happy to hongi the Mayor, and so he did. I thought the room would explode, so loud were the cheers and drumming feet of the crowd!

One more thing I must write about from those months. One afternoon when we had arrived in Bath for a meeting and various other appointments, Jenkins took Reihana and me on a special visit to Kingswood School. This school was situated high on a hill above the town, and accessible only by a muddy track that looked like a road in New Zealand. But this was a place Jenkins had always wanted to see, he said, for it was founded more than a hundred years earlier by John Wesley himself.

Reihana – only accompanying us, I think, because everyone

else was going to a tea with an excess of ladies – preferred churches to schools. He often spoke of his plans to build churches all over Northland when he returned home. But I never saw any church in England that I liked more than Kingswood School. Its golden stones glowed in the afternoon sun, and I thought for a moment that Jenkins had brought us instead to a castle, or some great man's house. The gravel drive swooped across a lawn so green, I imagined I was home again. I had never seen so large or handsome a school.

We were met by the governor, a Reverend West, and the headmaster, who was so short that, were it not for his substantial whiskers, he might be mistaken for a pupil. The boys themselves we met in the great Schoolroom, a long panelled room with many windows, set with dozens of tables. The boys all leapt to their feet when we entered the room, so we walked past row after row of dark suits and white collars, each boy standing perfectly still. Such discipline and respect! Such a large airy room! Every school should look this way. How much would other children learn if they could study their lessons in such a room? 'Train up a child in the way he should go: and when he is old, he will not depart from it.'

As usual, Jenkins spoke for too long, and Reihana spoke for even longer, though I cannot imagine the boys of Kingswood were interested in listening at such length to his account of a visit to Bath Abbey. Wesleyans do not go to such churches, for they prefer the plainness of their chapels, and if they did wish to visit Bath Abbey, the boys could simply scamper down the hill and see it for themselves. I tried to keep my remarks short, for Jenkins was already muttering that we must return to the city soon, to prepare for that night's meeting. I stood before the boys and reminded them of the Bible's exhortation to apply their hearts unto instruction, and their ears unto the words of knowledge.

When we went to leave, the boys gave us the most resounding cheer. Jenkins and the Headmaster conferred, and agreed that the boys might come close to bid us farewell, and then several hundred seemed to rush forward at once. We could not leave until we had shaken every hand. Some of the boys were smiling, some were solemn. But none wished for us to go without bowing to us, and shaking hands. Truly, this was one of the happiest afternoons I spent in England, with these fine boys, in this great place.

That was the day I understood why I had come to that country – besides meeting the Queen, of course. To receive new shoes, a copper kettle and the like was all very agreeable, but these things wear out in time. A school goes on, and is of use to generation after generation of mokopuna. John Wesley founded Kingswood more than a hundred years before our visit, and every year the school had grown bigger.

Let Reihana build his churches. I was determined that when I returned to New Zealand, I would build a school. It would not be a castle, and it would not be filled with the sons of Wesleyan ministers, for we have neither the materials for castles nor an abundance of Wesleyans in Tutukaka and Ngunguru. My school would be open to Maori and Pakeha children, and within its walls they would learn all they must know to make our country as great as England. This plan was ambitious, I know, but why should we expect anything less than greatness? When our ancestors sailed across the ocean into the unknown, were they not dreaming of paradise?

The Bohemian wants to know why I'm staying in Auckland this week. I tell him I thought I was going to the Native Land Court, to talk about Hauturu and who can sell it.

'Do you want to sell it?' He sounds surprised.

The Crown want to buy it, I say, because it's a good island for prisoners. It's hard for boats to land, and for prisoners to escape. Most islands are hopeless. They make it too easy for prisoners to swim or sail away.

The British know all about this, because when they put Napoleon on an island, he escaped. They had to find another island for him, in the middle of the Atlantic Ocean. These fighting men are too wily and dangerous. Look at Te Kooti Ariki-rangi. When he was imprisoned on that cold place, Wharekauri, he stole a bugle and lots of guns, took over a schooner, and sailed back to the East Coast with several hundred of his followers. He's still running around the country now, almost twenty years later. They've given up trying to imprison him. He's not starting any more wars these days, you see. He's too busy with his foolish religion.

While Hongi was sailing back from England in 1821, crossing the Atlantic as we would many years later, Napoleon died. Some people said that Hongi's ship passed the island just as Napoleon's spirit left it, and that the spirits of the two men were fused there in the middle of the ocean. This is why Hongi was such a great tactician, and so tenacious and aggressive in battle. He'd always admired Napoleon, and spent much of his time in Cambridge examining the maps from Napoleon's campaigns.

I don't know about any of that. I don't think Hongi needed the mana of Napoleon to become a great leader.

'When the Crown buys the island, I will still live there,' I explain to the Bohemian. 'They won't need the whole island.'

'Britain is an island,' he says. I wait for him to go on, but he says nothing else. Britain is too full an island: that is the problem. There are too many people in it, which is why they all dream of coming here. Over there, cities are like monsters, devouring the land, filling the sky with smoke. We'll never see such places here.

The Bohemian will understand this when he arrives in England. So many people, and the skies so grey. For all its wonders and greatness, England can be a dark place. When the winter sets in, the darkness lasts all day long.

For every kind of beasts, and of birds, and of serpents, and of things in the sea, is tamed, and hath been tamed of mankind:

But the tongue can no man tame; it is an unruly evil, full of deadly poison.

JAMES 3:7–8

I have left something out of my account of our time in Bristol and Bath, because it's an unpleasant thing, and I was not sure if I wanted to write it down.

At a museum or some such place, when we were being shown around, I saw a creature they called a crocodile. This was a scaly lizard with a long jaw, and it once lived in water, like a taniwha. The others in my group looked at it without fear, for it was no longer living, but I wouldn't go anywhere near it. These creatures bring illness. They can destroy us. They can climb inside us while we sleep, and eat away at us from within.

I'm not saying that this crocodile could do this, or that it had been sent by the ancestors to punish us in some way. It was already dead, not crawling across our path. But if I were an English person, I would not keep such a creature in my museum. I would burn it, or have it cut into pieces. I wouldn't touch it, as some of the others in our party did. I would not take it in my hands, as Hapimana did, just to show off in front of women. What happened to Hapimana – did it begin on this day?

Certainly, it was not a good omen, seeing this crocodile. When Jenkins told us that Kihirini was too sick to travel to Birmingham, but was going to stay on in Bath to take the waters, I wasn't surprised. Kihirini stood too close to that crocodile lizard. He could not have been ignorant, as the younger ones were, of its dark power.

Those of us left of the original Maori party – six men and two women – travelled on to Birmingham. This was another great city of many thousands of people, all employed in the making of things to be sold around the Empire, and we were told there would be much here for us to see and learn. We would observe the making of guns and brass, and pins and buttons, and perhaps even drinking chocolate. We would stay there for a while, touring the district, and then move on to Manchester and Bradford.

But in Birmingham we were to be stuck fast for some months. The days already seemed dark when we arrived, though it wasn't yet winter. Many mornings we awoke to rain, and even when there was no rain, we couldn't see the sun. Birmingham was a city of thousands of tall chimneys, all bellowing black smoke into the sky. The cobbles in the road were dark and greasy with dirt.

By the end of October, almost all of us were sick. Ngahuia now complained that she wished she had stayed in London, for she did not care for this dark place where everyone was at work all the time and there were no parties. Why was Hariata Pomare permitted to live with Mrs Colenso, near all the shops and theatres, when she and Haumu must sit all day in this smoke-filled city? When we received word from London that Hariata Pomare had a baby boy, Ngahuia insisted she be sent there to help care for the mother and child.

'She has Mrs Colenso and her daughter,' Mr Lloyd told her. He was no friend to Ngahuia, not since the scene at the Strangers' Home when he was obliged to leave her in Limehouse. 'You would be of no use to them.'

I felt of no use to anyone at all. Whenever I stepped outside the house of Mrs Johnson, my landlady, the dirty air would sting my eyes. Even inside the house, the damp made my bones ache. The gloom of the weather settled around me, like a heavy cloak, and I felt too tired to walk. I didn't want to end up like Kihirini, wheezing and exhausted, but now we were facing many months of winter, and I wasn't sure when our spirits would lift. None of us had much energy for meetings, though Hapimana seemed much cheered when he discovered many beer shops and public houses in almost every neighbourhood, and learned that unless it was Sunday these places were open every hour of the day and night.

There was much talk among us now about returning to New Zealand. We were all comfortably lodged in a row of terraced houses on Bath Row, which was a respectable place near the big hospital and the church of St Thomas. Mrs Johnson's house had its own narrow back yard, not a court where dozens of people hung their washing and shared the privy.

But after a month in Birmingham we had not visited a single manufactory or workshop. All we did was go to meeting after meeting, where most of the talk was in English. Sometimes Jenkins talked for an hour before we were invited to stand and address the assembly, and I remember finding it hard to stay awake, especially in our second or third meeting of the day. Mr Brent had gone home: why couldn't we go home as well? Mrs Johnson told Wharepapa that this was just the autumn, and the days would grow much, much colder in the winter. At the time

I couldn't fathom such a thing. I'd never been so cold in all my life.

Jenkins would not listen to any talk of returning to New Zealand yet. He seemed much at home in this city, for he'd lived here as a young man, and when we first arrived, he was happy to renew the acquaintance of many of his Wesleyan friends. All the meetings he arranged for us took place in their homes and chapels. We had no big civic reception, as we had in Bristol and Bath, but we didn't mind this much. We were kept occupied visiting Walsall, Kidderminster, Worcester and many other towns whose names I've forgotten. Now all I remember of many of these visits is the bright, curious faces of children, and ladies with lace collars peering at us over their teacups. We became quite accustomed to taking omnibuses and trains. On many nights we arrived back at our lodgings very late, Mrs Johnson, a candle held aloft, running up and down the stairs in her nightgown and shawl, her hair twisted with papers.

It was in Birmingham that Reihana finally stamped his foot and refused to wear a cloak at all. Jenkins had called at Mrs Johnson's to collect us, carrying three cloaks – one for me and one for Wharepapa, for we had none left of our own, and one for Reihana, who had not brought any in the first place. Jenkins laid them on the table while he talked to Mrs Johnson in English.

'I never wore a cloak in New Zealand,' Reihana told Wharepapa, his face grim. 'And I'm not wearing one now.'

He gathered them up in his arms – quite a feat, for he was a short man and they were long and voluminous – and threw them into the hallway. Jenkins and Mrs Johnson stopped talking at once. Our dear landlady didn't understand what was taking place. She stood with her mouth half-open, petrified, like Lot's wife.

'If you make us wear these cloaks, we will go home,' Reihana said. He had always quarrelled with Jenkins, but in Birmingham he seemed to look for ways to defy him. 'None of us want to wear them.'

Really, I didn't mind wearing a cloak, especially now the weather was so cold. But we had to agree with Reihana, for our loyalty had to lie with each other, and none of us felt much pity for Jenkins. This was unkind of us, I think, but at the time our minds were full of suspicions. We hadn't received any of the promised weekly money since we arrived in Birmingham. Jenkins told us that there was none, even though we appeared at meeting after meeting, and saw Mr Lightband taking a collection.

'Let you, Mr Jenkins, also wear a kaitaka,' I suggested. This was a good resolution, I thought. 'We will all wear them together.'

I don't remember what we agreed that day. There was no time for Jenkins to return to his lodgings, so he couldn't wear a cloak, even if he were willing. If this took place before our first meeting at the Birmingham Town Hall, which I think it did, then Reihana was certainly wearing a cloak by the time he stood on the platform. But this was the last time he wore one. Jenkins didn't argue with him again on this subject. They had other things to argue about.

This Town Hall in Birmingham was a splendid place. It rose high above the street like an ancient temple, making the dark rows of houses and lanes surrounding it look even more mean and airless. It was so large that Jenkins was quite hoarse at the end of the meeting. Dr Miller, the Rector of Birmingham, had arranged the meeting, and it was the afternoon, so most of the audience were children marched in from their schools.

Two thousand people were present that day, the Rector told us. But none of them were the great men of the city, and we received no invitations to any of Birmingham's grand houses. Wharepapa had become an adept spy, and he listened carefully when Jenkins talked with Mr Lightband, or with some of his Birmingham friends. There was talk, he said, of the Mayor receiving letters from London, perhaps sent by Mr Ridgway, which contained many slanderous statements about Jenkins' character. These letters said that Jenkins was only interested in fame and glory for himself. He was only interested in money. He forced us to dress up, like tame monkeys, and paraded us from place to place. Jenkins was very unhappy about these letters.

Wharepapa told us all this, and he also told our landlady, Mrs Johnson, and her friend, Mrs Strong. We were drinking tea together in the parlour, and Reihana was there as well. He'd been talking for some time that afternoon about the death of his son, and the ladies seemed very sympathetic, though I noticed that for every fifty words Reihana said in Maori, Wharepapa told the ladies only five in English, so they were not hearing very much of his sad tale. When Reihana finally stopped talking, closing his eyes to reflect upon his grief, Wharepapa began speaking of Jenkins. The ladies had quite a lot to say now.

'Mrs Johnson says it is wickedness,' Wharepapa told me, 'to keep us here against our will, far from home. Mrs Strong says that this is not Christian. We should not be monkeys, dressed in a costume.'

Wharepapa said that the ladies wanted to know what I thought. I didn't know what to say. The fire crackled and spat, and although the heavy curtains were drawn back, the window admitted no light. It was still the afternoon, but the days had grown indistinguishable from night. I wanted to say that we needed to travel far, far to the south, to see light again during the day, and the stars at night.

Whenever I couldn't sleep, and sat looking out my window, the sky was choked with cloud or smoke. All I could see was a drunkard or two staggering home, or the night-soil men lugging their pails from the courts. Sometimes they poured the contents onto their carts, and other times they dumped dark heaps on the road and salted it all with lime. I wondered how many of these carts moved around the city at night, and how many men were needed to carry away the excrement and ash of such a place.

These were not subjects you can discuss with English ladies. I have no recollection of what I said that afternoon. What I do remember is that before long Wharepapa too refused to wear a cloak at any of our meetings, and that Jenkins' face showed us that he was most irritated by this, though he said nothing.

Reihana now felt more confident about his protests – or perhaps now that Wharepapa had joined him, Reihana needed to stand out in some other way. The missionaries used to tell us that it was not enough to be a Christian. We must call out to others with the message, to make them see the evil of their ways. Reihana was determined to do this. The missionaries would have been proud of him, though I must confess to finding it tiresome.

We were at a meeting where several hundred people were present. In my memory it was a cold chapel with plain windows, where people stood against the walls and filled all the pews, but that could describe any number of meetings we attended in Birmingham. Reihana was in a fury. He'd confronted Jenkins that afternoon when we were collected from Mrs Johnson's house.

'There is much wrongdoing going on,' Reihana told Jenkins. He wouldn't even get up from his seat at the table. Mrs Johnson stood holding his coat, looking at us all in some agitation, for fear we'd be late arriving at the meeting.

'We can talk of this later,' Jenkins said sharply. He was looking exhausted in those days, worn out with the endless meetings, and the bleak weather, and our shenanigans, I suppose. The letters sent to the great men of Birmingham, attacking him – these preyed on him, too. By now he was talking of them openly, not just behind his hand to Mr Lightband. Jenkins felt them to be unjust and some days he spoke very bitterly. He would not only lose all his money in England, he said, he would lose his good name.

Reihana cared nothing for Jenkins' troubles.

'Later you will disappear off for supper,' he went on. 'Or you will go to visit one of your minister friends, and nothing will be said.' This was quite true. Jenkins never lodged with us, and the only time we could be sure to find him at his own lodgings for a korero was on a Sunday afternoon, when he wrote his letters and answered invitations.

'Then say what you have to say now, but say it quickly.'

Reihana was always telling me and Wharepapa that he was a quiet man who hated to quarrel, and that he thought for a long, long time before saying anything. I don't know about that. But certainly, he never said anything quickly.

'Many times I have had great sadness,' he began. 'Many times I think of all the falseness among us, and the wrongdoing, and I feel this sadness.'

'What wrongdoing?' Jenkins snapped. I wondered if I should sit down again, because I was very tired, and the cloak I was carrying was heavy.

'We all know that three of our group are acting in an improper manner,' said Reihana, his face mournful. 'We have spoken of this before, in Bristol. Yet still you permit those who do wrong to stand up in churches and speak.'

'You talk of Hapimana, I assume.'

'Friend, it is not just Hapimana, though he does much wrong, on almost every night of the week. My heart is filled with sadness thinking of his deeds. There are the deeds of Takarei as well, and the deeds of Horomona Te Atua.'

Jenkins gave a long sigh, and Mrs Johnson asked a worried question. She no doubt thought that Reihana was unwell, or perhaps unhappy with the mutton and potatoes she'd served at dinnertime.

'This is true,' Wharepapa said, nodding in a slow, solemn way. Of course it was true. Since Wiremu Pou had left us to join the Maori Warrior Chiefs, and Hare Pomare moved to Mrs Colenso's house, Horomona Te Atua was sad and often lonely. He was lodging with Hapimana and Takarei, and would not always wish to sit at home while the others ventured out to taverns and music halls. If Jenkins wanted to watch them, or prevent them from going out, he or Mr Lightband or Mr Lloyd should have shared their lodgings. And why would the Pakeha imagine that we Maori would only see the greatness of England, and wish to sample nothing else?

'Even Paratene,' Reihana said, speaking of me but not looking at me, 'has succumbed to the temptation of drink. We are all sinking low in this place.'

I felt myself bristling with anger, my face hot as though I had pushed it too close to the fire. On one occasion in a Limehouse public house I may have had one or two drinks too many, and on just one night in Birmingham, when we were entertained by Mrs Johnson's neighbour, a gentleman who worked in a brewery, I may have drunk a little more than was good for me. I was not alone that night. Wharepapa sat by my side, jabbering away half in English and half in Maori, and toasting the health of the Queen many, many times.

'I know all this,' said Jenkins. 'What is your point?'

'It's wrong to take these men to meetings, especially to Christian places of worship, when they act in this manner against Christian morals.'

'Do you say we should tell Paratene to stay at home tonight?'

'Not Paratene,' Reihana said, as though he were bestowing a great favour upon me. I wished I was holding a patu in my hand, so I could knock Reihana about the ears. I was very, very glad that Mrs Johnson couldn't understand what he was saying, though I think she must have had some idea of our merry evening in her neighbour's house. She opened the door to us afterwards, and smiled when Wharepapa stumbled into the umbrella stand. 'But the other three are bad week after week, and they should not talk at our meetings.'

'What if someone asks a question of one of them? Are we to say that they are not permitted to speak?'

'Yes. We will tell the people of Birmingham why, so these three sinners are humbled.'

'We will do no such thing.' Jenkins was angry now. 'I will not stop anyone from addressing a meeting, and I won't speak of any of these accusations. Can't you see what harm it would do? People would think ill of your Maori party. Our enemies would say that this trip to England was wrong.'

'You speak of enemies,' Reihana said, 'but you don't understand that our most dangerous enemy is the Devil, and he has captured these three young men, and led them into wicked ways.'

I think it was Wharepapa who brought an end to this conversation, reminding us that the time was late. The longer this talk went on, the more likely his own sins would be raised by Reihana, though I'm sure Reihana had no idea of half of what Wharepapa got up to.

Reihana came to the meeting that night, but he was still seething. After all the usual preliminaries of introductions and Jenkins' speech, it was our turn to talk. Horomona Te Atua stood, and spoke for a while about the great kindness of the English people, and how we had learned so much during our visit here. I can't remember what he said, really, or why it seemed to annoy Reihana so. Perhaps it was simply that he was speaking, when Reihana wanted him to be humbled and not permitted to speak.

As soon as Horomona moved to take a seat again, Reihana stood up, his face very severe. But Jenkins said to let me speak next, and Reihana sat down, clearly vexed. I spoke in his place, though I was uneasy about what had just occurred, and fearful that Reihana would be even more angry now.

By the time three or four of us had spoken, Reihana had disappeared into a small room to the side of the platform. Later he said that he was cold, and went into the room to warm up. Hapimana told him he'd be warmer if he wore a cloak, but Reihana was in no mood for such jokes.

We'd sung something, and then the younger men arrayed themselves at the front of the platform and began the haka. I pulled my chair back to keep out of the way, and from that place I could see Reihana. He was standing in the doorway to the small room, arguing with Jenkins.

'They must stop,' he told Jenkins. 'They are godless men performing this godless thing, here in the house of God!'

Jenkins held up a hand, and I thought he was going to push Reihana back into the room.

'You stay there,' he said, and he said some other things, but I could not hear them over the roar and thumping of the haka. Whatever he said did no good, for Reihana slid past him and charged onto the platform.

'This haka is no good!' he screeched at the crowd, pushing between Hapimana and Takarei. They both looked startled, but kept going, shouting even louder to drown out Reihana's voice. 'This is a wicked thing! It is sinful!'

He swung his arms in the air in a wild way, smacking Horomona in the arm. Still the haka went on. Reihana was shouting in Maori, so of course no one sitting in the pews could understand him. They probably thought it was all part of the haka: the young men were to shout, and leap about, and widen their eyes, while the old man walked among them, shouting his heathen encouragement. Jenkins did nothing to dispel this idea. He leaned against the wall, his arms folded and his lips set tight.

'This is some business,' Wharepapa murmured to me, but he did not move from his spot either. What was to be done? Reihana was still ranting when the haka finished, but the audience was applauding, drowning him out even more. Perhaps they thought he was drunk, or not right in the head.

Outside in the street, waiting for cabs to take us home, Reihana was still talking.

'I will tell Mrs Johnson everything about the sin among us,' he said to Jenkins. 'I want no part of your secrets and deceit.'

'As you wish,' Jenkins said, sounding utterly fatigued. I don't know how Reihana was planning to say so much to Mrs Johnson. The only English words I'd heard him say to her were 'good' and 'bacon'.

'And I will travel to London to see Mr Ridgway, to tell him my opinion of things. I will speak to him of our unhappiness here, and say how we are brought low, to wickedness.'

This had more of an effect, as Reihana no doubt intended.

'Go,' Jenkins said, and there was much contempt in his voice. 'You're no good to us here. Your opinion means nothing to me. You can say whatever you like to Ridgway, and it will leave no mark on me. The only people harmed are the ones who leave me, not the ones who stay.'

'You harm us all with your lies,' Reihana told him. It was raining now, and the rain had teeth, biting our faces. Everyone huddled around, miserable and cold, listening to Reihana and Jenkins. 'Where is the one pound five shillings you promised to pay them? This was an agreement made in London, but you don't honour it. You are not a truthful man.'

Jenkins didn't reply. He turned away from us all, and walked a few steps down the street. I wondered if he was leaving us, abandoning us here on the street in Birmingham because we were all too much trouble. I can't remember if Mr Lloyd and Mr Lightband were there that night. I only remember Jenkins.

He didn't leave us. When the cabs rolled up, he gave our addresses to the drivers. Despite his big words that night, Reihana didn't say anything to Mrs Johnson. Wharepapa did. And Reihana didn't go to London. Jenkins did. Mr Lightband told us that Jenkins was tired of the letters addressed to the Mayor of Birmingham, saying that Jenkins was a showman and an adventurer who didn't look after us. These letters were from Mr Ridgway and a doctor who was something to do with the Aborigines' Protection Society. Jenkins travelled down to London to confront both men. When he returned, we did not ask many questions. I was tired of all the quarrels.

I remember that when Jenkins returned it was December, and the cold was very sharp. Kihirini travelled up to join us, which was a mistake. He went straight to bed at his lodgings. He needed to sit in the warm pools of Bath, not shiver with the rest of us in Birmingham. None of us were particularly pleased to see him, especially as we were all quite ill ourselves by this time.

He was not the only Maori arrival in the city, for the Maori Warrior Chiefs troupe turned up next. Mrs Johnson waved the newspaper at us, in much excitement at the notion of two Maori groups at large in Birmingham. They would be performing at Holders Concert Rooms before moving on to Coventry. This time Horomona and I did not go to see his brother, Wiremu Pou – or, at least, if he went he did not mention it to me. I did not have the spirit for such adventures, for every time I stepped outside, the cold felt like a tight band around my chest.

There was news from London that Pomare's baby had been christened in Tottenham, with stories in all the newspapers talking of the Queen's lavish christening gift, and this made Ngahuia even more discontent. Mrs Colenso had sent a letter, and we all read it. Hare and Hariata had been invited to see the Queen again, this time in Windsor, and would travel there with Mrs Colenso. They were looking forward to seeing the little princesses again.

'Why should they see the princesses again?' Ngahuia demanded, more petulant than ever now her nose was red raw, and she had to walk everywhere with a handkerchief clamped to her face. 'And Mrs Colenso says that more photos of Hare and Hariata will be taken, and more of these visiting cards will be made.'

'They're going to be in another painting as well,' Hapimana reminded her. He was not friendly with Ngahuia, especially since she accused him of mistreating poor Haumu, and he liked to see her unsettled and annoyed. Mrs Colenso had told us that another artist had approached Hare Pomare, and the painting he would make would show Hare, Hariata and the great Patuone, matua to Pomare. For the picture of Patuone, the artist would rely on a photograph, as the Bohemian often does.

I didn't care what was going on in London. I was beginning to feel like a trapped bird, waking up every morning to see the same things from my window, or to see very little, because of the fog and the smoke. Even though I felt unwell, I was relieved when Jenkins told us we must travel to Gloucester, another city, and see the sawmills there, and the place where railway carriages were built. I couldn't face another day of sitting in Mrs Johnson's house smelling nothing but damp, wet newspapers, and stewed meat, while Wharepapa scribbled letter after letter and Reihana talked of his deep sadness.

We spent one or two nights in Warwick, where the Mayor was very solicitous, giving each of us a fine bound copy of the New Testament. Kihirini could not accompany us, and Ngahuia was difficult there, as I recall, demanding her own cab when we arrived at the station, and refusing to take her place on the platform that evening. But the rest of us were happy to see something new.

Something old was waiting for us on our return to Birmingham. Hirini and Tere Pakia had decided to abandon the Maori Warrior Chiefs and throw themselves on the mercy of Jenkins. They didn't care for performing each night on the stage, they said, and had decided that Mr Ridgway was right. It was degrading, for no one understood who they were.

I knew exactly who they were, so it was no great delight for me to stand with them on the platform in Cheltenham, or to stay in a room next to theirs at the Temperance Hotel in Stroud. Wharepapa said that if he were Jenkins, he would not have taken them back. I think Mr Lloyd and Mr Lightband agreed with this sentiment, for all this return meant was more expenditure, and the likelihood of more trouble.

At Christmas all our Pakeha left us for a few days. Jenkins went to his brother's in Stratford, taking Hapimana with him because he couldn't be trusted to be left without a chaperone, and was a bad influence on others. Mr Lloyd went to London, and Mr Lightband went back to Worcester. They all had family in these places. The rest of us spent Christmas in our lodgings. Our spirits were very low. On Christmas Day itself, we knew that Hare Pomare, his wife, and their baby were sailing back to New Zealand on the clipper *Statesman*. They were travelling in a first-class cabin, with all their expenses paid by the Queen.

I'm ashamed to say this, but I envied them. They were going home, escaping the terrible cold of England, and they would be well looked after on the voyage, with plenty to eat and a cabin all of their own. No one could look down on them, or tell them not to walk here and there. No one would ask them for waiata and haka simply as a way of passing the time, or putting on a show.

True, they had not seen as much of England as we had, but that also meant they had not seen the fogs and chimney smoke of Birmingham, or felt its damp black dust settle in their throats. They had not made spectacles of themselves by cavorting about unclothed on the stage, like Tere and Hirini Pakia, and that bounder Wiremu Pou. They were returning with gifts from the

Queen herself, just as Hongi returned with gifts from her uncle, the old King George, and this meant honour for them and their families.

The rest of us were still in England, with no word of when we could return home. Kihirini was confined to his bed, moaning about his cough and his aches. Wiremu Pou was still touring with the troupe of so-called Maori Warrior Chiefs. Hapimana was with Jenkins, watched so he could not get drunk or arrested again. The remaining nine of us sat in our rented rooms in the dark city of Birmingham, waiting to be told of our next engagement. We were cold and we were homesick.

On the day after Christmas, I was sitting by the fire, straining to read the English words of the New Testament. I understood some of the words, but too many of them looked strange on the page, and too small to make out in the dim light of our room. Wharepapa was at the desk, where the lamp's yellow light was strongest, writing a letter. He was always writing and receiving letters. We all wrote letters, but no one but Wharepapa received one almost every day of the week.

The sound of excited voices downstairs was followed by the now-familiar sound of Mrs Johnson climbing the stairs; for such a small woman, she had a heavy tread, though her knock on our door was always timid. Wharepapa called out in English, telling her to come in.

She was breathless and red in the cheeks, and wanted Wharepapa to come downstairs at once. A lady was waiting there.

'A lady?' Wharepapa turned to me, speaking in Maori now. 'Who is this lady? I know no ladies in Birmingham.'

This was quite true. He only knew ladies in London – or one lady in particular, Miss Elizabeth Reid, and though he had not been in London for some months, I had seen him write her name on many letters.

Mrs Johnson talked for some time and later, when Wharepapa had recovered his humour, he told me what she said. This lady, she assured him, was quite unknown to him or to Mr Broughton.

That was me. She always called me Mr Broughton, for she found the name Paratene too hard to say.

Mrs Johnson's friend Mrs Strong had yet another friend, and this lady had met another lady somewhere about the town. I was quite confused by this part of the story, for there were too many ladies involved. One of these ladies had told the other of our plight. And now this lady was downstairs, and Wharepapa and I were to come at once.

Mrs Johnson was particularly agitated because the only one of us sitting downstairs was Reihana, Mr Richard, who spoke no English at all.

'She said,' Wharepapa told me later, choking back a laugh, 'that he was just sitting there looking very grave.'

When Mrs Johnson finished her speech, Wharepapa blotted his letter, and told her that we would both come downstairs at once. The lady's name was Miss Weale. Miss Dorotea Weale, a highly respectable lady, friend of the local magistrate, and superintendent of the Winson Green Road Home for Girls.

Of all the meetings we had in Birmingham, this meeting with Miss Weale was to prove the most important. I was about to say 'of all the meetings we had in England', but that would be untrue. Meeting the Queen and the Prince of Wales were the most important meetings, the ones we would speak of when we returned home.

Perhaps Wharepapa's most important meeting was in

London, the day he met Miss Elizabeth Reid. After our visit with Miss Weale was over, and we were alone together in our room, Wharepapa confessed to me that when Mrs Johnson announced the arrival of a lady in her house, he was very, very afraid. He thought, you see, that this lady was Miss Reid.

Of course he would have been most happy to see Miss Reid again, he told me, but if she'd travelled up to Birmingham and presented herself at Mrs Johnson's that day, everyone would have discovered the thing that Wharepapa had been keeping to himself for some time. Elizabeth Reid was with child.

The Bohemian surprises me. He was a fighting man himself once, so he says. Bohemia is part of a great empire, and he was summoned to become a soldier.

'I was no good at fighting,' he says. This part does not surprise me. 'They said I should paint the officers' wives, for that was my talent.'

I don't understand why the Bohemian would want to be a soldier when he had no skill or passion for it, but he explains that there was no choice.

'You cannot say no to the Imperial Army. When they called me to fight again, I decided to leave the country. I went to Germany, and looked for a ship sailing far away. I thought of America, but instead I came to New Zealand.'

The Bohemian washes his hands in the basin. He has an appointment with someone in the bank, and I'm not to return to his studio until later this afternoon. I drape the ngore over my chair, and gingerly make my way down the stairs. I'm going to walk back to the Maori market to find something to eat. The day is quite bright, with no rain, so I don't mind the walk. Once I'm in the street, I laugh to myself like a drunk man, for the idea of the Bohemian as a soldier is a funny one.

Henry Williams, the missionary, was a fighting man as well once. I'd forgotten that until today. He was a sailor in the British Navy during the long wars with Napoleon. This was something that impressed us in the North when we first met him. He knew the ways of war, but he'd turned away from them. This is what he persuaded us to do as well, though it took him many years. Very few of us would even consider it before Hongi died. Many were waiting for a great ariki to lead the way, so Mr Williams was very happy when Patuone agreed to baptism in 1840.

Henry Williams and his brother, William Williams, spoke very good Maori. They were almost as good as Mrs Colenso, who learned when she was a little girl. The missionaries gave us parts of the Bible in Maori, and taught us how to read them. For many years the only things we Maori had to read were books from the Bible and the letters we wrote each other.

Soon it will be fifty years, I think, since my own baptism. Both the Williams brothers are dead now. I won't have the privilege of dying the death of a warrior, as Hongi did. I'm too old to fight now, and all our battles are conducted at the Native Land Court. There's still business going on down in Taranaki, I hear, and that Te Whiti is up to no good. But the missionaries would say, no doubt, that he goes about things in the right way, not with guns but with words.

He giveth snow like wool: he scattereth the hoarfrost like ashes.

He casteth forth his ice like morsels: who can stand before his cold?

PSALMS 147:16–17

Birmingham. I have never been so cold, not in all my life before or all my life afterwards. Maybe this cold addled my brain, because much of those last months in Birmingham is confused in my memory. I remember the snow, which I was seeing for the first time, wondering how something so white could fall from so black a sky. I remember the jabs of the frost, and our endless illnesses. There were many letters, people coming and going. And Miss Weale taking up our cause, which is when things started moving quickly.

Mihi Wira, we called her. She was an unmarried lady of about the same age as Mrs Colenso, I imagined. She had a strong face and a strong voice, and knew a great deal about New Zealand, for she had travelled there herself. Bishop Selwyn was an old friend, she told us. At our first meeting she could tell us little else, because she could not speak much Maori, and though Wharepapa understood much English, he couldn't speak all the words. Later we learned that Miss Weale was from London, that her father had left her sufficient fortune so she did not need a husband, and that she was in charge of the Winson Green

Road Home for Girls, a place we would come to know very well. She was a lady of great energy, like a tiwakawaka, always busy and curious. She was very devout in her ways, too, so of all of us she preferred the company of Reihana, the Christian soldier.

The first time she and Jenkins met was in the parlour of our lodgings, and though at first he seemed grateful for her attentions to us, the smile on his face flickered when Miss Weale said she had spent time in New Zealand, and knew many important people in the Anglican Church. As usual Jenkins talked on and on while we sat in silence, and he only appealed to us to speak once.

'This lady says you all look dejected,' he told us. 'But this is untrue, is it not? Some of you are ill, and that is the beginning and end of it. Tell me what you wish to say to her.'

'Tell her that we have no business here any longer,' Wharepapa said, swiping a handkerchief at his running nose. 'Tell her we are heavy in the heart, because this is no good, this scheme, and we all long to go home.'

'This is no time for your tricks,' Jenkins said, his voice severe. His face was strained and pale, and I wondered if he too was ill. This climate was good for no one.

'This is no trick. We are tired of these lectures. We long to go home. Give the lady the answer she requests.'

Miss Weale could understand none of this, of course, but she looked from one of us to the next, trying to grasp our meaning by reading our faces.

'I have already explained to her that we would *all* dearly like to return home, but that this is impossible until we have made more money. Perhaps this lady can help us find money, but not if we say we're reluctant to give lectures to the good English people who wish to meet us.'

'Always the money,' grumbled Reihana, and only a coughing fit prevented him from continuing.

Our faces must have been easy to read, for the next time we saw Miss Weale, in the warmth and comfort of her own large parlour, she showed Wharepapa a sheaf of letters and told us she was investigating our situation. She'd written to old Te Taka, Reverend Stack, and to Mrs Colenso, and they had both replied. She also had a letter from George Maunsell, the son of the great Reverend Maunsell, who was in London studying, like his father before him, at the Church Missionary College.

After those letters arrived, she no longer trusted Jenkins. By the time Mrs Colenso herself arrived in Birmingham, and sat for many hours with Wharepapa while he wrote letter after letter outlining our complaints, Miss Weale no longer smiled at Jenkins, or made an attempt, as far as I could see, at the usual civilities.

Some of us were spending more and more time at her house. Ngahuia and Haumu sat many afternoons sewing with the girls and their teachers, and I tried to read my English Bible, though I was probably dozing much of the time. The illness made me tired and idle. Miss Weale suggested that we write letters to be translated by Mrs Colenso and sent to the *Birmingham Daily Gazette*. These letters would describe our meeting the Queen, and the kind reception we were receiving from her subjects, and perhaps the good people of Birmingham would be moved to help fund our return to New Zealand. I happily undertook my letter, because I needed to fill my hours somehow, and because with every passing day I was more anxious to be home.

Kihirini was very little at Miss Weale's, because his lungs were inflamed and he could not rise from his bed. Hirini Pakia and Hapimana were not often at the house either, as I recall, for a very different reason. Miss Weale had heard talk of their various exploits in the public houses of Birmingham, and frowned whenever they entered the room. 'Gross sin,' she called their conduct, until Hapimana told us his head was getting tired from pretending to hang in shame. Takarei stayed away much of the time too for, like Kihirini, he was often too sick to leave his bed. Tere Pakia said she preferred the small fireplace and big smile of her own landlady to the sermons of Miss Weale. Yet she was to move all her things to Miss Weale's house, when the time came, without complaint, and they seemed to become great friends.

When did we move there? Not soon enough. It was 1864 by now, the winter stretching on, and still, those of us able to travel were venturing out with Jenkins to other towns for meetings and lectures, and any other appearance he could arrange. We had signed a contract, he reminded us, and this was the only way money for our weekly payments, and our passage home, could be raised.

I must say that this was not the only reason we went to this place and that with him, however. It was dull sitting around all day, waiting to return to New Zealand. English rooms were stuffy, for it was too cold to open windows and doors. Parlours I found to be hot as ovens, while passageways were like ice-houses. I would much rather go with Jenkins to tour the vast factory of a ribbon manufacturer in Coventry, or to appear before a crowd of eager boys at Rugby School, or to view the glassworks in Birmingham, which resembled the fires of hell, than sit inside a house where the sounding of the clock was the only noise, and lamps had to be lit all day because no sunlight peeped through the curtains.

For however fatigued we might have been with England, England was not yet fatigued with us. The night we appeared at the Corn Exchange in Coventry, thousands of people crowded the place. This is not an exaggeration, you understand. Accounts were published in the newspaper, and told to us in Maori by Mrs Colenso. Only some of the people had chairs on which to sit. Most of the people there, including ladies, were forced to stand for almost three hours.

We always thought of these night-time events as meetings or lectures, but the newspaper called this one an odd word, a 'Conversazione'. This is the Italian word for korero, if I remember rightly. I don't know why we couldn't just use the English word for korero, but apparently this Italian word was something all English people understood.

This night I remember in particular, because of the enormity of the crowd, and because it was the night I finally saw things Wharepapa's way. Before this time I would hear the complaints of others and think that Jenkins was not so bad a man. He rarely snapped at me the way he did at some of the others. I was not in one skirmish after another with him, as Reihana was. I never tested him by staggering from a public house into the arms of a policeman, like Hapimana. He asked too much of us, perhaps, and thought too little, but I didn't think he had a dark heart.

For example, when we spent half a day touring a big factory where watches and clocks were made, surely this was for our benefit, not his? The making of watches was not new to him, so there was neither enjoyment or money to be had from such visits. Also, during these trips he had to translate questions and explanations back and forth. If we were tired after a day's activities, he must have been very tired as well. I could not feel rage against him, as some did, and I tried to understand him. In my English Bible I looked for the words the Reverend Henry Williams had often spoken, when he was persuading us to leave our warrior days. 'He that is slow to anger is better than the mighty; and he that ruleth his spirit than he that taketh a city.'

That night at the Coventry Corn Exchange, though, something inside me turned against Jenkins. We were not all present that night. Haumu, who could not be trusted at such public events, was spending the evening at Miss Weale's. Wiremu Pou was, of course, still away with the Maori Warrior Chiefs, disgracing his family by falling about on stage. Kihirini's illness was much more serious than any of ours, and Miss Weale had arranged for him to stay in a hospital in London. In fact, he had caught the train down to London a few days earlier, escorted by Horomona Te Atua and Hirini Pakia. Those two said they would spend a few nights at the Strangers' Home before joining us again in Birmingham.

Originally Horomona was to be the only escort, but Hirini insisted on going, for he had other plans. As well as his unspoken but obvious intention to carouse with low-life people and spend the money he had wheedled out of Mr Lightband and Miss Weale, he intended to visit Mr Ridgway in Leicester Square, and present our complaints about Jenkins to a sympathetic ear.

The programme in Coventry began as it ever did, with some minister or another leading the group onto the platform. This particular minister escorted Ngahuia on his arm, which she liked very much, for the crowd cheered and shouted as soon as she stepped onto the platform. We stood for a while, acknowledging the applause, then arrayed ourselves on chairs. Some of us wore cloaks over our usual attire, but not all, of course: Reihana and Wharepapa wore nothing over their coats, and in any case, we had just a few of these garments left.

The Reverend began his remarks by praising the beauty and manners of Ngahuia. Wharepapa whispered a translation in her ears. His knowledge of English was growing all the time, though he didn't share it with everyone. When the minister was smiling and gesturing at Tere Pakia, possibly saying fine things of her as well, Wharepapa sat back in his chair and gazed up at the ceiling, as though the words were beyond him.

After Jenkins started his long talk, Wharepapa drew his chair back so he and I were close. Jenkins always started by speaking of the great deeds of missionaries in New Zealand. Wharepapa had told me this before.

I started thinking about Henry Williams, the minister who baptised me all those years ago in Whangaruru. In the North we'd known him for some years, and had learned to trust and respect him. When he translated the Treaty of Waitangi, all the ariki and rangatira listened to him and most of them signed. They accepted the idea of allowing the Queen to govern over us all, in return for her protection from all the Pakeha arriving in ships, especially the French.

The Maori words Williams read out for everyone to hear meant we would be governed by the Queen, and this was acceptable to us. But later there was much talk among the Pakeha of something else in the English words of the treaty. What we rangatira expected to keep for ourselves, the English words had given away to someone else.

Hongi was dead by then. He would not have signed, I think. Yes, I know he wouldn't have signed. Mr Williams was a good and important man, a rangatira, and he talked a great deal of our best interests. But that's the trouble with missionaries, with ministers, with men like Jenkins. They're convinced they know what's best, yet most of them will never be rangatira. Why should a lesser man speak for those of us who are?

Wharepapa nudged me, and leaned to whisper in my ear.

'He says that Hongi was a cruel man,' Wharepapa said. 'He's speaking of the evil of Hongi and his wars. Hongi was thirsty for blood.'

I disliked this, as Wharepapa knew I would. I never like the way the Pakeha tell of the past, implying that Hongi acted unusually, or with unusual cruelty. In fact, he acted the way he was raised to act, the way he was bound to act by custom. He didn't create wars, as Napoleon did, in order to grab land from this one and that, and raise himself up high.

'Now he's speaking of the cannibal acts,' Wharepapa went on, but he didn't have to tell me this. The English loved to hear of these cannibal acts, and I knew when Jenkins had begun to speak of them, because of the looks on the faces in the crowd. The ladies were gasping and horrified, and the men grew very quiet. Some looked a little afraid. Often they all seemed to stare at me, because Jenkins would gesture at me, just as he was doing that night.

Wharepapa had told me on other occasions what Jenkins had to say. I was one of Hongi's notorious fighters, a ferocious cannibal warrior. But since the missionaries baptised me, he told crowds here and in Bristol and in Bath, I had learned more civilised ways and now I was a good man.

At one point in my life, I would have felt this to be a compliment, but after the fiftieth of these Conversaziones I was no longer sure. Everything was made too simple; everything of the past was denigrated too readily. Who was Jenkins to stand in judgement over a great man like Hongi? Who was he to dismiss the service of my youth, my service to my people, as the acts of a simpleton, or a savage?

'He says you feasted many times on the flesh of your enemies,' Wharepapa whispered, and I felt my face growing hot. I forgot the words of the New Testament, to put away all bitterness and wrath. But I am no Reihana Te Taukawau, eager to shout my anger from the platform. When Jenkins asked me to lead the speaking that night, I didn't show my displeasure. I wanted to show everyone in the assembly that I was a Christian man, just as they were.

'Listen to me,' I said, with Jenkins shouting my words out in English. His voice was hoarse. This was not a good room for speaking, especially with so many people crowded in. 'Listen to me, you thousands of people, all of you gathered here today. I want to speak of Christian love, the best thing in the world.'

Some faces before me were smiling, nodding as they heard my speech translated into words they could understand, but some looked disappointed. This was always the way. They wanted the Maori Warrior Chiefs with their chest-slapping and wrestling. They wanted to hear gory testimony of killing another man and roasting his flesh over the fire. We were carnival exhibits, and they wanted to be shocked and entertained by us. They wanted to gaze on the savages, and hear of our terrible exploits in the heathen wilderness.

'For God so loved the world,' I said, my voice shaking, 'that he gave his only begotten son, that whosoever believeth in him shall have everlasting light.'

Reihana told me later that I should have said everlasting life, but I meant what I said – everlasting light. In those dark winter days, I would think of the heaven waiting for me, and imagine it as the opposite of places such as Birmingham and Coventry, with their endless chimneys bellowing smoke into the sky.

'We are all of that number.' I gestured at the crowd, and at those of us on the stage. 'All of us. I don't think I need to say any more.'

Not only my voice was shaking. When I sat down, I was tired and finding it hard to breathe. With too many people in this room, it was very warm and close. Although I wasn't as ill as some of the others, I was older than the rest. The wonders of England had worn me out, and so had the noise and excitement of these meetings.

I think about that evening now, and I wonder what I was really trying to say. I don't give such speeches any more. I leave preaching to ministers. And sometimes I wonder if Jenkins really said all those things about me, or if Wharepapa was making a little mischief. He wanted all of us from the North to be united, and he was right in that wish. If only I were not so obliged to rely on the speech-making and understanding of others!

After I sat down, Wharepapa spoke at much greater length, and with much greater eloquence, about the wars going on back in New Zealand, and how he was ashamed that the Waikato Maori were fighting the English at the very moment we were shown such hospitality. This was all well and good, but I wished he would not talk so much of Maori as wild beasts that needed to be tamed.

By this time in the trip he had grown fond of making the audience laugh, so when someone asked him to speak of the marriage customs of the Maori, he saw the chance for one of his jokes.

'Some adopt the English custom and marry the English way,' he told them. 'But others, who have no consideration for what is good and proper, keep to the old Maori ways. They marry in much the way the lions and the bears marry.'

While the room shook with laughter, I could not help

thinking about Wharepapa and Elizabeth Reid, who appeared to have married in the manner of lions and bears. But if anyone noticed me smiling that night while a morose Reihana gave his drawn-out account of our meeting with the Queen, including a list of every item on the luncheon table, they would have had no inkling of the cause.

Jenkins was not in a good mood the next day, because, he said, only twenty pounds had been taken that night, despite the vastness of the audience. We weren't sure whether to believe him. Now I was suspicious of everything that Jenkins did and said. There was an uneasy truce between us all for a while, when we did not complain. But just as he left us alone at Christmas, Jenkins was soon off again without us. He and Mr Lloyd hurried down to London for a meeting at the Colonial Office, and when they returned he was very, very angry.

Wharepapa, Reihana and I were still living in our lodgings at Temple Place on Bath Row, so perhaps this is where he shouted at us. It may have been at the house next door, where the others were housed. I can't remember who was there exactly, apart from Mr George Maunsell, who I was meeting for the first time that day.

His presence in Birmingham was one of the reasons that Jenkins was so angry. Mr Maunsell had arrived there the day before, catching the train from London with Horomona Te Atua and Hirini Pakia. The Church Missionary Society, at the request of Miss Weale, had sent him to act as our interpreter. They'd gone to the Strangers' Home, and talked to Colonel Hughes, and that was that. Young Mr Maunsell was to be part of our group from now on. His Maori was very good, as you might expect from the son of Reverend Maunsell. His father, young Mr Maunsell told us, was staying in Auckland, driven out of the Waikato by the terrible fighting there.

When Jenkins arrived, he was not pleased to meet Mr Maunsell, or to see Hirini and Horomona sitting with us.

'We went to the Strangers' Home to find you,' he said to them, 'but Colonel Hughes told us you'd already left for Birmingham, with *this* gentleman. Why do you need another interpreter when you have me?'

Mr Maunsell, listening to this but saying nothing, turned quite pink around the ears and throat.

'May we Maori not have many friends?' Horomona Te Atua demanded. 'Must we speak to only one Pakeha, a man who can twist our words?'

'Is it a friend you need?' asked Jenkins. 'Or is it that Miss Weale needs an interpreter of her own, someone who can twist *your* words against me?'

'Sir, I must say . . .'

'Forgive me, Mr Maunsell.' For a few moments they spoke in English to each other, and from the sound of the words and the looks on their faces, I could see no real ill will between them.

'I am under a great deal of strain at the moment,' Jenkins continued, his voice creaking, 'because of our very delicate financial situation, something the party assembled here in this room has never understood.'

'He must talk of the money every day,' Reihana complained to Mr Maunsell. 'He must keep telling us that we don't do enough, and that we are obliged to him, and that we have signed promises. But he was the one who made us stay in the big hotel in London, and have our photographs taken, and many other things that must have used up all the money. We know nothing of the money, of course, because he tells us nothing, except that we have none.'

'Colonel Hughes,' said Jenkins, looking sternly around the room at everyone apart from Reihana, 'who you all know, told me other unpleasant things. The Church Missionary Society have warned him of many malicious rumours reaching London from this place. It is said, so they allege, that our own Ngahuia and Haumu have been seen drunk in the streets of Birmingham!'

This was a terrible and untrue accusation, and we could not think who had made it. While Hapimana may have been seen drunk in the streets of Birmingham on many occasions, no one could mistake him for one of the ladies of our party, unless he was going about dressed in Ngahuia's bonnet.

'It is also said, the Colonel tells me, that I am grievously mistreating you all. This rumour has reached him from Birmingham, and I have no doubt of the source of the rumour. And then, when Mr Lloyd and I visited the Colonial Office, we learned from the Duke's secretary that you, Horomona, and you, Hirini, had been brought to that place just a few days ago. Do you deny it?'

'We go about London, and do and speak as we please,' said Hirini, staring at Jenkins with great contempt.

'So when Mr Ridgway tells you to complain about me, and offers to take you to the Colonial Office, you are willing to go with him and to do as he asks.'

'Mr Ridgway is a friend to us,' Hirini said sulkily.

'Ridgway is not to be trusted. He set himself against me from the first, and wants nothing more than to see this whole expedition end in disgrace and disaster. Lloyd and I were in a very embarrassing position, forced to defend ourselves at the Colonial Office. This is grievous ingratitude. It's especially aggravating given the purpose of our visit to London. We have been making arrangements to take you all home. My friend,

Mr Riley, offers us passage on a ship in June.'

'June!' exclaimed Wharepapa, and several other people groaned. We had been in England for more than eight months at this point. Another four months in England seemed a very long time, especially when it would take us an additional three months for the journey home.

This conversation did nothing to lift our spirits, and then something small, mentioned in passing by Jenkins to Mr Maunsell, made everyone angry all over again. Jenkins had left the house by the time it was discovered. Really, it was such a small thing, I'm ashamed now to speak of it. At the time, however, we all perceived it as yet another affront.

When Jenkins was in London, he had visited the studio of the artist, Mr Smetham. This was the man with wild eyes who'd taken sketches of us, preparing for a big painting of us all to commemorate the visit to England. None of us had seen the painting yet, or knew much about it. Jenkins was one of the figures in this painting, and this was why he had visited the artist. He wanted to look upon his own face, and see if the likeness was good. It was good but not good enough, he told Mr Maunsell, so he sat in the studio for some time while the artist made changes.

As I said, of all the things Jenkins did or did not do, this was hardly the worst. But we were all upset to hear of it.

'Such presumption!' Miss Weale said when we told her, and that was precisely it. We Maori were all to be drawn as the artist chose, and would have no chance to see either the painting or the artist again. Yet Jenkins made a point of returning to have his own private sitting, like the ones I'm having this week with the Bohemian. Was the painting to commemorate our visit, we wondered, or his?

'Man looks on the outward appearance,' said Reihana, his illness making his voice low, like a foghorn. 'But God looks on the heart. Jenkins will be punished for the darkness in his heart, and for his vanity.'

I felt very uneasy, for this anger building up among us was dangerous as fire. When we were all invited to speak our minds at the home of the magistrate, Mr Thomas Sneyd Kynnersley, it burned out of control.

The magistrate was, as all important people seemed to be, an acquaintance of Miss Weale's. He also took a particular interest in New Zealand, for his eldest son had recently retired from the Royal Navy and emigrated to Pelorus Sound in the South Island, to try his hand at farming.

One frosty morning in late January we were taken to Mr Sneyd Kynnerlsey's big house on the edge of the city. It was the biggest house we had visited in Birmingham, in its own park, though of course it was not as grand as Marlborough House in London. A number of carriages were needed to carry us there, because in addition to the Maori party Miss Weale wanted to come, and that meant Mrs Colenso and Mr Maunsell must come as well.

Mr Lloyd, Mr Lightband, and Jenkins were waiting for us there. Mr Lloyd looked as though he had an urgent appointment at the races, for all day he was pulling at his pocket watch or drumming his fingers on the desk. Mr Lightband smiled and shook our hands, but he too seemed very anxious for the whole encounter to be over. Jenkins was far more grave. When we walked in, he stood erect and silent by one of the windows, framed by its heavy curtains. This had the unfortunate effect of reminding us of his recent visit to the artist Mr Smetham, and thus of his selfishness and conceit.

The room in which we were all to speak was lined with books, and Mr Sneyd Kynnersley's servants were hurrying in and out, bringing more chairs and arranging them in a manner acceptable to Miss Weale. Mr Sneyd Kynnersley himself was a tall, distinguished gentlemen, his whiskers grey, and his voice surprisingly high-pitched for one with so solemn a face. He had written to the Duke of Newcastle, he said, and understood certain facts about our plight. Today was a chance for us all to speak openly, and let our feelings be heard. This applied to Jenkins and Lightband and Lloyd, he said, as well as us. We were all to be frank and honest.

Much of this frankness took the form of long speeches accusing Jenkins and his company of making money and not sharing any with us. Jenkins insisted this was not the case, and Mr Sneyd Kynnersley agreed with him.

'Mr Lightband has shown me the company's books,' he said. 'I assure you all that there is no impropriety there, and the financial situation is exactly as they describe it. Your expenses exceed your income.'

This statement didn't stem the flow of accusations, especially once Reihana stood to speak. Jenkins was debasing us by forcing us to dress in cloaks, and to perform heathen haka and waiata for English audiences. He had wasted the money we had been given by English people with his extravagance in London, and with his constant travels to one place or another. He and his minister friends liked to appear with us on platforms, but they never visited us at home to pray with us. He had refused to take the advice of the Duke of Newcastle, keeping us here for months and months when we were all ill and desperate to return home.

I would like to say this was the only meeting of this kind in Birmingham, but sadly, over the next two weeks, there were several more. Sometimes Mr Sneyd Kynnersley was present, and sometimes he was not. When he wasn't there, the words on both sides were angrier. Jenkins denounced Miss Weale, insisting that she had turned us all against him. Reverend Stack, visiting from London, denounced Mr Ridgway, saying his interference was the cause of all our ingratitude. Wharepapa and Reihana denounced Jenkins, saying we could not believe a word he said, and that he was probably defrauding Mr Lightband and Mr Lloyd of money as well.

At one of these meetings, Mr Lightband mentioned that Jenkins had met with the gentlemen of the committee, and that they all supported him. This was the group of important and wealthy men assembled by Mr Sneyd Kynnersley to look into our affairs and to arrange a farewell meeting for us at the Birmingham Town Hall. None of us were permitted to meet with them and state our case, and for this too Jenkins – perhaps unfairly – was blamed.

Truly there was no point to these meetings, I must say. On and on they went, for hours at a time, with no one satisfied and no issues resolved. Instead many bad things were said that could not be forgotten. On one particularly bad afternoon, Ngahuia was told she was a vixen who would agree with anyone if she were promised enough clothes and fripperies, and Hirini Pakia was told that with his drinking and money-grubbing he was lower than a cur in the street. Privately, I did not think either of these statements untrue. But public insults of this kind must have consequences, and therefore should not be uttered. When Jenkins told Wharepapa he was in league with Miss Weale, and no better than a monkey dancing to the tune of an organ-grinder, I knew at once that there could be no more lectures or tours. This was the end of things. Our alliance with Jenkins was broken.

This is the last day I will visit the Bohemian in his room, because soon he must sail to England.

I don't know how to ask him to keep our conversations a secret. I don't speak English to anyone else. He may not have been raised as I was, with a respect for secret knowledge. They must have their tohunga in Bohemia, I suppose, but the ways of foreigners are often strange.

Like me, the Bohemian didn't grow up speaking English. He tells me that when he arrived here, ten or so years ago, he didn't know a word.

'I don't talk too much English,' he says. 'Not then, not now.'

I don't ask him why. I don't need to ask.

English is our weapon, hidden deep within the fold of our tatua. We reveal it only when we need to, because a surprise attack is often best.

For by thy words thou shalt be justified, and by thy words thou shalt be condemned.

MATTHEW 12:37

Now when I think of those times, I remember myself as an observer, saying very little. But perhaps this is what I want to remember. Maybe I too said severe and ill-considered things. We had all grown too desperate – Jenkins to make back his money, and the rest of us to return home.

Men who are desperate sometimes act heroically, but none of us were heroic. When Miss Weale heard of Miss Elizabeth Reid's interesting condition, Wharepapa told her that his intention all along was to marry Miss Reid. Jenkins, he said, had forbidden it.

I may have told her that Jenkins pretended, back in Auckland, to be a minister, in order to persuade us to sign his pieces of paper.

Enough of what might have been said. At some point in February, when the days were still short and melting snow was turning to gravy in the streets, Mr Sneyd Kynnersley summoned us all to his great library once again. Jenkins said very little in this meeting, though his face was defiant.

The magistrate had papers for us to sign. This, he said, would represent our separation from Jenkins. The papers we signed in Auckland and in London would be cancelled. If we signed, we would no longer be bound to Jenkins, and could leave England at any time. Jenkins would no longer be bound to us, and was no longer obliged to pay us a weekly sum, or any other amount of money. Miss Weale would take care of us, and arrange for us to travel home on the *Flying Foam* in early April. If we chose not to sign, Jenkins would still be responsible for our lodgings and so on, and we would sail home with him in June, in the passage arranged by his friend Mr Riley.

'Kihirini has already signed,' Mr Maunsell told us. He'd taken the papers to Kihirini's hospital bed in London. 'He is very eager to return home, before it's too late.'

I thought of the boy Wiremu Repa. It was too late for him, and I didn't have much hope for Kihirini.

'I will sign,' Wharepapa announced, and Reihana followed. I signed, and so did Hirini and Tere Pakia. Horomona Te Atua hesitated before he signed, and said he was thinking of his brother, the missing Wiremu Pou, and wondering if it was wrong to abandon him here. He had not seen him at all for several months, because the Maori Warrior Chiefs were now touring the cities of the north.

'I will find your brother,' Miss Weale promised him. She said she would see Wiremu Pou and persuade him to follow us home, and that she would not rest until every member of that Maori Warrior Chiefs troupe had renounced their debauched life on the stage and returned to a Christian life in New Zealand. I believed she would succeed. All those strong warriors would be powerless in the face of Miss Weale.

'I will not sign!' Ngahuia declared. She was still furious with Jenkins for calling her a vixen. 'I will sue this one here and his friends for their broken promises. They owe us money. We have lived on nothing, nothing but charity, when we were told we would receive one pound a week. Haumu will not sign either.'

Poor Haumu shook her head, glancing all the while at Ngahuia to make sure she was doing the right thing. But when Mr Sneyd Kynnersley talked in a stern voice, and Mr Maunsell explained once again that there was absolutely no money in the company coffers, and nothing to be gained from a legal suit, both women signed. Ngahuia made as much fuss as she could, breaking the nib of the pen and throwing it down onto the desk.

'I don't care for all this talk of money or no money,' Hapimana said, suddenly haughty. He and Takarei were sitting a little apart from the rest of us, muttering to each other all the while. 'I will not sign. I will stay with Jenkins, as we agreed, and return with him in June.'

Takarei said he would stay as well. This would have been a moment of triumph for Jenkins, I think, if Mr Lightband had not immediately announced that he himself was planning to return with us on the *Flying Foam*, for Miss Weale had been very kind and offered to arrange his passage as well.

So Hapimana and Takarei alone would stay, though we all felt they should have come home with us. That evening we tried to say this to them – Wharepapa tried, and I tried – but they were unmoved. Sailing home at once with Mr Lightband was fine for the Nga Puhi, they said, but they were not in such a hurry to return home.

I wasn't surprised by Hapimana's decision. He and Takarei were from other places, other peoples, and they were outsiders in our group. Jenkins had sometimes taken them places without us, as though he were eager to secure their loyalty. Perhaps this was why he took Hapimana away at Christmas, when the rest of us were left in our lodgings. At the time we thought that Jenkins wanted to keep an eye on him, because Hapimana could not be trusted. Now I wondered if there was another motive in his mind.

All who signed now moved into rooms at the Winson Green Road Girls' Home. Our landlady, Mrs Johnson, was very sad to see us go.

'I'll be there at your farewell meeting, that I will,' she told us, brushing at our jackets as we stood about in the passageway, waiting for the carriage taking us to Winson Green Road. Mr Maunsell was there to interpret, so she took the opportunity to say many other things to us, about what fine and decent gentlemen we were, and not savages at all, whatever people said, and much more accomplished at reading and writing than half the folk of Birmingham. We had nothing much left to give her as a parting gift, but Wharepapa had a bone earring he presented, and I gave her my English copy of the Book of Common Prayer.

'Very genteel of you, to be sure!' she exclaimed, sniffing back tears. Mr Maunsell spent half the carriage ride to Miss Weale's house trying to fix exactly on the meaning of the word 'genteel', for we were all quite taken with it.

The short weeks left to us were quiet, if living in a house full of Maori and their interpreters, not to mention thirty girls and their teachers and many servants, can be considered quiet. We did not see Jenkins at all in this time, but we heard his name often enough. Miss Weale was outraged by his demands, for he was asking her to pay for our stay at the Strangers' Home in London the previous year. I'm afraid he was not the only person asking her for money, for Hirini Pakia was constantly pleading for an allowance. Even Tere Pakia had the grace to be embarrassed by this.

We Maori seemed intent on disgracing ourselves in every possible way. As well as Hirini and his pleas for money, there was Wharepapa and his personal business. He had been forced to tell Miss Weale about his marriage in the manner of lions and bears, because Miss Elizabeth Reid was threatening to arrive on the doorstep with a sad face and a swollen belly. It was a risk to tell Miss Weale, because she had seen off Jenkins, and was unlikely to be afraid in any way of Wharepapa. He was very worried that she might decide that he was sinful and no longer worthy of a cabin on the *Flying Foam*, and then what would he do? Seek out Hapimana and Takarei in their lodgings, and plead for Jenkins' forgiveness? Fortunately, Miss Weale was too great a Christian to throw him out into the streets, though she twisted her mouth in displeasure whenever Wharepapa's 'situation', as she called it, was mentioned, and on more than one day Wharepapa was obliged to put on a great show of wailing with contrition.

Our problems were our own business, until we heard from Mr Maunsell that Hapimana had disgraced himself once again, just as he had in Bristol. This time he was to stand in front of a judge in the Birmingham court, charged with behaving in a drunk and disorderly fashion.

'So much for the care of Jenkins,' said Miss Weale, and she looked pleased. When she had left the room to give orders to her housekeeper, we asked Mr Maunsell if Hapimana might be sent to prison. This was unlikely, he said, but Mr Lightband would have to find some way to pay his fine. Hapimana and Takarei still had their contracts, and the company had to meet all their expenses. But now Mr Jenkins had little hope of the Colonial Office lending him their support. Hapimana's conduct reflected poorly on Jenkins, he said. It suggested that he was not responsible enough to take charge of us, and that he lacked judgement. These were the things of which Mr Ridgway had accused him, and perhaps now the Duke of Newcastle agreed.

It seemed wrong to blame Jenkins for the behaviour of Hapimana, who was no doubt as foolish and reckless in New Zealand as he was in England. We are not different people in a different country, any more than I am one person in Tutukaka and another in Auckland. Hirini Pakia would be trouble everywhere. Reihana would be a bore. Wharepapa would be Wharepapa.

Yet in some way what his enemies said of him was right. Jenkins lacked judgement. If I doubted this for a moment, then I would have known it as a certainty at our farewell meeting in March, at the Birmingham Town Hall. This was to be our last great triumph in England, a chance for people to hear us one last time and to present us with gifts to take back to New Zealand with us.

And such gifts! Many kind people and many companies in the city had piled a stand beneath the orchestra with all manner of things for us. Before the event began, we stood about in a room behind the stage, and Mr Maunsell ventured out to look. There were tools of every kind, he said, and nails, and ploughs, even engines of various sizes. There were toys, dolls, and writing slates, and cutlery, and many coffee and teapots. He'd seen beautifully wrought workboxes, and a heap of glass beads, and a travelling rug for each of us. It was all very respectable, and showed how well we were thought of in England, and in Birmingham in particular. When we returned home with these gifts, our people would be very impressed with the bounty of England, and everything could be put to good use at once.

The Town Hall itself was packed. People were seated upstairs and down, Mr Maunsell said, with flags and banners hanging from the railings as though the Queen herself were coming. We could hear the strains of a quadrille band, and the hum of many voices. The dignitaries were drinking tea, Mr Maunsell said, and examining the array of gifts. The best people in Birmingham were here. Everyone wanted to say goodbye to us.

When we walked onto the platform, in the shadow of the great organ, applause thundered through the building, filling it the way a choir's song fills a cathedral. Before me was a swarm of faces, and I felt both relief and regret that this was to be the final public event of our visit. We had spoken in front of so many audiences in this country, but tonight it was all at an end. I planned to repeat my message of Christian love, to thank them for the kindness they had shown us, and to say that we were all the same, Maori and Pakeha, united by God's love.

The platform was crowded with chairs, and other people were joining us there, climbing up the steps on the other side. Many were ministers, some of whom I recognised from one meeting or another. Mr Sneyd Kynnersley was there, of course, and a number of other gentlemen who I presumed were members of his committee. Then I saw Jenkins take a seat on the far side of the platform, followed at some distance by Hapimana and Takarei, who did not look at the rest of us or acknowledge us in any way.

Jenkins! Truly we had not expected to see him here. Miss Weale said he would not dare show his face, and Wharepapa had said that there was no reason for him to be present. The people of Birmingham were bidding us farewell and giving us gifts. Jenkins was no longer anything to do with us. We had signed Mr Sneyd Kynnersley's papers, and the separation was complete. He no longer spoke for us. Our fates were no longer bound together.

Yet there he was, sitting in a chair between two ministers, with Mr Lloyd shuffling into place behind him. Mr Lightband was there too, clearly unsure of where to sit, and drifting towards the back of the platform. All in our party, including Miss Weale and Mr Maunsell, sat on the opposite side of the stage from Jenkins.

'What is that man doing here?' Miss Weale asked whoever would listen, and this thought was on my mind as well. Why was he here, sitting at the front of the platform, for all to see? If he must be here, why could he not sit with Mr Lightband at the back, to watch the proceedings without making something important of himself? He could not learn new tricks, it seemed. He must return to his old tricks all the time.

The man who was the new Mayor stood up to call everyone to order, which was no small feat. There were many rumblings and some laughter from the audience, for they were all in high spirits. We, too, had been in high spirits just moments before, but now there was uneasiness on our side of the platform.

'What good can come of this?' I whispered to Wharepapa. 'Surely he will not try to speak, will he?'

'If he does, we will shout him down.'

I had no appetite for shouting, and hoped there would be no call for it that evening.

The Mayor talked for some time, with Mr Maunsell translating for us on the platform. He was delighted, he said, to see so many people there to wish us well. He hoped that presently, when we returned to New Zealand, we would have a better impression of England than we ever had before. He said much else, but it was all along the same lines as these.

The next speaker was Reverend Winters, who we had met several times. He was eager to tell everyone that this meeting had very happy circumstances. Not only was it the first anniversary of the marriage of the Prince and Princess of Wales, it was also the baptismal day of the infant Prince. This baby, we had heard, was named Albert Victor, just like Hare Pomare's baby.

'Also, the most delightful news of all,' said the Mayor, and I wondered what he would say. That Wharepapa and an English girl had married in the manner of lions and bears? 'This very day, we received the news of a cessation of hostilities in New Zealand.'

Everyone in the hall was very happy about this, cheering and stamping their feet, as though they themselves had been threatened by the Waikato. We were too distracted to join their applause, because Jenkins was walking to the middle of the stage, clearly preparing to speak. Even when we saw him take his seat near us, we didn't expect him to talk. The pieces of paper we had signed with him were torn up, and new pieces of paper signed. We were no longer bound to him, or he to us. Yet there he was, once again in the centre of things, addressing the people of England.

As Jenkins spoke, Mr Maunsell translated for all of us. He was much better at this job than Wharepapa. Maunsell knew all the words in English and Maori, so, for the first time since we arrived in England, we were all able to hear and understand everything that Jenkins was saying.

I think it would have been better for everyone if we had not understood.

As I remember it, Jenkins made a few remarks about how well we had been treated by the people of England on this trip, and how great an opportunity it was for the Maori in our party, and so on. This was not so terrible, I suppose, but it annoyed Wharepapa.

'Why is *he* thanking the people of England?' he asked Maunsell. 'Have we not mouths to speak for ourselves?'

If Jenkins had stopped talking then, and returned to his seat, and if Wharepapa had been permitted to stand and give one of his orations on victory in the Waikato, and the greatness of the English, and the wickedness of the Maori before the missionaries took charge of us, then perhaps the night would have been unremarkable, apart from the vast quantity of gifts which would have to be transported down to Gravesend.

But Jenkins had much, much more to say. Most of it was about money. Many unfair accusations had been made, he said. He and his associates had raised £1600 in New Zealand, their own money, in order to give us this wonderful opportunity. He also spoke of the contracts we signed back in Auckland, which made him responsible for our maintenance while we were in England, and meant that we were bound by honour to follow his directions. I glanced over at Hapimana and Takarei at this point, and noted that they were nodding at everything he said, though I doubted they could hear Mr Maunsell's translation as we could.

The longer Jenkins spoke, the more agitated some on our side of the platform grew, with Miss Weale the most agitated of all. His plans for our trip to England, he said, were approved by Governor Grey, by the Duke of Newcastle, and by the Prince of Wales. When the group of important men led by the Earl of Shaftesbury wanted to send us home, we refused to go. We all wanted to do our duty, as promised. So off we went with him to Bristol, where at last he could hold public meetings and charge admission, without interference, so the company could begin to recover their money.

'But in Birmingham,' Jenkins said, 'I found we could no longer meet our expenses in this way. Certain people had spoken against me, without any justification.'

'For shame!' cried Miss Weale. 'He has a face of brass!'

She said so many other things, in so loud a voice, that some of the gentlemen on the stage turned to frown at her.

'Enemies of this endeavour,' said Jenkins, 'had sent letters to men of importance here in Birmingham, and interfered with the great mission of this visit.'

I only knew a little of these accusations and enemies of which Jenkins was always speaking. With everything he said, it was difficult to know what was certain and what was one of his loose truths. He spoke of us next, and this was what I mean by a loose truth, a part of a story. Many of us had grown tired of this life in England, he said, and were taking up the offer of a benevolent lady to return home at once. For himself, he would stay on with some of the rangatira, the ones happy to abide by the original agreement and eager to learn more of England. With their help, he said, he and his associates would try to make back some of their lost money.

After Jenkins sat down, Mr Sneyd Kynnersley stood to speak, with Mr Maunsell again telling us every word. He would not have chosen to speak of this matter, the magistrate said, but as Mr Jenkins had raised the subject, he must.

I can't remember all that he said now. The words, English and Maori, were swimming in my ears, and it was hard to hear over Reihana's exclamations about Jenkins and his presumption. I think Mr Sneyd Kynnersley talked of the inclement weather in Birmingham, and of our lives that were one day too dreary and the next too exciting, and that this was why so many of us were anxious to return home.

He sat down, but still it was not our turn to speak. The Mayor stood again, to make a fine speech about all the gifts given to us by the great merchants and manufacturers of Birmingham. The committee men and ministers on the stage sat smiling, and the audience applauded, this almost drowning out the sound of Takarei's hacking cough. On the other side of the stage, we were talking openly among ourselves now. Would we not get a chance to say anything? Was Jenkins, with whom our connections were severed, be the only voice heard?

Before anything was agreed, Reihana stood up, his face grim.

'I will address the crowd,' he told us, waving away Wharepapa's objections. Wharepapa knew, as I did, that Reihana's words would be angry, and that Mr Maunsell would translate every one of them.

'Friends, hear what I have to say,' he shouted, striding to the front of the stage. Young Mr Maunsell had to scramble to his feet to stand beside Reihana, and the Mayor backed away in some confusion, stumbling into his own chair. The audience, still smiling and clapping at this point, soon fell silent. 'This is what I have to say to you. I did not at all desire Mr Jenkins to speak tonight. Not ever do I wish Jenkins to speak. He stands here and claims to speak for us all, when Wharepapa and I have no faith in Jenkins.'

'Hear, hear!' cried Miss Weale, and this we could understand, even if Mr Maunsell was too busy to translate it. It was not hot in the Town Hall the way it was in the Corn Exchange in Coventry, but Mr Maunsell was damp with sweat, bellowing Reihana's words out to the crowd.

'Jenkins only tells one side of the story,' Reihana continued. 'Let I, Reihana Te Taukawau, tell you all *our* side.'

'Sir,' said Mr Sneyd Kynnersley, standing up himself and

tapping on Reihana's arm. Mr Maunsell stepped back, mopping at his pink face with a handkerchief. A lot of the gentlemen on stage looked unhappy, and more than one was standing up. I wondered if they planned to rush Reihana and remove him from the scene. Hapimana and Takarei, heads together, were engaged in frantic discussion. 'Dear sir, I wonder if this is the time and the place for such sentiments.'

Other gentlemen on stage started calling out, and even Mr Maunsell was now whispering to Reihana, as though persuading him to desist. The audience, however, were eager to hear more from our righteous friend, calling out all manner of things, drumming their boots on the floor, and booing Mr Sneyd Kynnersley when he took Reihana's arm again.

'They say, let him speak!' Wharepapa told me. 'They say, let the chief speak!'

I did not like this turn of events at all. This was the first time something of this nature had ever happened during our trip to England. By that I don't mean Reihana complaining about Jenkins, or denouncing him from the platform, because that had been going on every week since we arrived in Birmingham.

But prior to this, no one in the audience could understand what Reihana was saying. This battle with Jenkins was a private one, conducted in our lodgings and in the rooms of Mr Sneyd Kynnersley, or in letters back and forth to Mrs Colenso. Tonight, all of our discontent was made public, shouted by Reihana through the hall and repeated, in loud English, by Mr Maunsell. I didn't care for these revelations to the people who had welcomed us, and who were this very evening demonstrating their Christian good will by giving us so many gifts. The faults of Jenkins, and our dispute with him, were neither here nor there. Most of us would soon be sailing home, and this evening and its shenanigans would be the lasting impression on the people of England.

'Since it seems to be unpleasant for you, I will say no more of Jenkins,' Reihana announced, which induced loud laments from the crowd, and some half-hearted applause from the gentlemen on stage. I couldn't see the face of Jenkins himself, only the back of his head. He sat rigidly in his chair, not moving at all. 'But I will say this. We have heard tonight that certain gentlemen raised the money to bring us to England, and that this money is gone. Wharepapa and I say, rather than give us these gifts tonight, divide them between Mr Lightband and Mr Lloyd and Mr Brent, so they may make up the money they lost. These gentlemen have been ruined by Jenkins – ruined, I say! Ruined by his vanity and ambition! So we will not accept these gifts. We cannot. Let them go to the gentlemen who have lost all their money bringing us here.'

Before Mr Maunsell could finish speaking all Reihana's words, while the people in the chairs below us gasped and shouted, Hapimana leapt to his feet and started ranting and gesturing like a man possessed, pacing up and down the stage. He was so eager to take Reihana's place, I thought he might push him onto the orchestra below. All the while he spoke so rapidly that Mr Maunsell simply could not keep up.

'I have confidence in Jenkins! I have confidence!' he was shouting. 'Don't listen to Reihana. Don't listen to his stupid talk of returning presents!' I couldn't see Reihana's face, because his chair, to which he'd returned, was in front of mine. Perhaps the words of Hapimana upset him, but I doubt it. Hapimana was no one to him. Hapimana was just a boy, an Ati Awa, a drunkard, a sinner.

'We've worked hard here in England,' Hapimana was protesting, wheezing with the strain of his shouting. 'We can't go home without something to show our people! They'll think that here we were treated as low-class Maori, not respected by the English. Let Reihana Te Taukawau give his presents away to Mr Lightband and Mr Lloyd! We will take our presents, I tell you. Mr Maunsell, tell the people that we thank them most heartily for these presents and that I, for one, will take mine home to New Zealand.'

But no one could hear what Mr Maunsell was saying, because now the hundreds of faces before us, below and above us, were laughing. This was the worst thing of all. This is, I think, my worst memory of the time in England, worse than any day I spent coughing and shivering in my bed. The people in the crowd couldn't understand much of what Hapimana said, because his voice was shrill over Mr Maunsell's. All they could see were his violent gestures; all they could hear was the flapping of his tongue. Reihana had silenced them, and then shocked them. Hapimana made them laugh, and not because what he was saying was a joke. *He* was the joke. The Maori language he spoke was a joke. Some boys in the audience started mimicking him waving their arms and jabbering nonsense, and this made the crowd laugh even more.

I sat unable to speak, while all around me was in uproar. Almost nobody on the stage was still seated. Tere Pakia was crying, probably because she was hoping to get her hands on the fine ladies' workbox donated by a Mr Cartwright of Edgbaston Street, and now Reihana had said we were refusing all the presents. Ngahuia wandered off the stage, half-dazed, and the next time I spotted her, ten minutes later, an English lady was comforting her, and handing her a cup of tea. That sly Hirini Pakia was nowhere to be seen at all. Hapimana and Takarei were shouting at Reihana and Wharepapa, and Horomona Te Atua stood near them, his face sour. He could not take Hapimana's side in all this, of course, because Hapimana was not Nga Puhi. But not only was Horomona going back to New Zealand without his brother, and without the cloaks he'd carried over, now he would be going back without anything at all to show for himself. People might not even believe he'd been in England. They might think he'd only been to the South Island.

Meanwhile, all sorts of speeches were still going on, though very little could be heard. I can't remember the exact order of things or the names of the speakers, because there was too much noise and confusion, and Miss Weale seemed to be arguing with some of the gentlemen sitting on the stage. One of the ministers stood up to suggest that the presents be divided among the Maori willing to accept them, if only Reihana didn't want them. Mr Sneyd Kynnersley spoke up again, insisting that Reihana was very sensible to the kindness of the people of Birmingham, but he was acting out of honour and honesty. Reihana, he said, simply wanted the men who funded the visit to make back their money.

Whenever anyone spoke, different sections of the audience would cheer or boo, as though they were watching boxers fight, and had placed bets on one or the other winning. Mr Sneyd Kynnersley suggested that we Maori should all go home to our lodgings and talk of this again in the morning, when perhaps we would reconsider this decision to hand over the gifts, but this idea was roundly hissed by the crowd. Other gentlemen stood to speak, but I could no longer follow what anyone was saying.

At some point I understood that the Mayor was trying to send everyone home, but many in the crowd had become raucous and disobedient. Some of the ladies were leaving, but other people appeared to be surging in through the doors, some jockeying for position near the unwanted presents as though they planned to grab them for themselves. Chairs were overturned, and cups were smashed in the mêlée. The musicians gathered up their instruments and dispersed. This was not a meeting any longer. It was mayhem.

I sat in my chair, like a man who stays very still to avoid the fury of a swarm of bees. I couldn't decide if it was worse for the people of Birmingham to be insulted by Reihana's rejection of their gifts, or us Maori to be insulted by their laughter. Two of the committee gentlemen started beating on the heads of lads launching assaults on some of the arrayed presents, and I overheard Tere Pakia asking Mr Maunsell why Miss Weale was shrieking.

'Her bag has been stolen,' he replied, looking as though he wished he were back in London. Jenkins was still on the other side of the stage, conferring with some of the gentlemen, so not even he could be accused of this particular crime. I have always suspected Hirini Pakia, by the way, though I have no evidence other than the jingling of coins in his pockets the next day.

An account of the event was published in the newspaper the next morning, and read to us at the breakfast table by Mr Maunsell. It was not so bad, I thought, because there was no mention of the laughing and booing, or the stealing of ladies' bags. Still, Miss Weale declared it all a terrible business, and complained that she was being accused of instructing Reihana in what to say. The doorbell was ringing constantly, announcing ladies who had come to visit, or letters that had been delivered. Poor Haumu, who had not been at the meeting and seemed mystified by our discussions of it, retreated to her bed, and

Ngahuia reported that she had vowed not to leave it until it was time for us to return to London.

Letters were published in the newspaper every day of the week, arguing this or that about our visit to England, and Mr Maunsell was forced to spend all his mornings translating the letters for us, and our reactions for Miss Weale. One of the first letters was from Mr Lloyd and Mr Lightband, to tell the people of Birmingham that they were not at all ruined, whatever Reihana said, and that neither they nor Mr Brent, who had already left for New Zealand, were willing to accept the gifts meant for us. They called Reihana 'the dissatisfied chief', and when Mr Maunsell said this Reihana seemed almost pleased. For a moment I thought he was smiling, but then I saw he was just opening his mouth wide to eat his bread and butter.

'We are all dissatisfied,' said Wharepapa in his most solemn voice. He was solemn all the time now, caused, perhaps, by living too long with Reihana, and always trying to prove to Miss Weale that he regretted his wrongdoing with Miss Elizabeth Reid.

'I don't think we should have refused the presents,' muttered Tere Pakia, who hadn't stopped sniffling since the night of the meeting. 'If we're dissatisfied, it's with Jenkins and his trickery, not with the people of Birmingham! This is what we should have said. Jenkins is bad, but the English and their presents are good. We could take the presents, and just make sure that Jenkins doesn't get any.'

'I will accept no presents,' Reihana said, his mouth full, though he had nothing to say later, when Mr Maunsell read a letter from the gentlemen of the committee complaining of what they called the unfortunate and ill-timed address of Reihana.

'I'm glad that Mr Lightband is not ruined,' said Ngahuia, and I was glad as well. We all liked Mr Lightband, and were pleased he was sailing home on the *Flying Foam* with us.

The next day there were more letters to hear, but fewer of us to listen. Four of our party left early that morning to return to the Strangers' Home in London and prepare for the journey home. Ngahuia was eager to be back in London, where I think she imagined Mr Ridgway might buy her some more dresses and bonnets to parade about the streets of Auckland. Haumu had to go where Ngahuia went, because she could not be left alone for more than an hour at a time, and Miss Weale's maidservants were worn out with watching her, especially with all the visitors and letters coming and going from Winson Green Road. Hirini and his silly wife insisted on accompanying them, of course, because there was much more debauchery to be found in London than in Birmingham, far from the watchful eye of Miss Weale, and he, at least, would not be satisfied until he was embroiled in it.

I don't remember why we all didn't leave together. There was no reason for four of us to linger in Birmingham, unless it was considered less of an expense for Miss Weale to keep us there. I do remember sitting at the table once again and listening to a letter in the newspaper from Mr Sneyd Kynnersley, such a long letter that Mr Maunsell was engaged all the morning in the reading and translating of it. This letter made Miss Weale very happy, and her constant interjections made the reading of it take even longer.

Some of the things he had to say, as I recall, were that Jenkins had brought no letters of introduction with him to England, and that most of his experience of Maori was in Nelson, in the South Island.

'There are no Maori in the South Island,' said Wharepapa, looking as though he'd swallowed something very sour. 'And if there *are* any to be found, they are inferior and not worthy of mention.'

Mr Sneyd Kynnersley also wrote that one of our original party was dead, which excited the four of us a great deal. Who had died? Was it Kihirini Te Tuahu, who had been carried off to hospital? No, Miss Weale assured us, it was not, for if he were dead she would know long before Mr Sneyd Kynnersley. He was terribly ill, but still determined to travel with us back to New Zealand, and she had received correspondence to this effect from his doctor that very morning. So was it poor Haumu, who we thought had left that morning with the others, but perhaps had died in the night, out of her mind at the prospect of the long voyage home? No, Miss Weale had kissed Haumu goodbye and seen her into a carriage just a few hours earlier, though she wished the poor woman had better chaperones for the train journey than the ones setting out with her.

We decided in the end that Mr Kynnersley meant Wiremu Pou, who was not really dead at all, but performing with the Maori Warrior Chiefs. At this Horomona Te Atua grew upset, and raged about Mr Sneyd Kynnersley insulting his brother by declaring him as good as dead, and it took much convincing from me and Wharepapa that the magistrate was misinformed, not malicious. Our cause was not helped by Reihana.

'I said all along that this trip would bring misfortune,' he announced. 'And now it is quite likely that Wiremu Pou is dead – or dead to us, at any rate.'

Mr Maunsell suggested we return to the letter in the newspaper, because there was still much to be heard. Most of this was of our disagreements with Jenkins over money, and about wearing cloaks in every public place. Reihana nodded through all of this.

'I objected to wearing cloaks all along,' he said, and started describing, in detail, his dream and premonition on board the *Ida Zeigler*, when he knew that this visit to England would come to no good. I noticed that Mr Maunsell did not translate any of this business of bad omens for Miss Weale, and he soon interrupted Reihana's recitation yet again to continue with Mr Sneyd Kynnersley's letter.

'He says you all grew dispirited in the cold weather, and suffered severely,' Maunsell told us, and we all agreed with this. Our lives back in New Zealand, according to the magistrate, were spent boating, fishing, and lying down.

'*You* must have told him that,' Horomona Te Atua said to me, and perhaps I did. This was not my life as a young man, but times had changed, and I'd grown old. At that moment I felt an intense pang for my life at home, and a longing to be close to the sea again. I was even looking forward to the voyage back. There was no coastline in Birmingham, no beaches or coves. I needed to smell the sea again, to feel the waves rise and fall beneath my feet. I'm used to moving from place to place depending on the time of year, or – quite frankly – my whim. I don't like to be confined in rooms, and certainly not in cities, for long stretches. Certainly, I'd never spent a year away from Hauturu or any of my homes.

I can't remember much else of that long letter, apart from Mr Sneyd Kynnersley describing Jenkins' scheme as ill-advised, and Mr Maunsell saying that many words had been misspelled by the newspaper's typesetters. Reihana was referred to throughout as 'Heirana'. Horomona Te Atua burst out laughing at this, and

I have to say that Wharepapa and I joined in, even though it was just a piece of nonsense. Reihana sat in stony silence, looking aggrieved, and that face I can remember precisely, twenty-two years later. It still makes me want to laugh.

Before the four of us left Birmingham, yet more letters were published in the paper. One was from Jenkins, declaring that everything that Mr Sneyd Kynnersley said was wrong, and others were letters we had written ourselves some days earlier for Mr Maunsell to translate into English. Miss Weale had urged us to write these letters.

'Let your voices be heard!' she said, and we all agreed. This was the day before Hirini Pakia left for London with the ladies, so he set to work on a letter, as did the other men. Ngahuia had planned to write a letter, but Miss Weale explained that ladies in England only wrote to other ladies, and to gentlemen they knew very well, not to newspapers which might be read by any Tom, Dick or Harry.

When they were printed in the newspaper, Reihana's letter was published first of all, which pleased him. I think that all along he'd seen himself as our natural leader, the highest born, and had been offended that Wharepapa, who was younger, spoke for all of us and was proclaimed the 'head chief'.

I must say that I am not at all sure now that writing these letters was the right thing to do. We were all so enraged because Jenkins had dared to stand and speak for us, but now when I think of him I see him for what he was – a headstrong man, not an evil one. Jenkins was not a good businessman. He should have waited to acquire letters of introduction from Governor Grey before setting off with all of us across the oceans. He should not have mortgaged his house and his business in Nelson, as he told us he did, to fund our passage. Mr Sneyd

Kynnersley once called Jenkins an adventurer, and perhaps that was the right word for him. He wanted an adventure and he wanted to make money. In this he was no different from the rest of us.

Things were undone between us because he wasn't straight with us, and because he was using us to rise up in the world. Jenkins wanted to meet the Queen for himself; he wanted to have his photograph made, and his portrait painted. None of this would have happened if he had returned to England alone, as a simple Wesleyan, not even a minister. His mana depended on the association with us, but ours did not depend on him.

That was the root of the problem. There was no reciprocity in this, no equality. His manner, I think, always suggested that Jenkins believed he was superior to us because he was born an Englishman and a Christian, and because he spoke English, and understood money, and knew about such things as catching trains. But he didn't realise that we rangatira wouldn't bow to an Englishman just because of the place he was born. Up north, we've had Englishmen around for almost as long as I can remember, and for every government person and missionary there were ten scoundrels, deserters, and drunks.

We Maori can become Christians; we can learn to speak English. Look at me, old as I am, speaking it now every day when I visit the Bohemian. If we had stayed longer in England, we would be jumping onto omnibuses by ourselves, without needing anyone to buy tickets for us or show us the way. These days, we can ride the new tram to Onehunga the same as any Pakeha, though why anyone would want to, I don't know. I'm not going to clamber out and start pushing that tram up the hill whenever the horses get bogged down in the mud.

These things that the English invent and bring to our

country are good things, but they don't make us want to become English. Jenkins had worked for years down in Nelson as an interpreter, but perhaps Wharepapa was right, and the Maori are different down there. For Jenkins didn't understand this, the most fundamental thing about us. Who we are is determined by our birth, our inheritance, our connections, our whakapapa. Through marriage or adoption, Pakeha can be woven into our net. But the sweep of our net is broad, and it stretches back to the beginning of time. It can never be cast aside.

Jenkins was our guide and chief interpreter, and when we stopped trusting his words, our relationship rotted. I think perhaps that Jenkins, like some missionaries, didn't respect us, and thought too much of his own ends. This is what Hongi warned us against. The missionary sought the role of the translator, the negotiator. How were we to know if the truth was told when someone was always standing in our way?

When Hongi talked of all this it was a long time ago, a different time. But when I was in England, I thought of his words a great deal. Jenkins was the one speaking for us, and most of the time there was no one except Wharepapa to know what he said. But Wharepapa only knew so much English, and he wasn't always there when Jenkins was talking and smiling, telling us what so-and-so had said, and whispering with Mr Lightband about the money collected. Wharepapa was off writing letters, signing his autograph on banknotes, and getting himself into trouble with English maids.

In Birmingham I felt anger towards Jenkins, but now I wonder if this was wrong of me. Everything that made us unhappy there seemed to be the fault of Jenkins, as though he were a god conjuring up the fog and the smoke and the snow! I was discontent because I was sick much of the time, and wishing myself home on Hauturu, where the air would be fresh and I would see sunshine every day. The money I brought with me to England was almost gone, and we were told there was too little in the coffers to dispense the weekly money promised to us in London. When those around me said that Jenkins had tricked us, I nodded my head. It was easier to say we had been tricked, than to say we should not have agreed so rashly to come at all.

So when Miss Weale asked us, I wrote that second letter to the Birmingham newspaper. I wanted to tell the gentlemen of the committee that we Maori, not Jenkins, should have all been permitted to speak to the people of Birmingham. The mouth was stopped, I said, lest it should speak forth. That's how I talked in those days, I suppose. The only thing I had to read in Maori was my prayer book and the New Testament. I don't use the language of the missionaries so much any more.

Now I could say: Miss Weale was to blame, or Wharepapa was to blame, or Reihana was to blame. They were the ones who filled my heart with righteous indignation. But in truth I was happy to follow their lead, and to write one of these letters. I did not hesitate to denounce Jenkins' character in the city where he had once lived and worked, and had many acquaintances. If people laughed at Hapimana when he ranted at the Town Hall, or if they mocked all of us as a group of savages and cannibals, these were insults we could leave behind us when we sailed for home. We had no ties with the place, and would soon be on the other side of the world. But this was Jenkins' home, the place he'd left to seek his fortune elsewhere, and the place he'd returned years later, still seeking fortune and status. If anyone was cruel on the trip to England, we were.

We wrote those final letters to the newspaper because above all things we wanted to have our say. Mr Maunsell spent many hours working with each of us, making sure the English and Maori words matched, taking great pains to show us words in his grammar book to ensure there could be no mistaking our meaning. We trusted this book, because it was the one Hongi and Waikato helped write in Cambridge, when they visited England with Mr Kendall back in 1820.

However, some improper things were said in these letters, things for which we can't blame Mr Maunsell. Hirini Pakia, for example, wrote that men who wear white ties in order to appear as ministers are deceivers. When Maunsell read this out to us, I felt ashamed. I too had thought Jenkins was a minister when I first met him back in Auckland, and perhaps in Birmingham I had agreed with others when they said that Jenkins meant to fool us, and that he had pretended to be a clergyman. But to see this accusation in writing in the newspaper was another matter. No one in England thought Jenkins was a minister, and to say this made us Maori seem foolish, and Jenkins devious and false. We should not have written those unchristian letters. There was something undignified and unworthy about the whole business. A rangatira must know when to speak, and when to remain silent.

I must have felt some guilt about my conduct at the time, for without letting Miss Weale or any of the others know, I wrote another letter – this one to Jenkins himself. I paid a boy to deliver it to the house where Jenkins was lodging. For all that had occurred between us, Jenkins had brought us to this country. Without him, we would not have travelled to England and met the Queen. We would still be at home, knowing only the places and people we'd always known. It seemed improper to leave England without bidding him farewell.

Enough. Enough of Birmingham and its shame and sadness.

We had worn out our welcome, and made a spectacle of ourselves, each new battle in our petty fight with Jenkins printed for all to see in the newspaper. We had seen the greatness of England, but now we were sick, and cold, and had very little money left. There was nothing to do now but return home.

Today we must finish early, because the Bohemian's wife needs him. Their boxes must be packed and taken to the wharf. He has to clean all his brushes, for he's taking all the contents of this room with him as well. When he comes back from England, he and his wife will find a small place in the countryside, he tells me. He won't paint in Auckland any more.

I unwrap the ngore for the last time and walk around to look at the painting, which is still wet and sitting on the easel. There I am. I'm looking straight ahead, my eyes a little red and rheumy. My hair looks soft and white as the snow that fell in Birmingham, and it's much tidier in the painting than it was the last time I saw it in a looking glass. There is no peacock feather sprouting from my ear. Although I always wore my coat under the ngore, the Bohemian has not painted my collar. Under the ngore, in the painting, my skin is bare.

My moko looks very bright and very green, my whiskers

peeping through its grooves. It's not quite right, the way the Bohemian has painted it, and much of my face is in shade.

The first time my moko was ever painted was when it was drawn on my face by the tohunga before he began to chisel. The rays on my forehead each have four lines, to show I'm a descendant of the first line. My signature can be read between my nose and my lips. From my chin they can see that I had been placed in charge of a tribal area.

You see, when Pakeha look at us Maori, they see brown faces – some browner than others, some ridged with moko and some smooth. Tenetahi and his sons don't wear a moko. When he stands up in court, many of the Pakeha don't know he's a rangatira, for there's nothing on his face to tell them. Anyway, these days there are too many new Pakeha here, who have no inkling of what a moko means. They think it's a decoration, and another sign of our savagery. Maori are Maori to them.

When I was young, there were seven or eight different ranks into which a person was born – including tutua, ordinary people. These ranks didn't include slaves, of course, because they had no mana and were not tapu. They had to earn status. I inherited my father's rank of noaia, though much depends, in all this, on the rank of the mother as well. This is a complex matter, with rules and precedents.

We are not so different from the English in all this, you see. We learned quite quickly that a Duke was more important than a Viscount, and that a Countess was more important than Lady So-and-So, if she were simply the wife of a baronet. We understood that Prince Albert could not be king, but that his eldest son one day will take the throne, for that inheritance, that mana, is on the mother's side. The English know that there are vast differences in rank between one man and another, and that when status and inheritance is at question, a strict hierarchy is observed within a family. This is our way, as well. Why would they presume all Maori are on one level?

'You like it?' the Bohemian asks, wiping his hands with a dirty cloth. The tohunga who carved my moko would be horrified, especially if he knew the Bohemian had been cooking toast over the fire a few hours earlier.

I nod at him and smile.

'I come to the wharf,' I tell him. 'I will bid farewell to you and your wife, and wish you well on your great journey.'

He looks very pleased at all this. There is no point in telling him what is wrong with the painting. The Bohemian is from another place, and never learned the language of moko. To him it is just a detail, like the pom-poms on the ngore, that make the painting beautiful. He can't read Maori faces any more than he can read Maori books. I'm not even certain that he can read English books.

I mean no disrespect to the Bohemian, you understand. He is an artist, not an historian. He has painted his version of my face, just as Mr Smetham did in London. I suppose that what I'm writing down this week is my version of the trip to England, and if Wharepapa were to read it, he would disagree with half of what I say. Ha! Wharepapa will never read it. My English gets better all the time, but his gets worse.

I must go back to the hostel now, and write more. Soon I'll be sailing back to Tutukaka, and there's no gas lamp in my house there. Despite its noise and other irritations, the Native Hostel is good for something after all.

And many of them that sleep in the dust of the earth shall awake, some to everlasting life, and some to shame and contempt.

And they that be wise shall shine as the brightness of the firmament; and they that turn many to righteousness as the stars for ever and ever.

DANIEL 12:2–3

Our last days in England were spent in London. It was cold and wet, and there was the sense among us that we were waiting to be gone, rather than enjoying the sights of this great place. On some days the streets were drowned in a swamp of fog, the lit lamps in shop windows flickering like distant stars on a cloudy night. The city smelled of smoke, and sometimes looked like smoke as well. 'A bush fire', Wharepapa called it, when we emerged from the train station, and found ourselves able to hear and smell the city rather than see it. At other times the fog was tinged with yellow, damp and tacky against our chilled faces and hands. We were warned not to roam too far, in case we fell into the invisible river. In this weather London was hidden from us and nothing seemed familiar.

Indeed, these days were nothing like our previous life there, when ladies and gentlemen were eager to entertain us at their grand parties. Since then we had visited dozens of towns, and given all of our cloaks and Maori weapons away. There were no more photographs to be taken, or haka to be performed. The months of lectures and tours were over.

We stayed once more at the Strangers' Home – Te Whare Mangumangu, the Negro House, as Hapimana had named it when we arrived last May. Hapimana was not with us now. He and Takarei were still in Birmingham, and we would not see them again.

It was in some ways a relief to be back in Limehouse, where men from many countries walked the streets, and we were no longer the darkest or strangest faces, as we were in Bristol, Bath, and Birmingham. Whenever the fog lifted, I spent most of my time wandering the docks, looking at the things I knew I'd always want to remember. There would never be such great wharfs and warehouses in Auckland, not in my lifetime, and such a forest of masts would never grow this thick in our harbours. We will never have the great wealth of England. Our towns will never seethe with so many millions of souls.

Even though it was very cold now in London, the mudlarks were still climbing down the stairs along the river, or down into Limehouse hole, and picking their way along the shore at low tide. I pitied the old women, up to their knees in the freezing water, or crawling like crabs in the mud. It will never cease to be foreign to me, this sight, and the thought that they were not seeking food, but foraging for rubbish.

The more brazen children could hoist each other onto barges to pilfer coal, but the old women with their battered kettles and torn shawls made far more modest harvests. I never saw so much as a piece of coal in their hands. Once I asked Mr Maunsell what they found in the mud, and he supposed it was nails, and chips of coal or wood. They would all be better off in New Zealand, I told him. He said that unfortunately the colony needed strong, skilled workers, and had no need for the destitute, criminal and infirm.

'Let them go to Australia,' said Hirini Pakia, and I'm ashamed to say that we all laughed at this.

We saw Mr Maunsell in Limehouse on many days, and one morning not long after we arrived, he and Reverend Stack called to fetch Wharepapa. They were going to the church of St Anne's, they said, and off the three of them walked. When Wharepapa returned, he was married. The ministers from New Zealand served as witnesses, and Elizabeth Reid brought along a friend to sign her name as well. Wharepapa said this friend was quite disappointed that no other Maori attended the wedding. She had heard that 'Mr Solomon', Horomona Te Atua, was very handsome as well, and had taken a great fancy to the idea of marrying a chief of her own.

Elizabeth Reid's parents and sisters did not attend the wedding either, though Mr Maunsell said that they knew of it, and did not think it such a terrible thing. Wharepapa was a rangatira, even if he knew only a little English, and was much older than their daughter, and looked quite strange and frightening with his moko. The worst thing was that he would take Elizabeth away to the other side of the world, and she would not be with her family again. For that reason, Elizabeth returned home to her parents' house in Marylebone for her last few days in England. We didn't see her until Miss Weale and Reverend Stack brought her to the ship at Gravesend, her belly huge with the child due to be born during the voyage home.

At the time I felt sorry for that girl. She was a pretty thing, young and sturdy, and always gazing at Wharepapa with wide eyes. He had told her all sorts of nonsense about how she would be treated like a queen in New Zealand, neglecting to mention that the Mangakahia Valley was nothing like Pall Mall, and that she would be trading her mop for a hoe.

I wondered what *his* father would have to say about a wife with no dowry, and no important relations, someone who worked as a maidservant in her native land. We're very particular about such things. Just as the Queen would not let Princess Beatrice marry a footman or a chimney sweep, we would expect the son of a rangatira to make a suitable match, of strategic value to his people. We don't just marry this one or that one, in the manner of lions and bears, however Wharepapa chose to carry on while he was in England.

While Wharepapa was out visiting his new relatives, Mr Maunsell escorted Horomona Te Atua and me somewhere we'd never been before: the studio of Mr Smetham, the painter. I remember that it was too far to walk all the way, so we took a cab for some part of the distance, and this cost Mr Maunsell a shilling. The studio was a large room high in a house, and the wife of the artist kept fluttering in and out, as though she was afraid we might attack her husband. Before we had a chance to see anything, Smetham and Mr Maunsell had words about the proposed title for the work.

'It is called *Maori Chiefs Converting to Christianity*,' Smetham said, and the way he ran his hands through his hair made it stick up in a wild kind of way. His hands were busy all the while we were there, often scribbling at tiny pictures in his notebook. 'Though there has been some suggestion it be named *Maori Converts to Methodism in John Wesley's House*.'

'But they are no such thing!' Mr Maunsell exclaimed. He grew red in the face very easily, I now knew. He told Horomona and me what had been said, and we shook our heads. 'I cannot speak for all the party, but these gentlemen of the North are all Anglicans, I can assure you.'

'We mustn't tell Reihana,' Horomona said quietly to me. 'He

will catch the train back to Birmingham to box Jenkins' ears, for now it will be said that he's a Wesleyan.'

By the time the two Pakeha had decided the painting should be called *The New Zealand Chiefs in John Wesley's House*, we were impatient to see the work itself. Mr Smetham had it stacked behind several others, and his stumpy hands shook so, Mr Maunsell had to help him haul it out and lean it against the wall. It was much bigger than I had thought likely, but then, there were seventeen people painted on it, and I suppose such a large number requires much canvas.

When the painting was revealed, Horomona and I stood for some time in silence, looking on it. I think he was as mystified as I.

Mr Smetham had sketched us in our lodgings, but here we were presented sitting or standing about in a room I remembered in John Wesley's house. I recognised it from the portrait of the founder of the Wesleyan faith. This was shown hanging on the wall in the centre of the painting. Beneath his portrait stood a piano, and this too I remembered from the house we visited. Standing in front of this, looking very true to life, was Jenkins. He was in the centre of things, and I remember thinking: Jenkins would like that. In this picture he was an important man. But the Maori standing across from him I didn't know at all, and Mr Smetham had to consult his notes to tell us it was meant to be Wiremu Pou.

'Even I don't know him,' Horomona Te Atua said, 'and he's my brother. Which one am I?'

Mr Maunsell thought he was perhaps one of the standing figures, holding the taiaha, next to an even taller man we agreed was Hare Pomare. I didn't want to offend Horomona, but I could see no reason on earth why his brother should stand at the heart of the picture, gesturing to the sky as though he could see a vision of God hidden to the rest of us. Perhaps he was thinking of the lights beckoning him from the Alhambra Theatre!

I'm afraid that looking at this painting I had many of these unchristian thoughts, for it was not clear to us why this or that person had been arranged in this or that spot.

Mr Smetham mumbled for a while, and Mr Maunsell told us that the figure of Wiremu Pou was pointing up at John Wesley's portrait.

'But he is no Wesleyan,' Horomona Te Atua said. 'I think the only Wesleyan among us is Hapimana Ngapiko. That's why he stays with Jenkins now.'

The groups in the painting were divided into two clusters, much as we had been divided on the stage in Birmingham Town Hall. Various Pakeha were seated to the right, and again, we were unsure of their identities. The gentleman was Reverend Jobson, Mr Maunsell told us, and after I peered a while at his whiskers and jowls, I did remember meeting him, at the house of John Wesley. The two ladies, with their ballooning skirts, I did not know at all, and I even imagined one might be Mrs Colenso until I remembered that she was not a Wesleyan.

Sitting in the front row with these unknown ladies was the figure of Tere Pakia, as Mr Smetham informed us, pronouncing her name in the oddest way, the paper shaking in his hand. She wore a fine dress of deep blue that I had never seen before, so this must have been a costume of Mr Smetham's devising. Behind this group stood two swarthy gentlemen, possibly Italian, like some of the sailors who walked the streets of Limehouse. But these dark fellows were wearing cloaks, so, said Mr Maunsell, they must be members of our party. One was meant to be Hirini

Pakia, looking far more upright and distinguished than he ever managed to appear in real life. The other man, who seemed youthful and wore his hair styled in the manner of the late Prince Consort, was, Mr Maunsell insisted, Kihirini.

'This is Kihirini here,' Horomona said, pointing to the group on the other side of the painting. 'Next to Ngahuia and . . . is that Haumu?'

'It must be Hariata Pomare.' Mr Maunsell was squinting at the painting just as we were. 'Haumu was never sketched by the artist, I believe, because she was staying in Bow. And that is not Kihirini next to them. It's Reihana.'

We disagreed with this, because Reihana seemed to be seated next to the piano, in the shadow of Wiremu Pou. But this figure, according to the artist's plan, was me.

'He has a full moko,' Mr Maunsell pointed out. 'So it must be Paratene and not Reihana.'

'But is this not Paratene here, in his dogskin cloak, trying to look over my shoulder?'

'That is Takarei Ngawaka,' Mr Maunsell said, consulting Mr Smetham's list. The artist himself appeared to have grown disconsolate, and had flung himself down on a couch, his notebook trembling in his hands. I didn't see myself at all in any of these faces, in part because the moko were indistinct, smudges on some faces, or scratches on others. Whether I was the one peeping over Horomona's shoulder, or the one seated on a low stool next to the piano, I don't know. Either person was evidently unimportant, given very little space. Even worse, both these figures appeared to be looking at Wiremu Pou.

Hapimana and Wharepapa, pointed out to us by Mr Maunsell, sat huddled near the doorway, like shrunken old men. The more I looked at it, the more I thought that Horomona was right, and I was the small figure on the edge of things. This looked more like me than it did Takarei, though the moko was wrong. But all the moko were wrong. Truly, if we were not dressed in our cloaks, and standing with Jenkins, we could have been a group of Lascars crowding into a chophouse.

The painting had been finished for some time, Mr Smetham told Mr Maunsell, but he was uncertain as to the plan of action as to where it would hang or to whom it belonged. There had been talk of an engraving made and sold around the country, but all had come to nought, and now we were leaving, he supposed there would be little demand.

Mr Maunsell asked if we wished to convey our impressions to the artist. We had no desire to complain, of course, and Mr Smetham was already fearful and agitated enough. So we praised the size of the work, the richness of the carpet depicted, and the detail of our cloaks, and said the ladies in our party would be most pleased to see themselves in such a setting and in such fine costumes.

'And Ngahuia and Tere looking so much younger than they do in life,' Horomona said to me, but Mr Maunsell didn't seem to hear.

'Jenkins stands before us again!' I declared, and when Mr Maunsell spoke, the artist looked happy. We left his house soon afterwards. When she heard we'd seen the painting, Tere Pakia demanded to be taken to Smetham's house as well, but Mr Maunsell said that Mr Smetham was not a well man, and his nerves would not stand another round of curious visitors from New Zealand.

There was little time left, in any case. We were to sail from Gravesend on the fourth of April, on the *Flying Foam*. That good lady Miss Weale had arranged cabins for us all, so this time we were not to be held deep in the ship, with the cargo and the rats. Instead we were 'saloon passengers', sleeping in airy cabins under the poop deck, and invited to sit at table with officers from the 40th Regiment, Lady Wiseman, and the missionary Mr Ireland and his wife, who were charged by Miss Weale with our care.

Kihirini, too weak to walk, particularly needed this care. He had to be passed up onto the ship like a bundle. I hadn't seen him for some time, as he'd been staying in the hospital. The sight was shocking. His face was sunken and yellow, his body wasting away. At least on this voyage he would not have to share a bed with Hapimana. He would have his own mattress and pillow, and fresh meat for dinner. I wasn't sure if that would be enough to keep him alive throughout the long journey home.

Mr Lightband was there as well, in his own cabin, as eager as we were to return home. It was at his suggestion, I think, that we set about composing farewell letters to the Queen. Mrs Colenso was arriving on the steamer from London to say goodbye to us, and would translate our letters and hand them to the Duke of Newcastle. Horomona Te Atua and I, who were sharing a cabin, set to work immediately.

I don't know what Horomona wrote, but in my letter I asked Her Majesty to show love to the Maori of New Zealand. I quoted the Bible verse about faith, hope, and charity, declaring charity to be the greatest of the three, and asked God to bless us and keep us all. I thought of the Queen and her sadness, and told her that God's love would last forever.

Before I had finished my letter, Reverend Stack was knocking on the door, announcing his arrival, and that of Miss Weale and Mrs Colenso, for they were all eager to say their goodbyes. Perhaps I would have written a longer letter if they had not arrived so soon. There are other things I would have liked to say to the Queen.

But no, this can't be the way it happened. I have the order of things wrong, I think, because later Ngahuia told us that in the letter she wrote, she thanked the Queen for the great gift sent with Mrs Colenso. For when that lady arrived on board, she was carrying a parcel from the Duke of Newcastle. This included something from the Queen herself for each of us – a piece of notepaper with a thick border of black, bearing the Queen's signature and the date of our visit to her at Osborne. We were all very pleased to get this, even Haumu, who was in the asylum when we all visited the Queen. She grabbed the piece of notepaper intended, no doubt, for the absent Wiremu Pou, and clasped it to her breast, crumpling it considerably.

Mrs Colenso also had instructions from the Duke to present Ngahuia with something very precious. This was a brooch, a cross of gold set with pearls and other jewels, and it was a gift from the Queen herself. That long-ago summer's day at Osborne, Ngahuia had given the Queen her greenstone heitiki, and now Her Majesty was taking the opportunity to reciprocate before we sailed away forever. She understood our ways, as they were her ways as well. For every deed, every gesture, there must be a suitable response.

So this is why we wrote the letters that day on board the *Flying Foam*, while there was still time to thank the Queen for all the kindness she'd shown us. When Reverend Stack knocked on my door, it was to say he and Miss Weale and Mrs Colenso were leaving, and the letters must be collected. Ngahuia had delayed us all with her excited chatter about the magnificence of the Queen's gift, especially as her tears of joy had set poor Haumu off as well. Miss Weale had spoken sharply to both of them, though her English words still meant nothing to them. Wharepapa told me once that Miss Weale thought Ngahuia too proud, and doubtless felt the Queen's gift would make this pride, this vanity, even worse.

No. It was Mr Lightband who knocked on our door, and said the letters should be finished at once. A further two people had arrived on board the *Flying Foam*, eager to bid us farewell, and he wanted us to see them.

These two people were Mr Lloyd, and Jenkins. We hadn't seen them in person since that terrible night at the Birmingham Town Hall, though Horomona and I had seen the painting of Jenkins, where he stood in the centre of us all, under the picture of John Wesley. Now here they were, many miles south of Birmingham in Gravesend. They stood on the deck wearing thick coats, for the weather was still cold. Mr Lloyd was no longer so nervous and unhappy, perhaps because he was not required to pay for our passage home. He shook hands with whoever stepped forward to greet him, and stood about laughing too loudly with Mr Lightband.

Jenkins stood a few steps back, watchful. He was anxious, I think, that we would denounce him once again, or demand that the captain throw him off the ship. We were all assembled there on the deck, apart from Kihirini, who lay coughing and shuddering in his bed, and Hare and Hariata Pomare, who had sailed at Christmas, and the three Maori of our original party who had chosen not to sail with us now – Hapimana and Takarei, and Wiremu Pou. We had one addition to our group, Wharepapa's young wife, who stood among us clinging to her new husband's arm, her yellow hair blowing in the wind.

Miss Weale was not happy. That was plain for all to see. Even Mrs Colenso, who was a kind lady, and had once been a friend to Jenkins, was frowning, talking in a low voice to Reverend Stack. They were afraid, too, I think, of an unseemly scene like the one they had read about in the Birmingham newspaper. But by this day none of us had the appetite for such carry-on, not even Reihana. Jenkins stood tall and erect as ever, but there was a sadness in his eyes. He had risked his all to bring a group of rangatira to England to see its wonders and its multitudes, and together we had climbed to great heights. None of us had imagined that we would tumble from those heights in such a manner, or that the trip would end quite this way.

I thought of the letter I had been writing, moments earlier, to Queen Victoria. As I wrote, I was thinking of the words from Corinthians. 'Though I speak with the tongues of men and of angels, and have not charity, I am become as sounding brass, or a tinkling cymbal.'

When Tere Pakia stepped forward and began to sing a farewell lament, all but Reihana joined her. I did not hesitate in adding my voice to theirs. We swayed together as though the boat was already surging through the sea.

Haere, haere, haere. Our great adventure in England was at an end. None of us would ever return. None of us would ever see Jenkins again.

The time has come for the Bohemian to sail. I walk along the wharf, looking for him, and he's easy to find, despite the press of the crowds and the great mounds of trunks and barrels still to be hauled onto the ship. No one else in Auckland wears a round hat made of a piece of carpet.

He shakes my hand, and introduces me to his wife, who wears a grey dress and bonnet. Her name is Rebecca, and her sharp face, as bird-like as his, softens when she smiles. She is his second wife, and not as young as I expected. Perhaps this is why they have no children. She is English, the Bohemian has told me, so she must have some idea what to expect of this long journey.

'We travel in second class,' he tells me, and I think that this is not so bad, as long as the biscuits are not rotten with worms, and the sugar doesn't run out. In one of our sessions the Bohemian told me that he travelled from Germany in steerage, so he is pleased that Mr Buller is paying for a cabin.

'My husband tells me your trip back from England was very exciting,' his wife says, speaking very quickly. 'A mutiny!'

I smile and nod, though I don't say anything. I don't want to be seen or heard chattering in English on the wharf. In our last meeting, I told the Bohemian some of the foolishness of our voyage home, and this is what his wife mentions now. I spoke of the mutiny as an amusing thing, but at the time it made everyone on board quite anxious.

It began when one of the seamen kicked a second-class passenger who'd insulted him, and after he was placed in irons and locked away, a number of the other sailors took up his cause. The regimental men in the cabins near ours took up arms at the captain's request. For a time no ladies were allowed on deck, and several passengers were paid to help the captain sail the ship. Some of the second-class cabins were turned into gaols, and the men confined within them made much commotion by shouting oaths, sawing through their chains and smashing up their stocks. For a time Mr Lightband was obliged to sit up through the night on the poop deck, keeping watch, and later, when more of the seamen joined the mutiny, he had to take his turn guarding the prisoners. Wharepapa was eager to fight them, or at least to be permitted to brandish a gun, but Mr Lightband said that this was not necessary. When we arrived in Auckland, more than a dozen mutineers were marched off to Mount Eden gaol.

'And there was a ghost,' says the Bohemian, mischief dancing in his eyes, for I told him this story too, of a spirit reported to haunt the female apartments of steerage. Later the ghost was revealed to be the ship's still-living third mate, up to no good.

'Such great excitement,' his wife says, and then the Bohemian talks to her for a while of Wharepapa's baby, born at sea.

Wharepapa is nowhere to be seen today, among the crush of people on the wharf, but of course he is a topic of conversation, as ever. Many Maori are here, inspecting and admiring the ship. It's a brisk day, with a good wind for sailing, and a number of them, I think, would like nothing more than to climb on board and set off across the oceans.

Wharepapa is from a soggy inland place, so perhaps he doesn't feel the same urge to sail away. Although I've had my chance to travel to the other side of the world, and have no desire to make that journey again, I know that feeling, of wanting to stand on a deck and course through the waves, however short or familiar the trip. I feel that way myself right now, because I've been stuck in Auckland too long. I'm surrounded here, and I don't like that.

After Mr McGregor takes me back to Tutukaka, I'm going to find a way to get out to Hauturu. I'll send a message down to Tenetahi's crowd at Omaha, and one of his boys will come for me. It'll be cold there, the clouds drifting down from the mountain, but at least the only noise at Hauturu is made by the birds and the crashing waves, and the tui will still be fat and delicious.

Before I leave the Bohemian and his wife, I whisper in his ear in English.

'May God watch over you and keep you,' I tell him.

'God and Mr Buller,' he replies. I know he means this as a joke, so I say nothing else. But I feel very strongly that the Bohemian and his wife should put all their faith in God, and none in Mr Buller, and not depend on that gentleman for everything in England. We can never know the minds and hearts of other men. We can never truly understand what drives them, or where their frailties and ambition may lead.

Late that night, in bed at the Native Hostel, I'm restless – half-dozing and half-awake, because it's hard for me to sleep through the night now. It's especially difficult at the hostel, with the hum of snoring, and too much laughter and talk. A distant boom sounds, and for a moment I think I'm back on the *Ida Zeigler*, or the *Flying Foam*, and we've run onto a sand bar. But I'm still in my bed, not shaken to the ground, and after a moment I realise where I am.

I don't know what that noise is. It resembles the sound of a thick stand of kauri falling all at once, or lightning carving a slice out of a tree. I wonder if it's the Bohemian's ship, but he sailed this morning, and should be well beyond the waters of the gulf by now.

Now it's impossible for me to sleep, because I'm wondering if I dreamed the terrible booming noise, and if, like Reihana's twitching hand, this is a bad sign. I hope no evil comes to the Bohemian on this trip of his. I want him to return home safely, as I did.

The things I told the Bohemian about the voyage home from England were true. There was talk of a ghost, who was not a ghost at all, and there was a mutiny, which was quite real. On our arrival in Auckland the prisoners were led from the wharf in chains and marched to Mount Eden. And, as the Bohemian was telling his wife, during the voyage a daughter was born to Wharepapa and his wife, Elizabeth. I had suggested they name the child Dorotea, to appease Miss Weale, but when the baby was born just as we rounded the Cape, they decided to name her Maria Good Hope.

I didn't tell the Bohemian the rest of the story of our return. It was a long time ago, and he doesn't know these people. They would be just so many Maori to him, like the photographs that stick to his wall, or the sketches he makes at the Native Land Court. But as I lie awake in this narrow and uncomfortable bed, their faces appear before me, as clear as though we returned just last week.

Not everyone arrived home. This may be the way always with these long voyages. People who are already sick when they board at Gravesend hope that at sea, far from the soot and fumes of England, they will recover. Kihirini Te Tuahu was one of those who hoped to reach New Zealand but did not. Like that poor boy Wiremu Repa, it was too late for him. In England he'd wasted away in the damp and the cold, and with every breath he drew he rattled. We had been waiting for him to die for so long, it was not a surprise when it happened, somewhere in the Atlantic Ocean.

We didn't mourn his death the way Mr Lightband expected. We didn't really like Kihirini, I suppose. He was very grumpy, even before he was ill, and too proud. It could be said that we Nga Puhi were too proud, but we have many things to be proud about. Mr Lightband was a good man, but he didn't understand much about us or our way of seeing things. We didn't mourn Kihirini because we didn't know him. He was from another region, another iwi. He wasn't one of us.

Hare Pomare and his wife, Hariata, were back in New Zealand long before we were. Their baby, Albert Victor, is full-grown now, like Wharepapa's daughter. Not many children have such auspicious beginnings and certainly, his was more auspicious than that of Wharepapa's girl. Albert Victor's christening was written of in the *Times*. As a baby, he was held by his godmother, Queen Victoria herself, and kissed by the Royal Princesses. He was presented with a silver mug, engraved with his name, and that of the Queen.

But there was much unhappiness in store for this boy when they returned to New Zealand. Hare Pomare died when still a very young man, just a few years after the trip to England. I heard that Hariata married again, but someone at the Native Hostel once told me that she did not live long either. The boy was placed in the Anglican Orphan Home, all the expenses of his keep and education paid by Queen Victoria. When Her Majesty's son, Prince Alfred, visited New Zealand, Hare Pomare's brother took the boy along to be presented.

When he was about ten years old, I heard, Albert Victor was given a place in St Stephen's Native School here in Auckland, the school begun by Bishop Selwyn when the city was no more than a fern gully and a fort. That was the last thing I heard of him for some time, until Wharepapa said that the boy had joined the Royal Navy. Perhaps Albert Victor is sailing in some distant ocean now. Perhaps he has been back to London, his birthplace, many times. If so, he must have walked through Limehouse, and seen, or even stayed at, the Strangers' Home.

Of some of the others in our party, I've heard less. Mr Lightband returned to Nelson, I believe, to do whatever it is that Pakeha do. Horomona Te Atua, who travelled back to New Zealand without his elder brother, Wiremu Pou, lives somewhere near Wharepapa's settlement in Mangakahia. All these years I've kept my distance from that chancer Hirini Pakia, and his wife, Tere, and thankfully they're rarely about the Native Hostel these days.

The last time I saw Ngahuia, she was flouncing away from the wharf in Auckland. Off to sell her pearl cross, Wharepapa said, but I don't believe she'd do that. She was a silly woman, I suppose, but not that silly. That cross was a gift from the Queen. If it had been handed to Wiremu Pou, he would have worn it on his coat every day and boasted that the Queen had implored him to marry her.

The other woman in our party on the *Flying Foam* was Haumu. That poor woman ranted and cried on the voyage back in much the same manner she carried on when we sailed to England a year earlier. She was not right in the head. All those months at the big asylum in London had not helped her. If anything, she was more afraid to stay on a ship, more likely to hear strange voices in the wind. Her people took her away when we landed, and I don't know what became of her, or of the little daughter she'd left behind.

Reihana Te Taukawau is dead now, though he was younger than I, and I'm still here. After he returned, he built a church, as he said he would, though his health was not good. His people worked as gum-diggers to raise the money. It's at Ohaeawai, near the old battle site. Reihana died before it was completed, and he's buried there. All this happened within five or six years of our return from England. I never saw him again, and I don't think this troubled either of us much.

Not to be outdone, Wharepapa built a church as well, in the Mangakahia Valley. Miss Weale sent him and Reihana precious things for their churches – a prayer book, I think, and a font, and possibly a fine altar cloth. I say that Wharepapa lives in Parnell now, but really he comes and goes, staying a great deal of the time up north. He's here in Auckland for most of the winter because it's too difficult to get in and out of Mangakahia once the rains set in. I've always lived by the sea, and would not like to struggle over hills and fight my way through dense bush just to get home.

Elizabeth, his wife, didn't like it either. She grew tired of the mud and the loneliness, and the endless fetching of water and digging in the kumara pits. She said she would not live with him deep in the bush any more. He bought the house in Parnell for her, and now she lives all the year in Auckland with her daughters. Sometimes Wharepapa talks of getting a new wife, one who will look after him in Mangakahia. He says that English wives are too much trouble. This sentiment is not something, I suspect, he would ever include in one of his letters to Miss Weale.

Thinking of Miss Weale reminds me of Wiremu Pou, who she promised to find. He didn't sail home with us, or even with Jenkins. He was too busy travelling England, performing on the stage with his new friends in the Maori Warrior Chiefs, greasepaint smeared over his grinning face. But Miss Weale found him, as we knew she would, and harangued him and the others members of his troupe, as we knew she would, until they all agreed to stop their carrying-on in theatres and permit her to raise the funds for their journey home. I think he sailed back late in 1864.

Wharepapa, who still gets annoyed at the mention of his name, told me that Wiremu Pou found himself an English wife too, and brought her back to New Zealand. He didn't want to slink back like a whipped dog. He wanted to come home with treasure to show off, and a big story. They got married in London, just before they sailed for New Zealand. Miss Weale was at the wedding, perhaps to make sure that the marriage was properly Anglican, and that Wiremu Pou didn't run off to join a circus afterwards instead of boarding the ship.

After he returned, Wiremu Pou, like Horomona Te Atua, spent a lot of time in Mangakahia, so Wharepapa knows all their affairs. When Wharepapa met this wife, Georgina, he could tell she was some kind of lowly servant girl, tricked into believing that her new husband was a prince like one of Victoria's sons, with carriages and servants. Unlike the Maori women in Mangakahia, who'd all been taught to read and write by the missionaries, this Georgina could not read a word of the Bible or even sign her own name.

Of course, Wiremu Pou was telling people that his wife had worked at one of the royal palaces, and that Queen Victoria herself had blessed their union. Wharepapa let him tell his story, and didn't say anything to contradict it, except for one night when he grew sick of all the boasting, and suggested writing to Miss Weale and Mrs Colenso to ask more about this royal blessing. That shut Wiremu Pou up for a while! At any rate, we all knew the truth. Wiremu Pou couldn't stand that the Queen had singled out Pomare and his wife, choosing them for special gifts and offering to be godmother to their little boy. The last thing I heard was that Wiremu Pou died around 1872, leaving his English wife to fend for herself in the bush.

The other two who refused to travel home with us, preferring to stick with Jenkins, were Hapimana Ngapiko, who was Jenkins' first recruit, and his friend Takarei Ngawaka. They both sailed from England in June, on the *Surat*, the same ship as Jenkins. We didn't realise it when we saw the last of them in Birmingham, but their illnesses were not just the winter chills most of us had. Like Kihirini Te Tuahu, they were suffering from consumption. Both of them died on the journey home and, like Kihirini, and the boy Wiremu Repa, they were buried at sea. This is a terrible thing, in my opinion – for your body to be dumped into the waves rather than returned to your ancestral home. I wouldn't wish this on anyone, not even my enemies, though I suppose when I was young, and away on a taua, it would have given me some satisfaction.

Wharepapa likes to mutter that it was good we didn't travel home with Jenkins, because obviously the man was bad luck.

This is true. I don't agree with all the things said against him, but Jenkins *was* bad luck. He was cursed in some way. When he got back to Auckland, he should have hurried home to his family in Nelson, to the wife and many children he always spoke of so warmly. But instead he stayed in Auckland, trying to sell some jewellery entrusted to him, so he said, by friends in Birmingham. I don't know who these friends were. Not Miss Weale or Mr Sneyd Kynnersley, to be sure.

But Jenkins had these things to sell, and a boy from Birmingham to help him. This lad had travelled on the *Surat* with Jenkins and Takarei and Hapimana, along with Jenkins' brother and his family, who had decided to make a new life in New Zealand. The boy, who was called Samuel Wakeman, had been sent by his own family, to make his way in the world. Jenkins was to be his protector on the voyage and in his new country. Well, we could have told Samuel Wakeman and his family that Jenkins was not reliable in this way.

Jenkins was not a bad man. Let me say that again. But when he was supposed to be protecting us, he was thinking all the time of making money. And this was no different when he arrived back in Auckland with this boy. They went from place to place to sell these trinkets, these pearls, and Samuel, who knew no one in the city, was sent out alone to try to effect a sale. Jenkins needed desperately to make some money, I suspect, because he had lost so much when we were in England.

After a day or two there was some kind of disagreement between them. Wharepapa read the story in the *Daily Southern Cross*, and told me about it. Jenkins accused the boy Samuel of trying to steal from him. They were in dispute over the jewellery, of what had been taken and what had been sold. This boy said he'd taken nothing. He was sad to be so far from home, I think, and the sadness turned his head. He went to a chemist on Fort Street and bought some kind of poison. By the next morning he was dead. Jenkins was called to the court to give evidence, and was not in Auckland much after that.

In fact, he was travelling about the country for some time with the man the Bohemian knows, Walter Buller. Jenkins was working again as an interpreter for the Native Land Court, and Buller – another Wesleyan – was a judge. They were down in Whanganui when Jenkins died. It was just three years after we returned from England. Jenkins was still a poor man.

So it is fair to say, I think, that none of us made money from that trip. Reihana said that Jenkins was lining his own pockets, but now I doubt that this was true. He was always *trying* to line them, but the money fell through. This is what I mean when I say he was cursed.

One other thing about Jenkins strikes me now. I judged him severely for not coming down to see us, or to pray with us, during the voyage to England. I thought this was evidence of Jenkins thinking himself in some way above us, or not truly caring about the Maori souls in his care. But over the past few days, as I've been thinking of all this again, I remember this one thing that Charley Davis told me. Not before we sailed off to England, but years afterwards.

He said that back in 1840 or so when Jenkins and his wife first travelled to New Zealand from England, they brought with them their two oldest children. These children, a boy and a girl, were still very small. On board the ship they fell ill, and first one, then the other, died. Jenkins' wife was already carrying their third child when they set sail, and she was delivered of this child safely as soon as they arrived in Wellington.

Jenkins was a young man then, a cabinet-maker, with no

wealth or connections. I think he and his family would have sailed to New Zealand in steerage, not a fine cabin. Perhaps this is the reason he could not bring himself to seek us out below deck. Seeing our dark, cramped berths, and the swollen belly of Hariata Pomare, and the children of the soldiers playing at our feet, he would have remembered too clearly his own voyage out – his own wife with child, his own children playing. Perhaps even the lingering smell down there, of smoke, grease, and rank bodies, would have reminded him of the children he loved, and the manner of their deaths. It's little wonder he stayed away.

You know, I couldn't read the story about Jenkins and Samuel Wakeman in the *Daily Southern Cross* back then, because I could not read English, or speak it. But when I returned home to Tutukaka, I knew what I wanted to do. Reihana and Wharepapa were building churches, but I wanted to build a school. My taina, Henare Te Moananui, and I gave the land for it at Ngunguru. The Church Missionary Society bought the planks of wood, and tin for the roof. It's not grand like the fine Wesleyan School I saw in Bath, and there's no room for beds or kitchens and such things, but it does the job. The school opened in 1870.

Maori children attend, as well as Pakeha children. There are more of them every year, girls and boys. The schoolroom is so full, there is almost no room for me to find a seat in there any more. But for more than ten years I visited the school whenever I was staying up there. Sometimes I would sniff the chalk or strum on the counting beads to make the children laugh. Usually I would sit quietly at the back, and listen to their lessons.

This is how I learned English. Though I don't have much chance to speak it, I know how. If I were to sail to England again, I would be able to speak to the Queen directly, and understand exactly what she was saying to me in reply. I wouldn't need Jenkins or Mr Maunsell or Mrs Colenso to tell me the words of other people.

I won't be going back to England, though. It's too late. I was old when I went in 1863, and now it's more than twenty years on. I pull the blankets high around my shoulders, because just thinking about England like this makes me feel cold. If I went back there, maybe I would see Pomare's son, Albert Victor, walking the streets of London in his naval uniform. Some people, you know, insist he's lost at sea, but then some people will be always making up stories to explain what they don't know. Someone in the hostel told me that Albert Victor was last seen in an American city, on the other side of the Pacific, and that he'd changed his name.

This too is ridiculous. This young man was held by the Queen when he was a baby. At her personal request he was given the name of Albert, the name of the husband she loved. His second name, Victor, was hers. The missionaries persuaded me to change my name, but no one will ever persuade Albert Victor Pomare to change his. I would rather believe him lost at sea.

I know of Miss Weale, of course, from her letters to Wharepapa. She left the Winson Green Road Girls' Home, and the city of Birmingham, not long after we returned to New Zealand. Her health was not good, so she took my advice to move closer to the sea. She lives in Dorset now, in the south of England, where there is less snow and fewer chimneys. Mr Sneyd Kynnersley, she tells Wharepapa, is retired and still living in Birmingham, with his many children and servants. The young Mr Maunsell returned to New Zealand, and has been working with his father, the Archdeacon, on a new Maori Bible. Mrs

Colenso left England as well, I heard, and is now doing good work at a mission on Norfolk Island.

Some of those who we knew in England are dead now. Reverend Stack, old Te Taka, died there three years ago. The Duke of Newcastle and the Earl of Shaftesbury are both dead. When I met those fine gentlemen I never thought that I would outlive them for, as I say, I was already old then, and they were not. That's the thing you don't know when you're young, that so much of your life will be spent being old. This is why you must do everything you can when your mind is still alert, your body still strong. Youth is the time to be a warrior, and a student, and a traveller. You have no time to waste for, like Prince Leopold, that serious little boy who shook our hands at Osborne, you may not live to be an old man. The prince died just a year or so ago, still quite young. Sometimes there's not enough time for everything we want to do, that must be done. I worry about running out of time now, just to sort out this business with my land, and I'm eighty-six years old, or something close to that number.

Eventually I fall asleep, and sleep for a long time, even though there is always too much noise at the hostel. Too much talking. Always too much talking. When I put away my writing and take a walk around the Maori market that afternoon, just to get a little air, no one is selling anything and no one is buying. Everyone is talking.

Wharepapa is there, speaking so fast I can hardly understand him. He heard the sound last night as well, the boom that I thought was a ship hitting a sand bar, or lightning slicing through a tree. I was wrong about these things. The sound we heard was Mount Tarawera, hundreds of miles to the south, erupting.

'Many people have been killed,' Wharepapa tells me, in that

authoritative way he has, as though he was personally at the scene. Before he can say more, many other voices chime in, for this is a story everyone wants to tell. The spirit waka was a sign, just as the old tohunga said. The volcano exploded some time after midnight. There was one eruption and then another, and another, throwing fire and rocks into the sky. The sky spat back lightning, and shouted with thunder. Hot mud and ash fell like rain.

Entire villages are buried now in this ash and mud, and whatever Wharepapa says, no one knows yet how many people, Maori and Pakeha, lie dead within them. Some people are crying for those who are dead, and some fear that the end of the world is upon us. The Bible warns us of a great earthquake, when the moon is filled with blood, and the stars of heaven tumble to earth. One old man shakes his head, his body crumpled in despair. Tarawera is the place Ngatoro-i-rangi fought the atua Tama-o-hoi, burying the demon deep in the mountain.

'This is the doing of Tama-o-hoi,' he moans. 'For centuries his anger has been building. Now he's pushed open the mouth of the mountain, and shown us his fury.'

Some are lamenting the end of the Pink and White Terraces. These, I hear, have been plunged deep into the lake, shattered into pieces like broken coral.

Into smoke shall they consume away . . .

I don't know what to think. I walk off down the beach, trying to escape the wailing voices. Whether this is God's vengeance or that of Tama-o-hoi, this eruption is a terrible thing. Demons may walk among us now. What will be unleashed next? I need to get back to Hauturu, to stand on the rocks there and look up at my own mountain, the place where our world touches the sky. I feel very far away from it, as far away as I did all those months in England.

I sit down with my back against the sea wall and close my eyes, listening to the call of the gulls and the rhythmic lapping of waves. This is the best way for me to go to sleep, and right now I long for the escape of sleep, even if it's only for a few minutes.

This is the moment I see it. I'm not a matakite, so this isn't a vision, and I'm still awake, so it isn't a dream. But I know that what I see before me is a sign.

I'm standing on a boat. Hauturu lies in the distance, a deep green, its trees quivering with birds. The wind blows from the east, filling the sails. I want to be ready to clamber onto the rocks as soon as we arrive.

But the island is receding, not getting closer. I claw at the boat, willing it to turn around, but there's nothing I can do. We draw further and further away, and I know that however long we sail, however far we sail, we'll never reach it.

Cloud draws around it, until I can no longer see the island. Hauturu is lost to me, as though the mountain has exploded like Tarawera, tearing up or burying everything below.

I have been to England, travelling so much further than our ancestors, those greatest of voyagers. I thought that home waited for me, unchanging, and that I could re-take my place there, tend my fire. But nothing is unchanging. I saw that when I was a younger man, and everything that I grew up believing and understanding was swept away. Even before that, I knew that a home could be invaded, or destroyed, or taken. I was one of the invaders.

I have stood on a beach, waiting to hurl myself at the palisades and plunge a spear deep into the belly of a man. I've trained my gun on a figure hurtling towards me, and clubbed a man so hard I sliced the top of his head away. I've eaten the body of a dead man to destroy his tapu, and set fire to a pa so its men and women and children would be forced to flee into the path of our guns. These things I did knowing that they had been done in the places I lived, to the people I knew, and that I could be the man turning the sand to rust with my blood. I could be the man whose pa would be burned, whose head would be carried on a stake and preserved as one of the spoils of war. Only when the weather was stormy could we live without fear on the shore of Hauturu. The rest of the time we lived high on the cliffs, defended by our trenches and the sea, and watched for the approach of waka.

There was much to fear when I was a young man, though I knew how to fight and thought only of how the day would unfold, not the century. But how can I fight the men of the courts? They're like warriors on a spirit waka – barely visible, untouchable. They glide in through the mist and we're helpless, able only to watch and wait. I don't know how to fight them. I see Hauturu disappear, and I know that the battle is already lost. For the first time in my life, I'm afraid.

This novel is inspired by the life of my tupuna, Paratene Te Manu, based on the account of his life he gave in 1895 at the request of James Cowan, published in *Pictures of Old New Zealand*. In this oral history, Paratene lists each of his eight taua in detail, and talks at length about the trip to England in 1863.

In addition to this account, I've drawn extensively from letters by Paratene, Kamariera Te Hautakiri Wharepapa, Reihana Te Taukawau and Dorotea Weale; from the diaries of William Jenkins, Reihana Te Taukawau, Elizabeth Colenso, and William Wales Lightband; and from articles, announcements and letters in the *Birmingham Daily Post*, the *Coventry Times*, the *Coventry Herald*, the *Coventry, Warwick and Leamington Times*, the *Bristol Mercury and Western Counties Advertiser*, the *Western Daily Press*, the *Illustrated London News*, the *Daily Southern Cross*, and the *Australian and New Zealand Gazette*.

Although I've been largely faithful to the chronology, personnel and locations of the English trip, much in this novel is conjecture and invention. Many liberties have been taken with history, particularly in the relationship between Paratene and Lindauer. The Lindauer portrait of Paratene Te Manu in the Partridge Collection was probably taken from a photograph rather than life, and I've uncovered no evidence that the two men ever met. In June 1886 Lindauer and his wife had already sailed for England to attend the Colonial and Indian Exhibition, for which Walter Buller had commissioned twenty of his paintings – one of which was presented to the Prince of Wales.

No engravings were made of the painting by James Smetham, and it's unlikely that any of the Maori party saw it in London. The painting was completed by January 1864, and William Jenkins met with the artist three times early that month, spending a whole day posing so his own portrait could be altered. Smetham suffered from many long periods of depression, and ended his days in an asylum. The painting was purchased by Thomas Hocken in 1881, and is now held by the Hocken Library in Dunedin.

The Strangers' Home for Asiatics, Africans and South Sea Islanders, its foundation stone laid by Prince Albert in 1856, was demolished in 1937 and replaced with a block of flats. The Alhambra Theatre burned in 1882, on a night so cold that the water froze in the firemen's hoses, and was rebuilt. Eventually it too was torn down – in 1936, to make way for the Odeon Leicester Square. Marlborough House, with its early eighteenth-century battle scenes painted on the walls of the Blenheim Saloon, is now home to the Commonwealth Secretariat.

Much of mid-Victorian Birmingham is gone, thanks to the efforts of World War II bombers and post-war urban planners. Gone forever are the grand house of Thomas Sneyd Kynnersley and the Winson Green Road Home for Girls. But Birmingham Town Hall, which has played host to Charles Dickens, Mendelssohn, and Jenny Lind, among others, still stands. It was closed in the 1990s, but reopened, fully restored, in 2007.

Kingswood School in Bath, founded by John Wesley in 1748, served as the headquarters for the Admiralty during World War II and is now a large co-ed independent school. Paratene's visit in 1863 coincided with a difficult period in the school's history: its strict governor, Reverend West, was unpopular with boys and staff, and the headmaster, Henry Jefferson, resigned in 1865.

It's also unlikely that Paratene ever learned to speak English, though local history in Ngunguru records him regularly visiting the school and sitting in on lessons. The drawn-out court battles over Hauturu (Little Barrier) are, unfortunately, based on historical record. In October 1886 the Native Land Court finally ruled in favour of Ngati Wai and named fourteen people, including Paratene Te Manu, as owners of Hauturu. The next ten years were characterised by fraught negotiations with the government over the sale price, mounting court costs, and the issue of a Maori reserve on the island.

By the end of 1886, the Secretary of the Auckland Institute was urging the government to buy the island as a bird preserve rather than a military base or timber resource. Later, the situation was complicated by a continued campaign by Ngati Whatua for ownership; by the government contravening its own 1891 agreement by trying to negotiate with individual owners; and by Tenetahi's discovery that timber contractors would give him up to £5000 for the island's kauri (versus the government's fixed purchase price of £3000).

Maori residents were accused of bird harvesting, though it's been argued that Walter Buller – a dedicated and ambitious ornithologist – and some of the Pakeha island custodians were the true culprits. In *Yesterdays in Maoriland*, Andreas Reischek, the nineteenth-century Austrian naturalist, recalls searching for the stitchbird on Hauturu in 1883 'partly at the request of Sir Walter Buller, for whom I procured specimens of which his collection was deficient'. (Reischek himself left a collection of 2700 – dead – New Zealand native birds, now held by the Natural History Museum in Vienna.)

Although Buller drafted Lord Onslow's memo to the New Zealand government arguing for native bird sanctuaries on islands like Hauturu, he continued to acquire 'specimens' of endangered birds, such as the huia, for his own collection.

Privately he believed that New Zealand's native birds, like its native population, were doomed to extinction.

Although Paratene agreed to sell his interest in Hauturu in 1892, he still expected all the owners to receive a fair price from the government. He also expected the government to honour Tenetahi's request for a small Maori reserve on the island. But the presence of Maori inhabitants – especially ones who might be cutting down kauri, or shooting kereru – wasn't compatible with the island's new purpose. As the lucrative tree-felling continued, the government decided the time for negotiation and conciliation was over. The Little Barrier Island Purchase Act, to compulsorily acquire the remaining shares, was passed by Parliament in October 1894, despite arguments against it led by Hone Heke Ngapua, the Northern Maori MP.

Rahui and Tenetahi, my great-great-grandparents, kept up the fight. Rahui returned to the Native Land Court, arguing that the sale price should take into consideration the value of the kauri, livestock and cultivations on the island, and Tenetahi wrote a long letter to the *New Zealand Herald* invoking Article 2 of the Treaty of Waitangi, but to no avail. The price was fixed, the sale was decided, and an eviction notice was served. All 'natives' were supposed to leave by 10 December 1895.

After one unsuccessful eviction attempt by the Crown – sending the steamer *Nautilus* to carry the Maori residents away, only to find they were all back within days – a more impressive show of force was deemed necessary. At 5 a.m. on 19 March 1896 the government steamer *Hinemoa* dropped anchor at Hauturu and landed two boats, carrying Lieutenant Hume, a Mr J.P. McAlister, the Crown Prosecutor, his dog, an interpreter, a police sergeant, and '21 men of the torpedo corps' each with '20 rounds of ball cartridge', according to Charles

John Alexander, a passenger on the steamer. 'From the ship', Alexander wrote, they could see 'two or three natives about their hut, and it appears that these are the people this small army has been sent out to evict'.

Five people were removed from the island: two women and three men. The women, Rahui and her daughter, Ngapeka, were dropped off at Little Omaha, where Rahui's son, Wi Taiawa, was arrested and brought onto the ship. The *Hinemoa* arrived back in Auckland late that afternoon, where the army was dismissed. The four male prisoners – Tenetahi, Wi Taiawa, Kino Tamihana, and Kiri Tenetahi (my great-grandfather, then about twenty-four years old) – were marched away by the police sergeant, charged with wilful trespass on Crown lands. Lieutenant Hume, Alexander wrote, seemed 'ashamed of the part he played in the comedy of "the taking of the Little Barrier"'.

The *New Zealand Herald* observed that there was 'something pathetic in this unfortunate Maori [Tenetahi] being dragged away from his ancestral rocks by force and arms', and suggested that the Crown appoint him 'caretaker of the birds and beasts' on Hauturu. But there was too much mistrust between the parties to make this viable. Rahui and Tenetahi proceeded to drive the government crazy: by making frequent returns to the island; by continuing to graze cattle and grow crops there; and, in October 1896, by (allegedly) demolishing the island's only remaining inhabitable dwelling.

The early diaries of Robert Shakespear, the first caretaker of the new sanctuary, are full of complaints about Tenetahi's constant visits to Hauturu, though he grew to like and respect Rahui, describing her as 'most interesting' and 'a plucky old thing'. As late as August 1897, she was still sailing to the island to harvest kumara, sharing with Shakespear her considerable knowledge of the history of the island.

Shakespear's dim view of Tenetahi was not shared by Hugh Boscawen of the Lands and Survey Department, who said, in 1893, that he could 'not speak too highly of the kindness I received from Tenetahi and his family . . . [He] was only too glad to explain and show me everything that he thought would interest me.' This, of course, was before Tenetahi's eviction, and Boscawen, unlike Shakespear, had not moved into Tenetahi's house and threatened to shoot him if he caused any damage.

Tenetahi continued to battle in the courts, petitioning the government in 1910 over the forced sale of Hauturu. He died in June 1923; the occupation listed on his death certificate is 'Master Mariner'. Rahui died in 1930, in her hundredth year. They are both buried in the urupa of the Te Kiri/Omaha marae, just outside Leigh. In 2011, as part of a $9 million Treaty of Waitangi settlement, the Crown vested the descendants of Rahui and Tenetahi with fee simple title to Hauturu, with the understanding that all but 1.2 hectares of the island were to be gifted back to the Crown, and that Hauturu would retain its status as a nature reserve run by the Department of Conservation.

Paratene Te Manu was not present on Hauturu for the final eviction, but he was living on the island a great deal towards the end of his life. James Cowan was visiting Hauturu in late 1895 the day Paratene, then aged in his nineties, received his eviction notice. 'The ancient warrior, bent with age, would not touch his summons so it was laid on the ground at his feet. He picked up a manuka stick and danced feebly around the obnoxious paper, making digs at it as though he were spearing an enemy. The old man said he was not going to court, and was not going

to leave the island; it was his, and he was going to die there.'
As we know, the eviction from Hauturu made this impossible.
Paratene died in Ngunguru in late 1896. Some say he is buried
out on the islands Tawhiti Rahi or Aorangi, the Poor Knights.

Ngunguru School, which Paratene Te Manu and Henare
Te Moananui founded in 1870, moved to larger premises
overlooking the water in the 1930s. Today 200 children attend
school there. A print of Lindauer's portrait of Paratene hangs
on the wall at the school, and the marae at Ngunguru is named
in his honour. The Lindauer portrait, held by the Auckland City
Art Gallery, is so rarely displayed that many of Paratene's iwi
have never seen the original.

ACKNOWLEDGEMENTS

I am greatly indebted to a number of libraries and archives, and the librarians who helped me navigate their treasures. In New Zealand, these include the Auckland Museum; the Auckland City Art Gallery; the Auckland City Library; Archives New Zealand; the Auckland Maritime Museum; and the Alexander Turnbull Library. I'm particularly grateful to Ngahiraka Mason, curator at the Auckland City Art Gallery, for taking my father and me to see – in storage – the Lindauer portrait of Paratene Te Manu.

In the UK I spent many fruitful hours in the British Library; the British Library Newspaper Reading Room in Colindale; the Birmingham City Archives; the Zoological Society of London's Library; the Museum of London Docklands; and Tower Hamlets Local History Library and Archives. I'm also grateful for information received from the Coventry History Centre.

I was able to walk in the footsteps of Paratene at a number of locations in England, including City Chapel and John Wesley's house in London; and at Birmingham Town Hall, where I was given an informative personal tour by Rebecca Buswell of its Education & Community Department. The tour of Marlborough House (now the home of the Commonwealth Secretariat) by Terence Dormer was exceptional. I'm also very grateful for the generosity of Osborne House curator Michael Hunter, who took me around the palace on the Isle of Wight, and provided a vast amount of useful information on the meeting with Queen Victoria; and to Chaplain Mike Wilkinson and Headmaster Simon Morris for the warm welcome at Kingswood School in Bath.

There are numerous non-fiction books without which this novel could not have been written. Chief among them are *Pictures of Old New Zealand: The Partridge Collection of Maori Paintings by Gottfried Lindauer*, with descriptions by James Cowan, and – of course – Brian Mackrell's informative and insightful book *Hariru Wikitoria! An Illustrated History of the Maori Tour of England, 1863.*

In addition, I returned on many occasions to *Taua* by Angela Ballara; *London: A Pilgrimage* by Blanchard Jerrold and Gustave Doré; Henry Mayhew's *London Labour and the London Poor*; and Victor Skipp's *The Making of Victorian Birmingham.*

Much of the information on the forced sale of Hauturu is drawn from Ralph Johnson's 'Report on the Crown Acquisition of Hauturu (Little Barrier)', commissioned by the Waitangi Tribunal. The quotes from the letter by Charles John Alexander, passenger on the *Hinemoa*, are from *Marine News* 48, numbers 2–4 (1999–2000). Thanks also to Ian Conrich for bringing to my attention 'The New Zealand Warrior Chiefs' by Francis T. Buckland in *Curiosities of Natural History.*

I was helped a great deal by the expertise and research of numerous historians and curators, including Carl Chinn at the University of Birmingham; Len Bell at the University of Auckland (in particular his essay 'Actors in a Charade: James Smetham's 1863 *Maori Chiefs in Wesley's House*'); Chanel Clarke at the Auckland Museum; and independent researcher Pam Gillespie, who provided invaluable insights into the testimony of Paratene Te Manu at various sessions of the Native Land Court.

A number of people gave me money to help me research and write this book. Many thanks to Tulane University, which – over three years – awarded me a Council on Research fellowship, a Lurcy Travel Grant, and a Phase II Research Grant. Without these grants, I would not have been able to make research trips to the UK. Much of the New Zealand-based research was conducted in 2008 while I was a Buddle Findlay Sargeson Trust fellow – an immensely productive and enjoyable fellowship. I'm also extremely grateful to my sister, Lynn-Elisabeth, and her husband, Stephen Hill, for coming to the rescue when everything seemed quite bleak.

Thanks to whanau and friends – Stephen Morris; Roi McCabe; Conrad Grey; Naphelia Brown; Vicki Taylor at Ngunguru School; Steve Braunias and Emily Simpson; Bill Manhire; Katrina Smit; and Hamish Coney and Sarah Smuts-Kennedy – for their support and encouragement.

This novel was simply a short story until Geoff Walker and Witi Ihimaera talked me into something much more ambitious, so to them I send many thanks. Many thanks also to the editorial team at Penguin – Jeremy Sherlock and Catherine O'Loughlin – and to my expert editor, John Huria.

As ever, I'm profoundly indebted to Tom Moody, who helped so much with this project – from taking photographs to searching through microfilm newspapers to scrambling with me up hills in Northland and along the banks of the Thames in London. He has lived for the past nine years with my obsession with Paratene's life and times. Without his encouragement I wouldn't have begun this book, or finished it.

For their love and unwavering support, I thank my parents, Kiri and Deborah Morris, to whom this novel is dedicated, with much affection.

Forbidden Cities

'Paula Morris is that rare thing among literary novelists – someone who can write with depth and subtlety and also tune up a plot . . . Morris has a nose for our times. Like Dickens, she can tell a great story but also "catch" the world we live in, with all its complications and ambiguities.' Lydia Wevers, *New Zealand Listener*

From Sunset Boulevard to the beaches of Auckland, from the Bund in Shanghai to the banks of the Danube, from the Brooklyn Bridge to the Hammersmith Flyover, from post-Katrina New Orleans to Fire Island . . . the stories of *Forbidden Cities* explore places of escape, transgression, ambition, delusions, and desire.

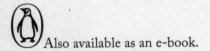

Also available as an e-book.

Hibiscus Coast

Emma Taupere has just returned to New Zealand from Shanghai, where her training as a painter has made her a copyist of incredible skill. Siaki, her ambitious and manipulative ex-boyfriend, has recruited her as a forger, shutting Emma away in a borrowed apartment on Princes Wharf. She works day and night copying one of the most valuable Goldies in the Auckland Museum, lost in memories of the two men who shaped her life in Shanghai.

When talent, hubris and greed collide with disastrous consequences, Emma has no choice but to flee up the Hibiscus Coast . . .

'*Hibiscus Coast* continues its predecessor's strengths of fine characterisation and evocative writing; and goes further by adding impressive qualities, such as dynamic plot and knife-edge storytelling . . . a weighty and wonderful book' *Christchurch Press*

Also available as an e-book.

Queen of Beauty

Winner of the Hubert Church Best First Book of Fiction, Montana Book Awards, 2003

Virginia Seton lives in rainy, seedy New Orleans, working as a researcher for an historical novelist with a 'strip-mined' imagination. On a brief trip back to New Zealand for her sister's wedding, Virginia is drawn into the family secrets, lies and tensions of both the past and the present.

A rich, moving and often comic novel, *Queen of Beauty* spans three generations of an Auckland family, moving between Northland in the 1920s, Ponsonby in the 1960s and modern-day New Orleans, and explores what it means to be Maori – and Pakeha – in changing times and places.

'Morris writes with great affection and empathy for her huge list of characters . . . it is Virginia's haunting grace and humour which provide a rich and almost spiritual anchor in this masterful work.' Penelope Bieder, *Weekend Herald*

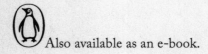

Also available as an e-book.